IMAGINING

JACK HABEREK

To order additional copies of this book, contact:
Bookwhip
1-855-339-3589
www.bookwhip.com

CONTENTS

SMYRNA

OUTREMER

MEISTER 1

am back in Thüringen and sitting here in the eatery of Otto's inn. Few sheets of paper—more and more of it seems to appear lately on the market. Is it better than parchment? Certainly a whole lot cheaper. And if stored between solid covers, it's no less durable. Enough of this though! I just had a sip of great cool wine from Otto's cellar, and I leant back trying to relax. I wonder, why actually am I writing this? I don't intend to deliver my story to generations after this one's time is up; well, my intention is not to deliver it to anyone in particular (Zweifler maybe). And yet I think I'd like it to be more solid, somehow, then just the whisper of somebody telling it to another—told, and there is nothing else, the sound of the words is over…Can we go back? If the fellow who was telling the story is there and didn't go to sleep (in this case me—still at the dark oak table whose surface got shiny from use over all those years and is still as solid as always two strong people would have a problem to lift it off the floor [I've seen it happen once during a cleanup]—drinking this cool Rheinlander), I think I like it, all of it. I like it better than anything else anywhere in the world, and this could be the reason as well. Good Lord…yes, trying to stop it to push away the nothingness only awaiting that we all turn around and let it eat away what we once called reality. But will it be the same story anyway, the second time around, if it is not written? Stories depending only on our memories tend to fluctuate. They change color. Temperature. Aroma. I think it is better for a story to be written. Any story. And mine I just like, I think it sufficiently important to justify this waste of paper (as said before, I write it on paper) and ink—the latter I make myself too.

Otto's daughter, Carla, just smiled at me, passing by. She is a tall big-chested woman now, although I remember her when she was little. I remember, in fact, her birthday. Otto still young back then, boyish, boyishly excited to the point that it was kind of hard to talk to him, his almost-white cowlick above his forehead bouncing up and down, his blue eyes unable to focus, he himself not accepting anything concerning the inn or the coach, his livelihood then, all devoured by the greatness of the event. His wife, Frieda—poor thing—had suffered terribly, the child being too big for her. Mathias saved her then (he is the kind of guy to take care around here of this kind of things), as she was held down to the bed she was on by four strongest male servants in the house. They must have been able to hear her on the other side of the Rhine.

They not only changed horses, which would have been the usual procedure, but because the right rear developed a squeak, they took it off to look at the bearing halves and put a new grease in. Then they did the same with the other one, just in case. They have finished the job—the wheels are back on, coach ready to go—but it's too late to restart the journey. The coach is not going anywhere tonight; we're staying right here. A room is being prepared upstairs for me as well as for the others.

Somebody just pulled at my sleeve, forcing me to look down only to get shocked how big he already was (at first I didn't recognize him at all: Carla's son, Günter). He seems now intimidated, looking at me, still holding my habit sleeve in his little hand.

"Gutta cavat lapidem," he says then with conviction. "De quibus suadeo vos sic habeo…"

I put my hand on the top of his head. "Quid agis, amico mio?" I ask.

And he answers, "Bene, Domine, benissimo…" He smiles and there is a spark of something in his face (if it weren't for his age, I'd say it's a spark of irony).

"Me habeo bene, benissimo in veritas…"

His mother apologizes right there, explaining that he takes Latin lessons in the monastery on the hill. Actually, it's not quite so; there's a monk who does that. He comes down here, in fact, the monk, twice a week, and gives the little guy lessons, unpaid for, just because the kid is so gifted, so incredibly quick, grasping everything in half a word. "We share our food with him," Carla says, with the monk, that is. "But that's it. That's all."

She asks me then if I would like some more ribs, pig slowly roasted and then smoked—incredible taste, tenderness. They use a kind of juniper that seems to grow only around here—and I was really hungry when we first got here. I nod now in the affirmative. She goes to the kitchen and then comes back with a big plate, still steaming. She pours me another glass of wine too.

I eat too much. This borders gluttony. It destroys one's health, and it is sin—and not venial, I know. This is serious. The little group on the other side of the room begins to be a little bit too noisy, it's the wine, I know, and yet it reminds me of a situation from long ago, in Paris. It was how I met Zweifler. Back there it seemed a lot more dangerous. There were knifes. I thought about dying, and then I saw Zweifler lifting them one by one, and then they were on the floor, immobile, kind of abandoned, it felt truly strange. Zweifler came to introduce himself, and only then, somehow, I saw the cape with the red Templar cross on it. Very much faded from the sun and wind, so I didn't see it right away. He sat at my table (at my invitation), and we had a chat. I've never been to Jerusalem and perhaps therefore simply love stories about the town, about that part of the world in general, and be it more bloody than holy—never mind that...

We spoke half of the night. I felt true friendship growing between the two of us. And suddenly, I feel a painful cramp in my stomach: it's overwhelming. For quite a while I can't move. God...

Carla comes to the table and she asks me if I'm okay. I answer in the affirmative, nodding, but only I know how false that is. Very slowly I come back to my senses. Am I okay? Lord...how can anyone be okay? I don't think we are down here to be okay.

The group across the room slowly calms down. They are obviously heavy with food and wine, and they have behind them the same long trip in the coach that I have. It is the sleepiness that takes over. One of them stands up and goes toward the steps; another one follows, and the whole thing slowly dies down. I want to sit down here for yet a while, now that it is so wonderfully silent, the night reigning, just slight murmur of fire in the chimney. I have some more wine. And then my hand touches the leather etui on the table. In it there is the parchment I obtained from Albert—a text copied on this rare, incredibly expensive parchment by himself. He didn't go to the copyists; he did it himself. It's only few pages, in beautiful calligraphy, on this parchment, which speaks by itself about luxury. I know it expresses his grief (reading it, I almost hear his lamentation caused by the death of his beloved pupil, who died way too young—Lord, and why is that? After which all the hearsay…). I would like to retain it here, for those who can read Latin to do just that—read it, try to understand what a great man once said about something which concern us all. To tell them we are here certainly is not to mock what has been mocked so many times before. And for those who can't read it, well, books have a lot of different adornments: pauses in their narration made of flowers, of scenes painted in colorful inks from the Bible's different editions, ornate and gorgeous bordures. Let's let it be it, then, a separation of one piece of the text from another…

My eyes move over the text one more time with sublime delight. And for those who care to understand, although Latin has remained outside of their lives, there is an index at the end of my writings.

> *Prima autem et manifestior via est, que sumitur ex parte motus. Certum est enim, et sensu constat, aliqua moveri in hoc mundo. Omne autem quod movetur, ab alio movetur. Nihil enim movetur, nisi secundum quod est in potentia ad illud ad quod movetur, movet autem aliquid secundum quod est actu. Movere enim nihil aliud est quam educere aliquid de potentia in actum, de potentia autem non potest aliquid reduci in actum, nisi per aliquodens in actu, sicut calidum in actu, ut ignis, facit lignum, quod est calidum in potentia, esse actu calidum, et per hoc movet et alterat ipsum.*

I see him now (Albert) telling me about ink—how important it is for the look of the document, that the ink doesn't bleed and how to prepare it that it doesn't. Listening to him, I hear what is said elsewhere about his interests in alchemy. He tells me all that because he knows I am not bored by it. I enjoy listening to him. Always did.

> *Non autem est possibile ut idem sit simul in actu et potentia secundum idem, set solum secundum diversa, quod enim est calidum in actu, non potest simul esse calidum in potentia, sed est simul frigidum in potentia. Impossibile est ergo quod, secundum idem et eodem modo, aliquid sit modens et motum, vel quod moveat seipsum. Omne ergo quod movetur, oportet ab alio moveri et illud ab alio. Hic autem non est procedere in infinitum, quia sic non esset aliquod primum movens; et per consequens nec aliquod alium movens, quia moventia secunda non movent nisi per hoc quod est motus a manu. Ergo necesse est devenire ad aliquod primum movens, quod nullo movetur, et hoc omnes intelligunt Deum.*

Slowly I put the parchment back into the etui given to me also by Albert, especially to accommodate the parchments. He had it made by a passing by cartwright staying in the same inn he was at the time himself. I know he paid in gold nuggets. Well, a sum…

I too now felt heavy with food, wine, and sleep. Just one more moment to cherish the memory that pushes back the shadows of the night.

OUTREMER

ZWEIFLER

I was born near Jerusalem, just outside the city, where my family had a household that could pass—turning to it a blind eye— even for a castle. There was nothing out of the ordinary in my childhood except the fact that very early in life, I have seen a battle, wounds from the sword and arrow, and garments stained with blood.

The house was built of stone, big yellow blocks of the stone so common in that area, windows with shutters, shut for the night, to keep the night's evils (thoughts of who approaches us only so rarely in the daylight) out. The night was something to be avoided. Loose troops would pass by, and we never knew for certain who that was and what their intentions were, until they took off. To us they looked like Turks, Mongols; some of them were Seljuks (more and more important in the area), or who knows who else. They would let us be though. Rarely they wanted something, like water, for instance, some food. But they were never aggressive, and Father thought we were lucky; if they change tactics, show for once what they really were or what were they really after, we wouldn't stand a chance, joining the long pageant of death the region was so famous for.

Father taught me to fight very early in life. I must have been seven, eight maybe. But it wasn't until twelve that I had a real sword in my hand (in my left it was a dagger, not that much smaller than the sword, both forged in Europe, in Spain, in Toledo—that I was dreaming of seeing one day—and both of them would easily cut local steel, nails we were using on our fence, for instance). It was a great pleasure to hammer a six inch nail, finger thick, into a beam, with one swift stroke just to shear it off flat with the wood, not leaving a trace on the blade. Father was proud of our weaponry. He had brought it here from Europe, and I envied him for the fact that he hadn't been born over here. I was always trying to imagine Champagne, Reims, the cathedral, and the town around it—all that, while I was listening carefully to him, devouring every word, promising myself to go there first thing when I am finally adult.

At home we spoke French, but outside I spoke Arabic with the kids and with my teacher; with Father Alonso, Latin. And then one day we had our confrontation: it was a troop of twenty Mamelukes on horses. It had to be fast—we were moving, I as well as father—among them as fast as we could, not stopping for one single moment. I got mine with the end of the sword, and I only felt it—a sudden jerk which almost ripped the sword out of my hand. I did not see him fall, and there was the second already running into me from the side, who I pierced also only half aware of it, so to speak, already engaging the third (I didn't have time to think about Father or what was he doing). And then my horse got a crossbow arrow in his chest, and I had to continue on foot. And I did. Toward the end of the skirmish, I saw Father, also on foot (that day, we've lost two good horses and quite a bit of blood). But they were all lying around, a whole lot of them. And our serfs helped catch their horses, as we—father and I—were already walking toward the house.

Mother was dead. There was a crossbow arrows sticking out of her chest, and I felt like those arrows were sticking out of mine. I just stood there without understanding. Just stood, watching how the arrows were cut off, one and then another, off her chest, that I used to suck not that long ago and now washed with blood. And I asked, kept asking God where has he been, why did he let that happen, what did my mother do to him or anyone else. The sky was bluish, cold, empty, except for a few clouds, almost not moving at all; and there was no answer to my questions, to my pain, to my tremendous surprise. None whatsoever. Even Father remained silent. And squinting at him, I was trying to figure out if he was only pretending not to notice me and my grief, or was it something else.

Now I'm not sure either.

Right about then, a huge guy with a cape on which there was a red cross approached me; he was actually my size (I already got used by then to the fact that most everything alive was shorter than me). This guy maybe even a bit taller, and he told me he saw me fight the Mamelukes back there, just the end of it (they—he and his companions—were arriving at the scene at just that moment to help, and although it has almost been over, there was enough of it left to now be able to say that it was good); truly good, my fighting, the way I moved, all that, and would I be interested in joining them.

"Joining whom?" was my question, to which he smiled.

"The Knights Templar."

"I'll have to talk to my father…"

"Certainly. I'll have to talk to him too. Would you be interested though? You'd have a chance to pay for your family. And do a lot of other good. Huh? What about it?"

Judging by his accent, I thought he was Parisian.

I still don't know why I said yes. But I did.

MARGOT

was born—well, can't possibly remember that. So I leave it out here too. What I will say is this, though: After I was born and lived for a while in the same place, I was sent on a long voyage to a distant country where the same language was spoken in a slightly different way (I was curious). Everything was almost the same, but there were things different too, and I shall never be able to forget Fra Anselmo, my caretaker and my preceptor—if I may call him that (different from everything and anything I ever knew before I met him)—who taught me most everything I know. I won't forget his room (or was it *his* room?) with a small window from where I could see the meadows down there and the grove a little farther up, the river, whose shimmering in the sun brought to me always the same disquietude of waiting—for what? But then don't we all wait for something? I lower my head. Isn't life waiting? In fact I thought about waiting a lot back then. I had no understanding of it yet, none whatsoever. Anselmo told me each time I'd ask to just pray, to forget myself and my waiting in prayer, and God would answer it sooner or later.

I just had to be patient. And then that it was another thing life was about: patience.

Not that much later, new groups were created, and the woman religiousness was, if not patronized, certainly encouraged. Groups that were created wander from place to place to teach about the true religion. Preaching was then seen as central activity, in contrast with the monastic stability and the bishopric preaching that couldn't reach too far. Classifications were created based on how deep a group would penetrate the society of the world, which is to say their distance from the center of population. That was also seen by some as religious awakening, and was oriented in rather than out of society. We, the women, were found as particularly responsive to the tendency and forms of service developed, which could be and were defined as women's movement. In 1216, Jacques de Vitry obtained the papal permission for organizing women's groups in Lowlands, France, as well as Germany, to live together; and thus the papacy has for the first time been confronted with such intensity of feminine piousness.

Early on, the Premonstratensians included women in their orders as itinerant evangelicals. Goes without saying I was one of them, trying all along to prove that these houses organized by the monks on the bases of that papal permission were not just a result of Premonstratensians propaganda but were an actual expression of a strong religious movement with its own internal drive. I would go from place to place, preaching, explaining, gathering people around me, noticing that they were truly listening to my words. I remember preaching in a small town in Northeast France when a woman in rugs touched my garment, after which she started shouting out claims she had regained her sight. Was she crazy, or has it been real? I'd never know, because there would be no way to find out, if it weren't for the fact that it wasn't just a single event. I had that quite a few times afterward in different places, including later on in Paris, in a public bath, where a guy couldn't stand because of his legs being completely lame and useless from the moment he was born. I asked him what was wrong, and he told me. And then I said—and I shall never be able to know why I said that—I just told him to pick up his bed, pallet actually, dirty and stinking from a distance, to pick it up then and walk home. And I'll be damned for eternity if he didn't do just that. I saw him walk, I saw him cry for joy, thanking me…Lord, why me? Do I deserve this?

In Valanciènne, a woman approached me in such a manner (I was speaking to people) that I couldn't see it and touched my garment, of which I suddenly knew because I felt that something came out of me. I said that, and then, trembling, she confessed: she had a blood issue for years that just couldn't be cured, and that just stopped—the touching me stopped it. She was cured, made complete. I granted her that. We went back to Paris, to our house there.

ALVA

I don't see much of my brother; he spends time during the day on physical exercises, fending, riding, shooting a bow, and such, or also reading—with Father or alone, reading whatever we've got here (and that's quite a bit; Father spent a fortune on collecting scrolls and whatnot—in our French or in Latin, in which brother's also getting steeper and steeper).

The day I'm talking about now, the day we will never be able to forget, was like any other day in its beginning; and only then, in its second half became a true nightmare. I was practicing my lyre when we've heard horses and riders enter our gate. Binah, our servant, went out to greet them, and we saw—my mother as well as I—how she was killed in that very instant, at one swing of the sword. Mother pushed me toward the entrance to the basement, and I knew at once, no words exchanged, that she wanted me to hide in there. In fact, we had a special place, a hideout, an entrance to where the piece of masonry was arranged in such a manner that if somebody didn't know, they wouldn't be able to see it. It was just even, evenly homogenous piece of stonewall; one piece of solid masonry on steel tracks so that it was enough to push it, lightly— one hand was sufficient to do it—enter, and then close it behind one in the same manner. I did just that. And then I was in there for the longest time without moving, without producing a sound.

Until my brother opened the entrance. He stood in it, and by the way he looked, I knew that something bad had happened.

He said nothing to me, but when I got up, I was sort of squatting on the floor and got up, making the couple of steps toward him. He just grabbed me and pressed me against his chest. We stood like that for quite a while, and I didn't dare to ask what really had happened out there. Then he let me go, motioning toward the basement steps. Outside I saw hell. Mother was dead. So were the other servants. The castle was all stone, so it was there, untouched. But all the auxiliary, wooden buildings, were gone—just stumps, irregular, blackened by fire, still smoking. On the gate's upper beam, our dog was hanging by her huge ears they had put together above her head and nailed to the wood. On the upper edge of the beam there was a piece of wood with and inscription burned into it: IHSV—just as it was once above our Lord's head. The author of the idea, before he died, explained to Father (a nick of time before Father pushed his sword into his chest) that the dog has been sent down here by the lord of dogs to redeem them all, to buy them back from the devil.

Their, Mamelukes', bodies were lying around too. That was the doing of both of them—father and my brother. With them there were two trusted helpers, Michael and Jean, now both slightly wounded. A quick thought crossed my mind: were we going to be able to stay here? I was born in this castle and I grew up in it, and I felt the blade of anguish enter my chest. I knew, or I thought I knew, that we would probably go away. Several days already agone, Father mentioned the kingdom of Acre—that it would take a lot of defending—so I thought now that the kingdom of Acre might be Father's ultimate choice. All of it based on a terrible miscalculation of the forces coming from Europe. They should have left the region right that very moment. It would have saved a lot of lives. Had we left on that day for Europe, a whole lot of suffering and disaster could have been avoided, so much the more so that there was not much, if anything at all, to still save. Next days, though, were spent on preparation for the moving to Acre. I was wondering if Father was considering coming back there, to our castle, at all. Most probably, had we managed to defend Acre, thus increasing our influences down there; the answer to that question would have been positive. But things worked out the way they did. Anyway, for now, we finally left the castle and started moving slowly toward the kingdom of Acre. In our way, we didn't see anybody, the land around us, everything on it, as if it had died from the bubonic plague.

In Acre it was the sight of the sea, which I saw a few times before, that filled me with awe. There is something in the sight of sea that speaks to me about our faith, about God, and how he created the world: the kind of painful mystery, the cross standing in the infinity of our expectations. The day was clear blue, the sky high, no end to it. I was praying silently.

They accommodated us in Monmusart, almost touching the tower of the Templars' ward with a window looking out to the same sea, so my feeling associating itself with the mass had not been interrupted. I sat on the base of the windowsill and thought about Father telling us about the cathedral in Chartres, about the creation of the world, the cross with its inscription, and other things which someday I hope I shall be able to see with my own eyes. There were moments during those months when thinking about anything was simply impossible. The Mamelukes' arrows were falling into the city almost as a solid block, and the mangonels wouldn't stop; the barbican, considered over time the weakest point, had been then set on fire and they let it collapse—God, if not stones falling off the sky, it was pottery filled with explosive. What seemed wonderful to me was the fact that the Templars fought right on the side of the Hospitallers, as if there hadn't been centuries of competition, now left behind for good.

We would get food from Cyprus on steady bases—I'm not sure if I mentioned that already, but I am here not to write a chronicle. There are the *Gestes* already written with the proper knowledge of the military material. I just write what I can't stop—sort of— because for instance, I bit my lips at some point so badly that I then couldn't talk. I was very young and when one is young like that, one hopes. It's only much later when the hope dies down when one just stops waiting for anything, except maybe for the final victory of some sort.

The Turks were well in the city; all was lost. Our only chance was now the sea and the bunch of boats we had there, and it was also then that the sign over the cross—*in hoc signo vinces*—would restore not so much hope, as a sort of waiting, which always gives life a little bit of a meaning again.

Suddenly, I thought about our poor dog, and I started crying—like a child. I suddenly hoped she might be in the paradise for dogs and I would see her whenever I get to ours. Whenever that is. Whenever!

WILLIAM

They brought the women from the side of the river, on a wooden platform with two huge wooden wheels—the whole thing pulled by an ox—both of them on top of it, chained to a wooden post the size of an old tree, crown cut off, fixed right in the middle of the platform. One, silent, as if apathetic, maybe not all there anymore; her head fallen on her chest, simply there and not even making the impression that she might be waiting for something. And the other one was very much alive, energetic, nervous maybe, almost all of the time since the cart could be seen approaching, mumbling to herself, shaking her head, as if denying or affirming something energetically. She had black thick hair, that hasn't been washed for the longest time and was now in long streaks of black color mixed with the rest: sweat and dust and the rest of what was in this air. Her eyebrows, as they could be seen, thick, black, joint together, giving her face the impression of a lion in a trap—sort of forcing one to think what will happen once she breaks those chains. And with that reflection, a shudder could wander down one's spine. Her body was covered with a cape, looking a lot like a monk's habit—dark brown, almost black too—at the height of her waist, held together by a string the thickness of a thumb, knotted together at her belly.

The executioner unchained them both and, with his helpers led them, their hands still chained together, toward the pyre, behind which the spire of Notre Dame was now sharply visible.

They had to climb the ladder to get up to the top of the pyre, which was a little bit awkward, and which was solved by adding another two ladders on each side of the first one. Once on top, they started chaining both of them to the central post, also about the middle of the pyre. At the beginning and then during the whole procedure, the silent one started to cry and never actually stopped, silently, passively, again as if not waiting for anything anymore but the worst that was certain to come. The other one seemed to be fighting something. The flame started to climb the dry wood, and once the heat got to them, the more valiant one started shouting at us, the people down here, gathered to watch.

"Pigs! All you know is eat, fuck, and shit! And twaddle about your stinkin' God!"

Her silhouette was now starting to vibrate because of the flames getting higher and higher, separating her from our sight. More definitely.

"The only thing you'll teach your little ones"—her eyes squeezed almost closed, her mouth deformed in her fight with heat, giving her the aspect of something strange, something truly evil—"shall be how to be stupid and obedient, how to work from the crack of dawn till sunset, never trying to even imagine another type life." Fire was beginning to take hold of her garment.

She moved convulsively, throwing her head back, as if there was a way away from the flames. "Pigs!"

Death rattle, just a sound, empty and senseless, and then her voice was suddenly strong again, as if coming from somewhere else.

"You, yourselves shall create commissions and committees that will write the laws, and those will make your life an ultimate misery. They'll be educating your little ones so that every thought of independence shall be killed before it even finds expression." Her voice was becoming an ever-more irregular rattle again, which she was trying to fight feverishly. A flame started at the left side of her face, frolicsome, then trying to escape up toward the sky—it was her hair, unwashed, greasy. And she, still shouting and still fighting, her voice becoming only that same death rattle again, chased the flame away with her hand—a short, abrupt gesture, as if it was only something bothersome of no real import. She pointed her hand then somewhere above our heads. "But it is coming, changes, new world. Annuit coeptis novus ordo seclorum." The heat made her face look that of the devil's, but her words were still perfectly understandable, although the stench of burning flesh was becoming more and more distinct, more and more offensive to the senses, and then plain invincible. The other one fainted a while ago. And now our stentor's head fell down on her chest as well. It suddenly became clear that, as scary as she might have been, whomever she might have been rendering her services to, she was first and foremost only human. She too was silent now. Just the food for fire, hanging immotile, sort of crookedly, to one side, skewed on her chain—an object which the fire controlled now completely, getting higher and higher every second, seeming to reach the sky overhead, seeming to take control of the whole piazzetta we were on, a tidbit reaching meaninglessness at an accelerated pace that it would in the end consume without a trace. We had to move back because the heat in our faces was becoming unbearable. Yet some time passed by, half hour maybe, certainly not longer than that, people started walking away, toward their respective shelters for the night.

It was over.

On my way back toward the hotel, I thought about our actual situation—the unpayable debts Philip has incurred with the order and what our options are, what could still be done, and what cannot even be thought of. The night was now in quick onslaught, the houses on both sides of the boulevard already dark; in the windows here and there, lights would appear, thus deepening the impression of darkness surrounding the carriage. The city was setting out for the night.

I thought about Philip, how weak he was—how provinces, more and more of them, were slowly more and more independent from the central power. A kingdom which is based on terror and theft, lies and delusion is no kingdom—it is a monster representing only itself and its weakness. People are afraid and hateful, and that is not a combination that would fly; sooner or later the whole of it hits the wall, and it's not the wall that gets damaged. Damage aside, it is the poor, regular people earning their bread with their hands who pay in the end for all the excesses and lack of balance.

Those who are left with truly nothing, whose basest needs get only exacerbated by any kind of change, their life afterwards even more offensive than ever before, those who for God only knows which time in a row get the explicit message that this is the valley of tears. For those who rule, they are simply the "stupid ones," unteachable and such. Father told me that whenever I get to hear something like that, I should know it's the devil who talks to me.

To our left they had a fire going, some street people—without a place, probably, to even try to go to. It's big. Last thing I see before we passed is a huge wooden wardrobe, which upon seeing, I ordered my coachman to stop; and we did too. I wish we had some guards here to investigate about the provenience of that wardrobe, but there's only my coach and me, so we leave it at that.

The fire slowly climbed up the dark silhouette and then got higher, now with multiplied strength fighting the night, of which some reflexes were reddish-golden elfins dancing on the river, where also a dark silhouette of a barge suddenly passed by. I have no idea why, but I suddenly reached to my right, and my hand touched my document case as if I was afraid of its disappearance; I was not. Under my habit, I had two loaded pistols, and they were still there, of course.

I had a book in there too, written in vernacular, although there is a use of Latin here and there. Quite learned, quite apt—well, the language of the book, its composition, the use of grammar, etc. Tell me there's a long educational process involved here. The author was from a household of substance. I'll read it again. I'll make notes. I knew that. I'll do all of it before I issue the order for arrest.

MARGUERITE

I love this area of Reims—the vineyards, that lovely green fertile land, inhabited by decent working people, and the town, whilst one walks through it—at first glance silent, peaceful, and yet as if stopped and given to thought—one seems to inhale the strangeness and grandeur of its history. I was talking there to people gathered in front of the cathedral, which by now is pretty advanced and may even come out more impressive than the Paris's Notre Dame— well, it probably will be that, once finished, whenever that might be. The last interdict period is not a good prediction for the future, and it put a halt to a lot of other things that could have grown in that time as well to the size they had been intended to grow up to.

Lot of people gathered there to listen to me, making me think that I did not waste my time writing my book about the mirror of the simple soul and then fighting copyists (it is always a fight, a true one, and I doubt if that will ever change) all along exchanging my fortune (my inheritance) for their work; my name slowly becomes known, yes, they come to see me and to listen to my voice, to what I have to say, and may they not quite like it.

Good Lord, please forgive me, it is my ego again; and I don't do it for me. No, none of it. I do it for you, Sir, that you may grow, whilst I decrease.

I would like to be a part of the process I write about in my book, the process of becoming part of God's will, whilst one's own will gets belabored in such a manner by life itself that it shrinks or disappears altogether, even before we get to depart. I know for a fact at this point that some in the clergy, since already quite some time, don't approve of my work—well, don't quite agree with my vision as to what human predicament is, what are we here for, and what will become of us at some point. They also seem not to like something that is a lot simpler than that: the fact that people gather to read (one of them who knows how to read and a physical copy of my book, gotten God only knows where and for what money) a copy of the book. And be it on paper only (which begins to show all over Europe since this century started, give or take) is still quite, costly and that they come, like here, to listen to me, even if not to any other sermon by anyone else, which I know ignites the hot points of hatred. It is a smell of success, beware!

Two Sundays back, I told them about the destiny, about not only possible but certain persecution, discomfort, and suffering, and that they, as Christians, most of them Catholics, should not be afraid of.

"Beware of men," I was saying, and my voice strong, unfailing they could hear it in the whole plaza. "For they will deliver you up to the councils, and they will scourge you in their synagogues, and ye shall be brought before governors and kings for my sake, for a testimony against them and the Gentiles."

A moan went over the crowd, the strong wind bearing my voice to the farthest corner. Some moved, like a sudden shudder of foreboding, this time making itself present this side through more than one person.

"But when they deliver you up, take no thought how or what ye shall speak, for it shall be given you in that same hour what ye shall speak. For it is not ye that speak but the spirit of your father that speaks in you. And the brother shall deliver up the brother to death, and the father the child. And the children shall rise up against their parents and cause them to be put to death. And ye shall be hated of all men for the Lord's name's sake, but he that endureth to the end shall be saved."

I wondered if they were wondering who might be talking here, whose voice was delivering to them the words spoken like that, in front of a church.

The day was clear with blue sky, and just a few wads of cotton up there were slowly moving across the blue. The ones closer to me, sheer poverty judging by their clothes, didn't hide their sympathy, although they themselves were visibly afraid by the perspective, which they did not yet understand. An old man was nodding, looking somewhere at the base of the podium I was upon. A big-chested woman beside him would look at him furtively now and then, as if looking for support in her fight with her fear.

"Even if you could understand the order of the world, which you can't, as you can't understand your own predicament in it, you couldn't grasp the meaning of any of it. Isn't that what the Lord says to Job? The only thing Job wants is explanation: the why. God answers him saying that he wouldn't mind telling Job just that. But could the latter understand that explanation? No! Job wasn't meant to. It is the trust that means everything here. The trust. Confidence that your pain is dealing here with sheer goodness and everything will turn out good for you, no matter how gloomy, how torturous it might seem right now."

That was two Sundays back. And today, I had the same crowd, right there, quiet, waiting. The crowd seemed homogenous to me, all of them, give or take, just casual listeners. Only two people were somehow jumping into my sight out of the mass. They were here not together, didn't come here together. Both of them in monks' Dominican habits, one looking straight at me (and in his case, I had the impression of sympathy, a hardly visible smile appearing on his lips), and the other one pretending I wasn't of any interest to him at all. The second one had face, smoothly shaven, intelligent, with thin (from up here bluish-looking but also almost invisible) lips, his skin bluish too from that fresh shave, almost transparent, which somehow gave me creeps—all of it, including his habit, the symbol of offering this life to the Lord, of having already given up this life's ambitions for good. What reigns is the strong and steady memory of transience of this life's things, waiting for what's to come, and trusting. And there was no trust here; and behind appearances of indifference, tension—a painful, filled-with-waiting invincible tension. A shudder went down my spine.

ALVA

think I mentioned our arrival in Acre and the room I have gotten, with the window looking out to the sea—a wonderful place for wondering and daydreaming. We sketched a bunch of pictures I like from the wall of my room in the castle we were abandoning, and now I called on my brother to help me hang them on these walls, built of mighty granite stones; only the mortar between them could have been used to hammer a steel hook into (one of those hooks they, Father and he, couldn't have decided to leave behind) upon which the picture would then be hanged. My brother laughed that it wasn't him we needed, it was Thor, the Viking god with the hammer, the one Father told him a lot about.

I was sitting there, looking out of the window, as Giscard dropped by. I can't really remember where we met him, but wherever that might have been, he seemed to have joined us, our family, like an animal does. He's just there, living with us, eating and sleeping, and the rest is history. Father says he is very intelligent. He speaks French with us—well, he is French, just like we are—but he knows Arabic. I saw him talk to them myself and willing to become a theologian.

He's learnt quite a bit of Latin and some Greek.

We consider our father a very learned person. Most of his life he spent studying stuff; he spent a fortune on texts, copies, originals—whatever he could lay his hands on. But here, I'd say, in Giscard, he found someone just like him: a person whose life passes studying stuff, learning as much as he can, with no reward in terms of degrees or positions. If there were no universities in this whole world, Father would say, his life would mean studying anyway. That's a curiosity we bring down here with us. It is on our shoulders just as a hunchback has. Not for us to decide what to do with.

He was sitting there now, smiling, I think looking at me and probably wondering how to start the conversation—since I knew him, he wasn't any good at that. "Are you reading something?" I tried to help.

"Yes," he got serious. "Aristotle your father gave me." And then, "Don't mean to bore you…"

"You're not boring me, at least not yet." "Will you tell me if I am?"

"Okay, I will." After a while of awkward silence, I tried to help again. "You said you were reading Aristotle? Did Father give you the copy?"

"It is not actually Aristotle himself. What your dad had was a copy by an Arab in Spain, in Cordoba. In Latin, he called himself Averroes. What your father gave me to read is a translation of *Poetics* into Latin too. By that very Arab.

I don't think I could do it in Greek, if there was a copy extant, see?"

"I should ask Father how he got that copy, where from?" "It's easier and easier. Western Europe seems flooded with copies like that. I've heard that in France, in Paris at least, the church authorities are confiscating those, if they can find it."

"Why?"

"Well"—he was touching the top of his nose and I thought it was funny—"we know Aristotle through Aquinas's work. The Christian church seems okay with that. They read it and reread it a countless amount of times. They got used to it. Now this, this Averroes starts showing here and there little differences, in the beginning seeming negligible. But then growing in importance, more and more people reading it, and it isn't exactly what it seemed to be delivered to us through Aquinas. The differences they call errors. Rightly so or not."

"How do they know what's got to us through Aquinas isn't an error?"

"I just said, Alva, rightly so or not. Up until very late, all we know is Averroes…" He sat there for a while, nodding, and then just looked up at me, smiling again; there is something boyish in his smile, something I truly like.

"It's got to the point where I can only be certain that if our Lord came back to us today and started teaching anew, it wouldn't take very long till he be declared by the church authorities a contumacious heretic with one possible outcome—the pyre, unless he'd finally use his divine powers changing those inquisitors into cockroaches or something like that. Why, besides, he didn't do it the last time he was here—oh, Lord, that truly beats me! I know one thing for certain: if I could do that, I certainly would, being in his shoes back then! Certainly! I have no doubts."

"What about the other cheek?" I wanted to know.

"He did just that now, didn't he? And we also know what the outcome was, don't we?"

"Now that's heresy, Giscard. You know that."

"Yes, I do. And yet it is so hard to accept the death of a God and the survival of boring and senseless mediocrity who made him die."

"Next you'll tell me that there's too many of us and some should die so the surviving rest may have more comfortable life. I've heard something like that not long ago."

"I've heard that too."

"And? Are you going to say it's right? Well, is it?"

"No, it isn't. I'm sure of that. Life is what it is, and we have to deal with it, certainly not through killing."

I nodded, and he smiled again. Looking at his face, I felt something inside me melt. I was looking then at the picture on the wall realizing that the boy the painter presented there was a lot like Giscard. The whole scene was located in some kind of a court. A matron in a sumptuous outfit was holding her hand on the boy's head, while he himself was looking out the window to the immensity of the sea, just as I saw it only a moment ago. The boy on the picture had almost no clothes on. I thought it was a great painting. I agreed here with Father, although I didn't remember the name of the painter. It just didn't matter to me.

Right about then, somebody knocked at the door to tell us that dinner has been served. We went over to the dining room where a whole lot of people were sitting at the long table. The main guy at the other end said a short prayer. It was soup at first, a poor thin soup with a few vegetables floating in it, almost tasteless. Then a small piece of meat. Way too small for my hunger. I thought I could eat the guy next to me and then some. By the same token, I knew to think without being reminded by anyone about Saladin's army outside the ramparts, with very small chances for any kind of help. The Lord would help us if we knew how to help ourselves, and gluttony certainly wasn't the way in question. We, and that all of us, were grateful for the little we had; at least we still had something. Days were slowly passing by, and we, I think also all of us, were beginning to wonder what is all this for if nobody out there seems to care anymore. I know there were talks; I know ours are right now trying to convince the European courts about the importance of our kingdom here, but nobody seems to really believe in that importance anymore, and that to the degree, we ourselves are beginning to have our doubts. Then what? Lie down and die? My family is ready to fight to the very end. I know that.

ZWEIFLER

mentioned that Father was very proud of our weaponry from Toledo, Spain, and it took him a long time, years on end, to admit to me that he made those swords and daggers himself right here, in the barn behind our lodging that, as said earlier, could be *cum grano salis* considered a castle. And right here, a reflection surfaces about the possible point of describing how he was doing that: what could the future generations' interest be in an obsolete technology (someday, it will be obsolete like everything else—I think we are a constant process, unstoppable, difficult, if not impossible to redirect)? Yes…but there are also things that stay with us— paintings, sculptures and such…

And I think that for the same reason, I will never forget the day when he showed me the remnants of the oven he built to smelt the ore brought here from somewhere around Damascus. I still see him here, like I saw him that very moment. The bricks were made here, and to seal it, he used the clay from the hill behind the house mixed with water in a proportion, which he himself worked out. Each time it was the same oven, the whole thing—the entire construction, each time, is built of new bricks with the same investment of human effort and patience, for just one single steel ingot. Bellows were made by Senna (local blacksmith—or maybe he, Senna, purchased them somewhere, who shall ever know; Father knew not). From the same clay he made the crucible in which the ingot was sealed in, ore with the just right amount of charcoal, and pulverized glass for helping remove the slag; in the end he would add certain amount of sand. The recipe he found on the old parchments purchased by him in Cairo for amounts of money that nearly exhausted our family resources. Each time, only one final product being the result, and it went on like that for countless amounts of years. Father became not only a great blacksmith, having built up the knowledge that would grow only over the years, slow as molasses, but also great swordsman, exercising methods of swordsmanship with his own product, developing in the end both to a true perfection.

For long hours they were operating the bellows to build up proper temperature, that is until the fire at the oven main entrance grew higher than the oven itself—bluish and voracious. I remember seeing a thread in it, like an evil joy, while it was looking at me (fire can look at you; there are moments it can). Senna would help him with physical work; it wasn't a task for a single human being to operate the bellows for so many hours. And then they would take the oven apart; take the pot—sorry, the crucible with the ingot inside it—out, break it to pieces with a hammer, and carefully liberate the final product: the steel for the sword. After that, it was days and days on end of hammering; but I associated the noise I have heard with the actual making of swords only after Father told me what it was. I was then still a little boy explaining to whom anything more serious and more complex would have been simply useless. It is only now that I understand why, after we have joined the Templars, Father became almost from the beginning a brother sword-bearer with all the honors related to the title. My memory back in the barn, I see the steel moving under the hammer in such a manner (inside of a steel through made of steel bars screwed together into one unbreakable piece, Father's basic tool at this point for a longer period) that it would remind me of a snake coiling upon itself slowly, from one piece already hammered into something, which would roughly remind one of a sword back into an almost cube, still red, emanating mysterious light, the soul of a steel ingot talking to us. And the hammering would then restart, all over again, go on for days on end.

In the battle for Acre, years later, I saw Father at the side of Konrad von Feuchtwangen (I was a bit back behind them) clashing with the forces of Al Ashraf Khalil; and I saw Father fighting one of the Saracens, at some point cutting the Arab's curved weapon in two, making Khalil's worrier fall to his knees and beg for quick death (which is what happened next).

I close my eyes—it's a way of coaxing my memory into cooperation…He made a hammer. I have no idea if it has any special name—from a piece of steel, over a period of many a day. He filed something that was half rounded to my eye and then used it to hammer on an anvil along the *statu nascendi* sword a channel. No idea if that's the right word; most certainly not—but it comes back to me now: something that's called the fuller that, as has been explained to me, allows for the blade to be longer and more resistant without increasing the weight. I don't know how much longer the blade could thus be, but as far as the resistance, I have seen countless examples.

After one of the days spent fighting for the city, yet before the towers started collapsing, they were sitting together at night and talking about Father's business, drinking cool Greek wine from the cellar under the castle stones, each of them having its own name, different colors, and different grades of coarseness were coming back to me, down to the one that reminded me of a bar of butter and smoothness of glass, in uninterrupted use for days and days on end, oxidation of steel slowly disappearing—the steel surface losing its imperfections and gaining the shine of the mirror in which you could see your face, the details of your skin. I already mentioned the iron nails hammered into the wooden walls, half of their length in and then, with one swing of that sword, cut off without leaving a trace on the blade surface; that was fun. There are some of the swords made in Damascus that can do that too—costing a fortune and really rare at that.

It was the Templars who would buy and sell his products. After Acre was lost, we were in the north part of the ramparts; but the news of the Accursed Tower falling into the hands of the Saracen got to us rather quickly, so we knew almost right away we too have lost everything. I'm not talking here about the darkness's onslaught caused by the news of the city falling into the hands of the enemy. I'm talking about the sense of impending death if we wouldn't move fast enough or with enough resolve. We escaped with a handful of other knights; and then on a small boat, absolutely not seaworthy, we took off and got away as far as we could from the city. The shore disappeared behind us, and I remember feeling the uncertainty of a human being lost in an infinite expanse of unchanging space, which I think we all shared at that moment.

We spent several days on the sea, in that tiny boat, going west, until an Italian trireme from Brundisium going to Smyrna picked us up. I slept. Right there, on the deck. And slept. And slept.

We had to stay a few days in Smyrna waiting for a ship going to Europe. Weather was beautiful, so we didn't go for an inn at first. We stayed on the shore, high, paved with stones; and only then that the ship was delaying did the simple need for a little bit of comfort made us go and get inn rooms, still on the peninsula, with a window that if opened (which it was at all times), would give at the isthmus. And downstairs, a girl I liked very much would serve us our food every day, as far as I can remember, at the same table. Our locomotion turned out to be the same trireme that picked us up, just going back to Brundisium. From there we had to make the long journey across the Italy to France, and once at the border, we decided to go at first to Avignon.

WILLIAM

had her followed and watched very carefully: every gesture and every word, wherever she might have been. The suspicion of heresy springs up quickly, and quick in their judgment are average people. Too quick. They are always ready, is my experience, to get the wood and build a pyre. I think because watching a witch die in this manner is spectacular in a way; and one of the most powerful things in this life, which gets a human being down and oftentimes turns him into a downright devil, is boredom. That, I think, is the main reason for the church to have created inquisition. Employ specialist interrogators to truly find out, to know before a condemnation is pronounced, to avoid hastiness of the mob, to make the sentence fathom all its own debt—so to speak—its own seriousness. The sadness in the eyes of God. I know I'm right here.

She was sitting now on the horse (we call *horse* a contraption built of wood, the two top boards fastened together at half right angle, forming sort of a dull wooden blade, on which the interrogated sits astraddle, completely naked; and on her feet there are two shelves, fastened there like tight shoes, almost, except instead of soles there are those shelf-like surfaces to add leaden weights. I've seen cases when a tough witch, capable of denying everything long enough, had been cut in two halves by the horse. It is sudden—there is sound one wouldn't wanna hear in no circumstances—and the witch goes quickly down. It is quick once the bones part, by the end of it lightning quick even, and then there is just meat on that stone floor, bloody mess, that has to be thoroughly washed before a new interrogation starts and what's left from the present one taken up to the small cemetery we have at the level of the main yard. It is then buried there. No coffin. No words. Who kills them? It's the world reflected somehow in the consciousness. Would it be consciousness then trying to preserve its own *status quo*? Because it can't be bothering God…huh? Why would God insist on burning witches? No, everything, give or take, is the anima, Þ ψυχ Þ, as the Stagira guy says. Everything. There's no active world outside it.

Today, she bit off her tongue right in the beginning. And after that, I couldn't quite understand her babbling interrupted by howling of a dying animal; so they brought a ladder, and I had a guy stand on it, listening to what she might have been answering to my inquiries. Oh, he is good; he didn't lose one word, I believe. Not a single one.

They added some more lead, and her voice got even worse.

"Good Lord, this isn't easy. You, sir, be my witness. Like I know you are. I do know that. I am certain of it if I can be certain of anything in this life."

My careful question to her was, "Your only access to the world partially lived, in small part explained, mostly misunderstood, in (is)yourself, isn't it? It sits inside this body like a sweet nut in the useless crust, which has to break in order for everybody to get to its content. And if that, how would you know that there is a world outside? Me, for instance? How would you know that I really exist?" Her answer came to me through my guy on the ladder. "When you were doing it to your mother's ass, was she squealing?"

I did not tell them to add lead to her "shoes"; I didn't want her to die too quickly. Concerning her guilt, I had no true information yet, none that would be of any judicial value anyway.

"The world in our life is there like a chisel to cut off what's not needed. You understand that, I know. You were voicing that opinion when they got you. But if that is so, that the opposite facet, how do you know you're not alone? Nothing there beside your sight, feeling, pain, pleasure? Yours only? How do you know there is something that is there without you, huh? Big guys broke their heads over that, you know?" I said.

"My ass is coming asunder, you halfwit, that's how."

I'm closing my eyes for a moment and see Clement talking about necessity of protection for the church, his hand—right hand—in the air, index pointing toward the ceiling. "Why is John saying what he is saying in what concerns additions or subtractions…huh? That anyone who subtracts or adds, who then changes his message in any way, be cursed. One has to be extremely careful what one says." Philip (the scribe) is looking now at me, trying to understand (I always feel a little awkward when people like that, not used at all to abstract thinking, to follow metaphors and comparisons are suddenly forced by the unforeseen, trying to put things together, sweating visibly, their foreheads wrinkled; and he is right now trying all right too), to get fully what I just have said. And I too, for whatever reason, suddenly feeling a little embarrassed.

"Do you think you could change the faith of an angel? Or maybe it is not even *faith*? Because how could one call certainty *faith*? But in our case you've gotta be gentle—you've gotta know how to handle the newborn. You can't manhandle a newborn now, can you? That's why we fight heretics: like with a newborn, so it is also with our faith (it isn't and probably never will be certainty). We are only human, and that means we can only believe, and that is what has to be preserved at all costs—when you put it down, you've gotta be gentle, you've gotta watch yourself. No damage tolerable. Anything which goes through your head has to be carefully examined first. You can't express an opinion because it just passed through your head and now shines, huh? If you put the newborn down too abruptly, he might be a cripple for the rest of his natural life. And it still pisses and shits, there's the same stench, the squeal that drives you crazy—yes, sir, and all that notwithstanding, you've gotta be gentle…"

How long has it…

Only now I've noticed that the woman on the horse is making a noise that reminds me of a little dog whose back has been broken by the wheel of the cart going down the street too fast. And I knew the story was ending abruptly. Here. And now. Was she still able to understand me? Or was her mind already gone? In which case, I would just be wasting my time down here. Which was it now?

"Do you admit that you now understand your practices are most of all damaging to our faith? I mean how delicate it is?"

She was shaking, and the squeal did not change. And suddenly the whole thing seemed, to me, simply absurd.

"Add lead!" I commanded. They did, and the horse cut her in two with a sound that made a shudder wander slowly down my spine. Her head remained on her former left, I thought, with the heart.

"Clean up and dispose the body," I said, already turning around toward the arch of the stone staircase.

I felt I needed air—fresh, unsullied by excrement—a silence not pregnant with moans and farts, and such. I suddenly wanted badly to see the light of day (maybe even sun, if I'm lucky), and even though the steps leading up aren't the most comfortable, I was going as fast as I only could. The guard upstairs saluted me, and I didn't salute back, not because I was pissed off or something, but because I was nauseous. I had to cough. And then breathe deeply. Is there a way to get used to it? Since I have to do it and there is no way around that, I wish there was…

ALVA

can't sleep because of the constant noise of the battle; day and night, down at the ramparts, it is raging, and only fewer and fewer of ours come back to the main dormitory where brother is now to sleep. Meantime, I got to know quite a few of the knights and their help, and I think I'm qualified at this point to make such a statement. It looks to me like the present *status quo* is not going to last much longer. We need help. We need to cry out to the world, to Europe, to the kingdoms over there that call themselves Christian. I know from Father that there were attempts to organize help, but they amounted to nothing because we are surrounded, from the side of the sea as well. It sound like that is all—hell, no! That's just one of the reasons and maybe the least significant. Politics, European big picture, boredom, the sense of suddenly feeling tired, our cause causes now whenever spoken about over there. The little ones and the princes, no matter. We all seem to have enough of certain things certain time come. And here inside there is almost nothing left to eat; we are hungry. I never knew what that means really, I mean the meaning that I discovered only now. Yesterday I left my palm toward the sun and I saw my own bones. I asked myself how can they still fight. Where do they find strength? I got down here today, and that's one flight of stairs only, and then I had to go back, climb that very flight back up—that was all; I hardly made it. I had to sit down and try to find some air in the room around me—that bad! And there was a battle going on at the ramparts; the noise of it not weakening at all, people still finding strength to hold them Arabs back. Out of sheer admiration God should give them help of some kind. Which? Where from? I've no idea…

And then we were in the small boat, on the angry sea, where the bigger vessels didn't dare to go out that day. and I didn't dare to ask where we were going or what chances did we have to get anywhere in the world. My main task was to hold on, stay inside the boat, don't let the sea wash me out. I did. I live long enough to see in the rain and foam enveloping our bodies, the hull of a ship that finally rescued us that day above us, gigantic, cutting us off the sky altogether, becoming the sky for us. Our people were like one shouting and yelling, obviously trying to get the attention of the crew, and then we were picked up, one by one, and lifted up onto the deck. And I can describe the feeling—the certainty, obviously wrong—that we now have escaped the death's claws for good. Joy? Is that it? The true joy…

The ship was going to Smyrna, and so we had no choice; we were going to Smyrna for a few days, at least. Not that anybody really cared after what we've just been through. Smyrna was fine too. Any place, I'd say, which wasn't water. At some point, the mighty voice of the poet resounded inside of me: Since we got here my spirit (just as were doing the spirits of others, as far as it was possible to get to know that then) roaming around, gliding invisible tracks along those ancient streets, stopping just for a moment longer in the squares imprisoned amongst houses so old there was no way to know even approximately how much time had passed since people (and just who were they?) brought the stone from the quarries in the mountains and built them down here. I felt all those years in my heart, and strangely, it would not contribute to heaviness life fills us with, in fact, the opposite. I felt suddenly lighter, unexpectedly capable of flight. And, by Zeus, I did just that too. I felt like moving, did not want to stop, but finally I found rest at the Tmolus. I had spent the night at the foot of the mountain in a small hut all in green brushes covered with flowers; there the small, as if shy, temple of Cybele gazed out from the elms into the shine of the high moon, which gave her a ghostly aspect I couldn't quite comprehend and which made me a little uncomfortable, to be frank. Through a thousand blooming shrubs my path lead upward and from the precipitous slope trees were pouring their soft flakes, now and then, over my head. I had started that journey in the morning, after the night and the dreams were over; and about midday, I was on top of it. Full of joy, I looked before me, and I could taste the pure air of the mountains, of this vertiginous height, in my mouth, which in turn made those hours truly blessed. I thought time became spirit and was running in my veins too. Down there, left behind me long, long hours, lay the land, from here reminding me of the sea, full of colors that the world had given back to it, assailing my senses from all sides, filling my soul with its own fullness. Flight—the only type of action that could be satisfying there and then. Not exactly the flight of a bird propelling the body with the movement of the wings, no, a flight where nothing moves gliding through, through the airs like angels do, no stopping, no engagement of the consciousness—pure movement without additions of any kind. The next day I come back to Smyrna, and yet there's time there (A is after B and B after C, and so on); we know not being outside of time. There's always next minute, next hour, next day; and if there weren't, no need could be satisfied. None. I walk from place to place. I think. I think about war and peace. The poet's voice talked about it, and at some point, they made an *Auswahl* for the troops.

And in the port, waiting on the cobblestone shore, we met Giscard, at least I think now that it was the case. Young fellow, French like us, who was in such a shape that trying to say something certain today is just out of question. Now I think that's how it was, but to know for sure, I'd have to ask Giscard himself, if he really still has the knowledge in question. I walked in the port quite a bit. Next day I felt a lot better. Smyrna is a town that gives me creeps too. It is impossible to know details of its history. (One may have access to sources, but then there are so many that the problem I'm talking about starts right then and there. Try to remember all that and build a picture guiding you through that history to the time you might be in, time that forms your present.) One realizes that even our puny being on this Earth of ours may assume appearances of infinity. The simple question "how far back?" isn't answerable in some cases. Smyrna is one of them. Right on the pier there were street stands with fish of which we bought a lot, being as famished as we were—too much as it turned out, we couldn't eat it all, and a lot went to waste. Father purchased a jar of wine from Cyprus, and later I saw him, for the first time in a long time, a little tipsy. I knew he had enough. I mean of the situation in which we found ourselves, stripped of any meaning, hardly big enough to see how small we were on this Earth of ours. I wonder. We, the believers. When I was looking there at a big Turk (I think) shouting, moving around like a windmill, his energy inexhaustible, just selling his mangy fish, I wondered. Why doesn't God try him for a change? Why is it always us, huh? We may not be weaker than them, but that's beside the point. Life comes and put us on trial, and it looks no good all along—like there was no big picture. And our believes were just that: believes and nothing else. The older I get, the more do I understand Father's admiration for the biblical Job: incessant faith, iron consistency in staying on the once-appointed path, no matter what kind of torture God allows Satan to use on you.

Still few days had to pass by, and we were back on the open sea again; yet some time ago, the ship would stop at Haifa. But not now; Haifa was not in our hands anymore, and we made a sharp turn to the west. From Smyrna hence we were going straight to Brundisium in Italy, leaving Cyprus to the left as well, straight where from we'd have to organize our trip to Rome and then Avignon, which was Father's wish—to go to the place of his birth. As said before, we were French. True. But I have never been so far to France, and the same goes for the rest of my family, as far as I know. This is going to be our first time together. Yes, for the first time in our lives we shall be admiring the wonders of our country, all of us in the same place. From Father's accounting, the most admirable should be the Paris Basin, should we ever get there. Chartres and Reims, then Amiens and the Notre Dame de Paris. I can't wait. I wish we'd already be there, standing in the front of the western façade of Chartres, trying to breathe normally…Suddenly, I wish Suleiman could see Chartres. I wish. He may just spread his famous blanket and lie flat there, praying for forgiveness for everything he ever did. For every blessed thing he's ever done so far. For our lives.

MEISTER

We didn't go this morning. Reiner, the coachman, said he was coming down with something, feeling really bad, weak, his knees trembling. No, he definitely wouldn't be able to drive us anywhere. There is no other coach. Besides, I'm not in a hurry. There's no particular place I'm rally headed to, so I've decided to enjoy myself right here, at this very same table—big, heavy and solid. I've just noticed that the old wood, shiny from such a long use, had metal incrustations in it: silver, or something like that, polished thoroughly with a rug. It would come up to the surface, like from a deep of a river, an announcement that there is something there, in the water, which is not just a stony or sandy bottom, something that is there and in our hearts at the same time, like a little touch of fear. Otto brought me a while ago a pitcher of Reinisch from the cellar, nicely cold, that I think does me a lot of good. I sip it slowly. I don't want it to end too fast. I know I would order then another one, and that is sin. I think we offend the Lord at each and every step, and it is better when one watches oneself.

Carla walks around among the tables with a rug, cleaning some of them from time to time, although they are clean—there was nobody there this morning. And it forces me to think about the past, about the time I was still young and she was a child, just like today walking around and cleaning. It forces me to admit that life as we know it is a mystery, about which we know nothing. Time's a-flying, ain't it? We try, try to tag it, get an idea, and it just mocks at our efforts.

They brought finally the horse for the trader from Erfurt, the only guy amongst the travelers who claims he can't wait. He bought it for an absurd amount of money, with the saddle and the rest of it. Packed light things most necessary, I understand, and now he just departed. The rest of us stay until Reiner gets good enough to drive the coach again. I still feel a little bit sleepy, and I begin to think that it might be the wine I've already drunk. I let my head fall back a little, closed my eyes…

Carla then brought me some soup. Light chicken broth, with a bit of carrots in it, did me a lot of good. I pushed the plate toward the center of the table and reached out for the etui. I didn't open it for a moment. I let the eyes of my imagination see Albert telling me about inks he makes; about what a complex medium that is; how many solvents, dyes, resins; how much of particulate matter; and how all that affects the appearance when dry. I've been, because he had invited me, in his lab; but it did not seem to be what a typical lab of our time usually is. I think in his case the research goes on more in his head than anywhere else. He seeks not a particular mineral, salt, etc. He seeks a recipe… yes, the final recipe, and I don't really know what for, what that is or might be that they are all after (should I perhaps say *we?*). I see him now: he looks ahead, at nothing in particular, deep in thought.

"Die-based inks are generally much stronger than pigment-based ones and can produce much more color of a given density per unit of mass. But if the solvent isn't quick enough, they bleed at the edges of the image. There are ways to avoid that, certainly, it's not impossible. But it's difficult."

I know he isn't talking about writing only. Drawing incunabula and such. No.

Meanwhile I opened the etui and pulled out the pieces of parchment with his writing on them. The lettering has golden hue; there is some red in there somewhere too. I wish he were here.

I read,

> *Secunda via es ex ratione causae efficientis. Invenimus enim in istis sensibilibus esse ordinem causarum efficientum, nec tamen invenitur, nec es possibile, quod aliquid sit causa efficiens sui*

ipsius; quia sic esset prius seipso, quod es impossibile. Non autem est possibile quod in causis efficientibus procedatur in infinimtum. Quia in omnibus causis efficientibus ordinatis, primum est causa medii, et medium es causa ultimi, sive media sint plura sive unum tantum, remota autem causa, removetur effectus, ergo, si non fuerit primum in causis efficientibus, non est prima causa efficiens, et sic non erit nec effectus ultimus, nec cause efficientes mediae, quod patet esse falsum. Ergo est necesse ponere aliquam causam efficientem primam, quam omnes Deum nominant.

I wish I could ask him about Thomas. And how he died. I know that, but I still would like to hear it from him one more time. One more time? We have actually never spoken about that. I never dared to pry into Albert's sadness depth. Never. Although had I asked him about the details, I know for a fact he would have told me at least what I have already known: his second stay in Paris and his quarrelsome time with the people who were *pro as well as contra* Averroistas, the second grand condemnation by Etienne Tempier which aimed at both—Aristotle as well as Averroes (God's doing reaches far beyond any principles Averroes' as well as Aristotle's)— and then Italy, where the weakness still developed, his levitations, and the incessant writing, finishing the *Summa Theologiea*, which he had the honor to have placed on the altar together with the Bible. Reginald de Piperno begging him to come back to work and he refusing to dictate. The straw. His levitations again. Talks. And then he died. All the talks about poison. And I see Albert's face looking into the depths of the past, trying to return the belongings of the death back to life, to see what could never be seen so far… Albert wasn't afraid to descend to hell or ascend to heaven. Hell no!

FRANCE

ZWEIFLER

Walking along these streets gave me, at some point, the impression, not quite clear at first (neither are these the words I would use to express it right then and there), that I was in the middle of exceptional beauty, unknown to me so far. We just got to Avignon. The day was cloudless, people were dancing and singing. We went all over to see, admire the seen, wanting more. It sure is one of the most beautiful cities I've ever seen. I thought that until now about Jerusalem and I have to say I didn't much change my mind up until now, and yet… I also realize that I left these parts when I was still a child, and how little a child sees (seeing reportedly so much!). And what is seeing? I'm trying to think what I would say… Certainly that it has to do with how the direct perception affects the long-term memory. There are those things that in our memory are more beautiful than the ones without a particular subject, and *vice versa*. I can remember sunrises, for instance, in places I could name now as well as I could back then, and I can remember with the tiniest details the sunrise in Smyrna that day after we had arrived there. I still see Giscard's face, his eyes, half-closed, his lids a bit swollen…

Then I was sitting with Guy at the table in the inn we ate in and would also later stay the night over, talking at the table with all those people around us, not giving a damn. And it was from him, Guy, where I got some idea of the city's history. We both spoke French, which I spoke ever since I was born—I think I mentioned that already somewhere, but this must have been the first time I really had a lesson in the history of France firsthand, as it was happening. I was listening to him with full concentration, all tense, as he was only now explaining to me that we have come to this country to maybe help those of ours who got arrested up there in the north, as heretics, who by torture were forced to confess to things that are really bloodcurdling, and the real mechanism behind all that is the fact that the kingdom of Acre fell, that our influence in the—what was called—Outremer, is now nil. That, and then, the debts, terrible debts of Philippe le Beaux (I've heard also *le belle*, which doesn't make much sense from the point of view of the French grammar, but just might express his real personality a lot better), debts which shall never be paid. There's no way, economically speaking, that he may find a way of doing it at some point in the future, so this is how he solves the problem: kill the creditor. They are now in the dungeons of Paris—Jacques de Molay, Godfroy DeCharney and a host of others who have been arrested under the same accusation. Worse, under torture they confessed, and it doesn't matter that under that type of torture anyone would confess to having done anything—including crucifying our Lord personally. There is, well, there was a papal bulla from the time when Bernard de Clairvaux was on our side, granting that we do not have to respond to any civil authority's accusations, but that's been done away with by Clement V. What chances do we have? Do we have any chances? I don't know.

Guy is silent for a while, just drinking the wine, and then looks at me again (looks me deep in the eye, and in his I see fear).

"I brought you here because, although born in Outremer, you're French, and you explicitly wanted to visit your country—"

I interrupt him. "No! and No! I was born right here, in Avignon. They came here, my mother with the big belly already. She let me out shortly after coming down here. Only after my birth, we're talking months here, taken over there by both of my parents. Just going back home. No, I wasn't born in Outremer."

"Oh!" he says. And then, "So much the more, as we talked on several occasions, we need to see Paris, see the cathedrals and other marvels only France has produced in the whole of Europe, and I agreed with you all the same in that you should." He has a sip, deep in thoughts. "See, from what I found out so far—and believe you me, it's not easy—people are afraid, even to talk about these things. We may not have any chance whatsoever, and the whole thing may turn out plain dangerous. See, there is the fear of death, which isn't that strong in our case." (A question I had all the time was why was he saying *we* all along? What *we* did he actually mean?)

"And then there is the fear of certain kinds of death, which most of the time we can't even imagine in a detailed way. Then when you get the leaks, just hearing the common whispers about it, you get goose bumps, and your hair stands on ends. I wouldn't wish that kind of death to anybody, even my worst enemy." He slowly lifts up his cup and takes a sip. Obviously, the place of my birth isn't all that important to him. "And this is what we are risking here. From the very beginning, which is to say 1305, the date of his coronation in Lyon, Clement V was subservient to the French monarchy. Which means, of course, Philip le Beaux, our mortal enemy—from the very moment he realized he wasn't ever gonna be able to pay what he borrowed, he modified the papal bullas in such a manner that they didn't mean anything anymore. St the times Bernard of Clairvaux was amongst us, we, the Templars, had certain prerogatives, get it? Then those prerogatives were gone for good. Question?"

"Have you ever been a knight?"

He suddenly doesn't look good. "You know, I mean general empathy to what happened to them…That's why I'm saying *we*… We, that's most everybody these days."

I just nodded. Didn't feel like a petty quarrel.

He regained his former composure. "Now we had nothing to protect us in judicial sense, good Lord, in any sense. Not a thing. From the moment the bullas have been tampered with, we are just people like everybody else, and they can deal with us as they please. And they do too. Most of us from among those more significant ended up in Paris's dungeons, and so we are back to the question of if we can do something about any of this and what, see? If there's an option, what is it? Regular fight would mean war with France, and we don't want that. We are no match any which way you slice it. And we don't mean any harm to our country now, do we? This is just one thief with the support of another. Just as St. Paul says, we are dealing with dark forces in high places. It's not the whole church, not all the Catholics, not the entire anything. In this particular case just two miserable ones, bent on destruction, because there is no other solution for them, no other exit out of the situation they have created by lack of moderation, lack of responsibility—like little children who want something right now, and they will get it, regardless if it is affordable for them or not. Worry they will later—well, actually parents are the ones to worry, parents, not they themselves. Now you can see how they worry—Jacques paying. And with him, we all are. And from what I found out so far here, in Avignon, your chances to join us, I mean the rest of us of what's left of the order, are growing. And growing. And, friend, my advice to you would be whoever exactly might you be, whatever your rank, take off those clothes. Put on something regular and inconspicuous, and don't say a word about Templars to anyone, not a word that you ever knew anyone of us. Goes without saying that you yourself have been one of us at a time. Terror causes mistrust, so I wouldn't trust anyone. You hear? Anyone!"

I told him Peter wept bitterly after the cock had cried for the third time, and I wouldn't want to repeat that.

"There is a chance," he said, pensive.

"Yes?"

"I've no idea if there really is anything to it, but see, I met this guy, some time ago, at the bridge, who had a lot of sympathy for the Templars—not really knowing much about us—and he turned out to be somebody of import in the castle. I told him most of what I knew. Of what I just told you. He looked sad to me, you know. Like he had compassion for us and wanted none of the Parisian Philip's court. I don't know…"

"Guy?"

"Yes?"

"Do you remember the guy back in Acre, or rather in our house there, remember Father's castle, nighttime, after super, I think his name was Armand…"

"Dead. Died in Acre's siege, on the rampart. I saw him die."

I didn't know what to say. We were just sitting there, he and I, two particles of sadness and anguish, both of us seeking feverishly a solution that didn't seem to be available at any rate. Just the night and its silence enveloping us, until Guy proposed a walk.

"To where?"

"Doesn't matter," he said. "The bridge…?" "Sure," I said. "Let's go!"

Outside, the spring night flooded us with the smells of budding life, awaking one more time to do what it's been doing for thousands and thousands of years: forcing one to reflect if there was a purpose, any purpose to it. Millions of stars up there, giving one vertigo. We were going down the street, and the view between the dark, sleeping houses on both sides was the only one available. And yet it was forcing questions, imposing anxiety, making one feel strange.

"Guy?"

"Yes?"

"Is there any grand picture to all that? What do you think?"

"See, that's giving up. That's giving in. That's sin. 'Cause if you say no to your question, then why bother? Job sits on the pile of dunk scraping pus off his body with everyone he ever cared about dead and the thought of giving up doesn't even cross his mind. Why? Because of the grand picture he believes in. That's faith. Strength. Sense. We—you and I—are right now here, not that far yet in any possible sense. All of it is just a beginning. Prelude to something we don't quite anticipate yet. And you're not a weakling! Hell, you're not!" I'm trying to think back about that day, that evening; and today it's hard to imagine how much perseverance his attitude must have had, considering what I found out about him later. I think it was Giscard who saw him right, somehow, from the very first moment. None of us did.

We were just about at the river. Rhone was almost ideally tranquil, reflecting the sky truly like a silver mirror, reproducing the miracle above us. The night was soft and warm. I felt his hand on my shoulder.

"Doesn't this tell you something? That there's gotta be something else, that it all has to have some sense." "Guy?"

"Yes?"

"It tells me—always did—that I am too small for anything. I am in the world that isn't mine. That the two of us have been mismatched. This world. This sky, this night, this spring has been organized for somebody else. See, Guy?"

"Yes?"

"How about you?"

"I think it's an illusion. It overwhelms for a purpose. It's not too big. It only makes impression that it is. For you to put yourself together. Get up and fight."

"And win?" "Sometimes…"

I asked him if he had ever known somebody, anybody, who would have won, and he answered me nothing. We were standing there at the river, near the famous bridge, surrounded by this warm spring night and its velvety softness did not agree with the situation that got us here. I thought about Paris, about the process, about Jacques de Molay. We were standing there at the beginning of the bridge, silent, but inside of me there was a quarrel going, which couldn't be quenched by soft nights in southern spring. People I cared about were dying because of ugly greed represented by just one fellow who happened to have been elected a king and who was no bloody good compared to those from the past who entered the history of the country as the ones to be remembered. This fellow was a poor dunce of no use to anyone. Then why? Why would great people, supermen like de Molay, die because a nothing like that wanted them to? This world, as I had known it so far, was no bloody good, but so far I haven't seen so much cruel nonsense that every fiber of my body would revolt against. Father would talk, and quite often at that, about the existence of God and how that very existence has been proven by this or that thinker against God's invisibility. Hell, the terrible nonsense is to me the best proof of it being used as a test ground—all this beauty, this overwhelming awe of what is out there confronted with the half-silent, stinking fart that our life is, proves to me everything. Basic product of life seem to be our tears, those that really roll down our cheeks as well as those swallowed down and never shown to anybody, under the sky which convinces us that we are no different than the ants dying under our shoe without even our knowledge about it. I told Guy that. He kept on nodding but for a while didn't say anything. Then he looked at me.

"Get going. Tomorrow, get rid of the cloak, never as much as mention the order, and get thee going. That's all." I had met Guy in Smyrna (before that, briefly, back in the castle of my father near Jerusalem), where he stopped for a while on his escape from Acre and from where we travelled together to Brundisium aboard the aforementioned trireme. Then to northern Italy, in a cart driven by oxen, only to cross over into France. Father bought at the border couple of horses, and we went to Avignon. That night, I spent the night in the inn we were together in. Next morning I took off for Paris. I never saw him again. But right now—I guess I'm wrong—shortly before we'd go, he related more to Giscard than to us…This encounter just stayed with me as a memory, which is rather pleasant and a definite part of the story I intend to deliver. To whom? I really didn't think about that. I just think that whoever might be out there should know about it. Should know what really happened. That somebody should separate chaff, of which there is so much, from wheat, of which there's so little. And nobody seems certain what is what here.

FATHER

There's something in the air; people talk about the devil, that his time has come, that we are in the days of the revelation. That's more or less what we were discussing yesterday at our night meeting. Is it possible? God allows the revelation of John to happen as reality, because he has mercy on us, wants us to get out of this valley of tears, to live like we once were meant to live, not in the swamp, trying to merely survive, defend what is divine in us in manners that are simply ridiculous at times. No, live: praising the Lord, in goodness, success, forgiveness, upliftment and completion. Those magnificent cathedrals—Chartres, Paris, Reims, Amiens, Rouen, Evreux—all of them built at the same time, does that have a significance? Maybe it does. Maybe it is just a defense against the shadows of the night; maybe they mean the white wings of hope, which shall carry us one more time to the very end?

The news from Paris is excruciating. There is no way that the kingly court could possibly satisfy our debt. We are all beginning to realize that there is no other way to interpret what is happening and that it may have only one outcome: wiping off the order. Wiping it off completely because we once have been this world's bankers, and our debtors are now bankrupt, and that with a bad name not for them but for us. We shall probably be the ones who invited the devil into this world on a grant scale, and it is thanks to us that he feels now quite comfortable in Paris. We have brought children into this world, which at the time seemed to be a good idea, a normal thing anyway. Am I responsible for whatever might be abnormal about their coming into this world? Maybe we should restrain? Not do the usual stuff we do? Huh?

There are those who work and there are those who never will. Those who work get roof overhead (somehow we are all afraid of rain) and something to put on the table (hunger is one of the more convincing things in this life, one of the saddest ones too). Strangely, those who work have no say, and those who never worked rule; they live in palaces, they represent the governments, and they will never give up what they've got—kings, popes, vicars of God—on Earth. Really? Did someone tell him about it, did he agree? Is there any way to ask him about his opinion in this matter? Meanwhile, having influence on the education, they turn it into a joke. Who, for instance, knows how to read Latin or Greek today? What the hell for? Can't you be intelligent without Latin or Greek? You sure can! Then why aren't you? Why in the earthly hell are you such friggin' piece of greedy stupidity? Huh?

Now a little bit about my own activities down here: our meetings, conferences, reports of findings. General analysis of our situation as of today. What might be still our chances of salvation? Can anyone thing of something?

Looking at all those people at the table since afternoon until late at night, I thought I was going to have to place an order for at least nice twenty-five wooden chairs, elegant and comfortable, just as I saw them displayed at the L'ébeniste shop all the way down, close to the river. The back support carved in just one piece of oak, with flower pattern—it didn't look comfortable to me until I myself sat down in it; it was really great. Under one's butt there's a leather cushion with some kind of a sponge of maritime origin. He told me he gets those from Marseille; his family has a business down there. He also told me those chairs are his mainstay; they are really sought after. He sends them as far as Bordeaux on the west side and Strasbourg in the east. I told him I needed few days to think. But already there, inside his shop, I knew I would get twenty-five of those. He'll need a couple of months to fulfill the order.

Getting up at yesterday's meeting, Lou, massaging his lower back area, told us—well, started to tell us—about Paris. We believe him, every word he says, because we know he has access to the kingly court and what he tells us is what had been pronounced before—by the people up there, people according to whose will things happen in this country. And not only in this country, everywhere but wherever it might be we can only follow. There were times—yes, times—when things were happening because one of us had said something. Those were times of Bernard de Clairvaux, when he was still alive and well. Those times are now gone forever. Finishing his report, Lou addressed me. We needed, if we were to see our assembly again, a set of new chairs—a hell of a lot more comfortable than the ones we had now. If you sit for a few hours, it's not your head that is at the lead—the opposite, the pain that dictates what is being said comes from the other end.

Brief laugh went over the assembled—like a wind in midsummer goes over a field of wheat, a sough, quick, frank—but also quickly subdued to what is a lot more important in being: what we are here for. I have children, and it's for them I do a lot of what I do, more important than anything else. They are the future of France.

This here is my town; this is—and I shall always remember that—where I was born. My first eye opening took place right here. And right here I remember myself running along the old, ancient street yet the Romans had built. Toward the river, there are other gamins just like me. The noise is universal, must be the same anywhere in the world. Then there is the miracle of the river, sun breaking in the wavelets, blinding. The water on one's skin with deep tan. That can't be easily forgotten. Would that be it?

We remember our beginnings with such clarity only when we touch our end. I went to Outremer. I lived there. I had a wife. She died. We had kids. We built our home there. With the oldest, we came back here so he may be born in France and not where the devil tells one "Good night." And yet our castle is there. Now destroyed. Burnt. And then we came here for good; we came because there was nothing to go back to, and all of it happened so and so many years ago. It seems like yesterday. Like there is a very little time between today and the day of our arrival here. And that's close to twenty years, goodness…a lifetime. I can feel it. I do. The end is approaching. We have no influence on the beginning, and we shall have none on the end—it will come, with prayer or with curse. And maybe that's the only thing that is up to us. I think I'll pray.

I'm here for the second time. Smyrna is for me what Father intended it to be: something unforgettable—not a city, more of like one in the Western world, with more or less tradition from the past, with houses concentrated at one point where certain amount of people live over a longer period of time, calling themselves inhabitants of this city. Hell, no! Smyrna is a place where everything mixes with everything else—there is a present (I am here now, aren't I?) but there is also a past as alive as I am, whose blood I can hear pulsate in the arteries of life as I know it.

I'm now in a narrow street the houses on which must go back so many years that a comparison with Paris, for instance, may seem only—I'd say—strange. I hear a laugh. Paris is not in the league. As are so many other centers of our European culture. I clear my throat. Shockingly many. I am here at the cradle. The world is young, doesn't know yet how to speak, and it has to be changed; its voice takes a longer getting used to. Oh yes, more effort, more patience than it usually does. Everything around seems virgin, including air we breathe; and although many a thing may seem laughable (as is usual case with life anywhere, now isn't it?) we suddenly prefer to preserve our seriousness.

There's a couple ahead of me walking in the same direction, a little slower than I do. I'll pass them in a moment, in a nick of time. But seeing the smoke, we all stop. Right up ahead a thick black smoke rising quickly up toward the sky is like a command for everybody in this ancient street to stop. Now I'm trying to deliberately speed up my pace to get the couple ahead to do some questioning, but they suddenly (seeing my intentions) speed it up too, and so does an old guy on the other side of the street. So that I am left with a youngster in the door on my side, who remains immobile, as if deliberately waiting for me is my impression. As I approach him, he says (seriously, not a trace of a smile on his face):

"You think is a fire, right? One of those old houses, dried up like pepper is burning, now wouldn't you says just that?" He speaks

Greek that is a little bit difficult for me. The very little I know is a lot more ancient. But I know *what* he's saying.

"And what is it?"

He nods at the same time squeezing his mouth almost in a single line, shapeless. "Sometimes it's just that, a fire. Certainly. Wouldn't be able to tell how many cases our fire department slept over because they thought just that. But no! That is something else!"

"Like what?"

"Who knows exactly? But it is here and now. And it never needed a definition to be anywhere. Just like us—it just is."

At some level up there seems to be a suck of some kind; that's where the soot-black stream of smoke suddenly ends. "Everything ancient enough attracts that presence. We can only pray. I tried to find another solution, but there is none. Not really."

"Everything ancient enough…" "Yawp!"

I was trying to look around, but he didn't give up.

"Did you now that Homer resided here? Homereum is nearby."

"Yes," I said. "My father told me that. He loves Greek and Greece. We finally talk Greek, don't we?"

"I was about to ask, where are you from?" "I'm French."

"Oh…"

ALVA

In Brundisium, Father bought a cart with a horse. (And right away a doubt appears: was it a horse or an oxen? I think it was an oxen; horse came in later—I'll get to that.) All our things went onto it, and so did we. And slowly, at the speed of a single-oxen carriage, we started our journey toward Rome. We stopped and stayed overnight in villages along the Via Appia until we got to the swamps, and there we had to travel for a while in the stench of decay, which I didn't think I was gonna be able to forget soon.

Father saw Rome before, so he wanted to just rest, whereas we were ready for exploration. We were warned about the thieves, most everywhere; everything that could be taken from us had to be secured with a string or something of that nature so the thief would leave it and run. We followed the advice and didn't lose anything. We stayed in Rome just a few days then we started moving west to Avignon where the Templars were supposed to meet (Father's group). That took again a few days. At some point, a guy grabbed me indecently, not realizing that I wasn't alone. And I saw brother grabbing him right under his chin and then somewhere at his belly, and then up he went, way above brother's head, where from he started flying toward the wall on the other side of the street. His body hit it, and down he went; he looked like dead, strangely bent on the stones. I told brother that I considered what I have seen a terrible exaggeration. In my opinion, it would have been enough to tell him off. Brother disagreed. He is strangely feisty for a man of his strength—only too often, I have to regret. When it gets rough, it is in a way only the other facet of getting smooth. We stayed there a bit longer. We kept on looking. I got the idea that Rome is a marvel almost at the same time we had to leave. Sitting on the wagon, I felt deep regret that we couldn't stay. But we could not! It was up to Father, and he categorically said no.

So we were again on the wagon, moving at the speed of a snail—this time west, toward Avignon. We've actually never found out why this particular group chose Avignon for the place of that meet-up. But they did. Our life there restarted as it had before— the monotony of long years we have spent there in Avignon. Our situation has never been clear; people have sources of income, they can explain if asked where their livelihood lies—yes, they can, for the most part. I didn't have the faintest idea. I for one certainly couldn't explain a thing. And then some, what, twenty years later, Father just disappeared. For a day at first and then for weeks, and then I knew that the curse of this place that I felt from the day one finally materialized: that something finally happened that nobody will be able to change—something like death, unchangeable, irrevocable, and making hair stand on ends. And then a rumor came (I couldn't tell now how it's got to us, but it did) that Father and a quite sizable group of people from Outremer were really already dead, taken out all at once or close to it, and burned at stakes outside of town. Who was I to complain to? Was it possible for me to understand something like that? A man I truly loved, a man who never harmed anything that lived without a profound reason for it, suddenly murdered like that—no court, no judge, and all of it in that terrible surreptitious secretiveness that spoke for itself. I felt ice around my heart. I felt horror-stricken. I felt that something was going on, which couldn't be explained on the bases of what we knew so far about life. And just what were we faced with here? What was it I was meant to learn? That our life now and then just doesn't make any sense?

I was taken then (it was several days after that) to a place outside the ramparts of the city where the stakes had been built and where they died. I just stood there—perhaps it was the first time in my life that I couldn't pray; I was just standing there, and everything around me was beyond my understanding, and nothing seemed to make sense. He came here, to his country whose business he was protecting, guaranteeing with his own life that it would go the best way it could possibly go. And this, a small pile of ash, was his remuneration. I didn't know which individual pyre had been his; there were several, so from the first one that was close to me I picked up a piece of wood carbonized by fire. That was going to be my reminder of him—keepsake. Later on I found out that it had happened the same way, more or less, in the whole of France. France expelled Jews and destroyed Templars. Not one of the people I got to talk about it to could agree with the next as to why.

Yet a couple of weeks later brother disappeared in the same manner. Just vanished. Nobody would inform us what actually was happening. It was Giscard who found out (however he did) that they took brother north, to a fortress named Chinon, for interrogation. He was tortured, until he confessed. Confess what? Whatever they wanted him to sign.

We packed up the same day and started the journey north, to where Chinon was. After a long push-pull, I got to the girl whose name was Simona and who agreed, for one of the sacks full of gold nuggets we had from Father, to get brother out. With that little gift, she was able to better arrange her life than I could with what we had left. But she did get him out; we were in a hug, brother and I, that evening, for a time unnaturally long—as Giscard, who was also there, described it to me. Then what was left was a plan for the immediate future: what would we be doing in France considering all we knew so far. We've decided that evening to go to Paris. In a city that big, it would be much easier to hide than in some kind of a small village where we would be picked up almost in no time. We were different than the people here—the clothing we had on, our customs, the way we moved and spoke (the last should probably be the first of all). But in Paris, nobody would notice; there were thousands upon thousands of students, adventurers, scholars, and such from all over the world, and it would really take a miracle to track us down. We started moving. There was nothing to wait for. By moving fast, we could only gain. And really soon after that, I saw la Notre Dame and la Seine. And so many other things. My God, so many…

MARGUERITE

Yesterday, the lords from the king showed up at the *beguinage* with the kingly warrant to enter our building if I didn't come out. But no harsh words fell; they were polite. The carriage waiting in the street wasn't also what they use to transport heretics—I don't know much about these things but it reminded me of the carriages aristocracy uses to travel in the city.

"The great William of Paris wants to talk to you himself," said one of them. "Your writing becomes famous. You can forget Cambray. Guillaume has been removed definitely from the whole thing."

The hotel they transported me to was also a palace rather than anything else. The walls inside were dripping of gold (plaster, I think, covered with gold leaf), and in the middle of that strange framework was Christ-crucified relief looking halfway as painting and halfway as sculpture, so touching that a simple look would materialize for you that horrible death: the body sheer bone, the ribcage covered with skin looking more leather than skin, his face, also bone and skin, simply sad—the sadness of death, all of it maintained very consequently in dark greens. I shuddered.

"You're impressed, aren't you? Unknown German master. My time in Köln. I bought it for here, because I got as impressed as you are now, or maybe even more than you just did. Then it was brought here and installed the way you see it. What do you think?"

I did not see him at that point; he was just a voice. "Magnificent. It's hard to believe…"

"It is, isn't it?" "It is."

He was watching me all the time was my impression—feeling, I should probably say. Like a hawk. He wanted to know everything about me, I thought. I felt very uncomfortable, maybe because I couldn't see him.

Under my feet was a floor such that I was fearful to walk on, simply enforcing carefulness on one's part. They (these carpenters) sure knew how to use wood, different kinds of wood, inlaid into one another, giving one the impression that one is walking in heaven already, that a sinner like me doesn't deserve such a place at all. Then I was left in the room all by myself, or so I thought. (Now I'm confused: was it the same room or have I been transferred somewhere else? If so, it was just like the rest of it so far, sumptuous, emanating luxury, a world totally different from everything I knew so far in my life. And there I was, left alone. Yes, I am a little bit more certain of my memory. Not that much later, though, a man entered—a man in a certain age: gray hair, gray beard, a brown habit on him (I think that's Franciscan habit, although I'm not sure; I couldn't tell). His eyes looking at me were reminding me of water reflecting sky on a day when blue turns almost gray; slight smile was erring on his lips, as if he knew something that I didn't. He was obviously measuring me up, calculating perhaps the rest of the visit, the conversation we would have. He sat down behind a desk that was in itself something I wouldn't be able to forget soon—a work of incredible complexity, not one piece of wood left in its straight functional form but all turned into scrolls, some of which covered with gold leaf and some left in black mahogany after black polishing, the top with papers, marble polished to mirror-shine. He was sitting behind it, I realized while I was taking in all the details, leaning back, looking relaxed, although I knew he wasn't that. He was seeking words, proper beginning of the conversation, of which he obviously wasn't certain. Then cleaning his throat, looking the other way, he said, "I asked you here because I wanted to know directly from you about certain things I keep hearing—well, hearsay means nothing. Nothing can be based on hearsay, so last week, I was at the western façade of Notre Dame myself, listening to you…"

He looked straight at me now. "D'you know what I'm talking about?"

"No," I simply said.

"You talk to people, to a whole lot of people, about God, about things holy, for which normally you have to have authorization of the church. Who authorized you or just had given you permission to talk about such things to a large gathering like that?"

"I read the Bible. I think I hear his voice. And what I hear I'm trying then to deliver to people. That's all."

"The problem here is a common one. How do you know it's his voice? How do you know—just how does one know, ever, in any of those events—it is God who speaks to one? Religion is like a child. It is fragile and can be injured, distorted so easily—well, that oftentimes it happens without our even knowing about it, you know."

"He never comes to me. I never see him like I see you now, sire, but I hear his voice exactly like I hear yours, and it is an experience of goodness. I think one can feel the difference between good and evil. It is given to us, it is part of our blood."

"When you listen to all those witches before they get burned, well, some of them sound like the devil himself, like what we find in the gospel in the description of the ones who are truly possessed and torn by the devil. But then some others sound quite differently, mild and soft, I tell you, and one would swear that they have nothing to do with evil. They say things which at first glance seem to proceed from good. You lack that type of experience, so it doesn't surprise me that you say what you just said.

You would need to be there and listen. That might be the learning kind of experience. That would, I bet, change your mind and teach you caution."

What I said to that surprises me now, and I didn't know back then, and I doubt if I shall ever know, why I said it. I said it nevertheless, as if I had no say at the moment. None at all. "You know how many there are who have no place to sit, except the naked ground, a stone, something like that, for you, one you, to be here and sit at that desk, on that chair. As he says in the gospel, woe to you Pharisee, lawyers, and scribes, hypocrites. For you are as graves which appear not, and the men that walk over them are not aware of them. Woe unto you also ye lawyers for ye load men with burdens grievous to be born, and ye yourselves touch not the burden with one of your fingers. Woe unto you! For ye build the sepulchers of the prophets, and your fathers killed them. Therefore also said the wisdom of God, I will send them prophets and apostles, and some of them they shall slain and persecute. And that is the case now, isn't it?"

He was looking at me. A moment longer. All of the weight of his sight, which reminded me of a pond on a gray day, concentrated on me, unchangeably. On the desk before him there was paper covered with writing, a huge glass inkwell with a feather. He must have been writing before I was brought in.

"I read your book. You proclaim the total loss of the ego. I'm not me, at some point, and you're not you. We join God. It's not my will, not anymore. He wills through us. Whatever I do, if I still do anything, I do because he wills it. If I'm not me, how do I know who that is? And who am I anymore? Huh? Our religion doesn't say anything about losing one's ego. Its puffiness yes, but not ego itself. Look, I don't want to join some cosmic monster I know absolutely nothing about, become one of his most basic parts. You got that? That's one of the differences. And that's why you're a heretic injuring the true faith. Because you make it repellant, repulsive, distasteful. Think about it for a moment. I know the ego is the problem. But without ego, none of us is him or herself. How then could we talk about continuation? And we want it to continue after we die, don't we? Somehow? We want to get compensated for all the tears, pains, humiliations, for all the moments when we said that it would have been better for us not to be born, don't we?"

He kept silent for a moment. Then picked up. "It's sufficiently difficult without your lies. Yours or anyone's. Then why lie? What is there that justifies you, the unlicensed, unwarranted preachers that make it all a lot harder by killing or weakening the only consolation?"

He picked up a silver bell from the desk and shook it.

The door opened, and a servant entered, bowing to him. "Bring in the meister!" he said, and the servant disappeared only to come back in a moment, ushering in a man—tall, gray-haired also, with a beard, and almost the same watery gray eyes. He stopped beside the desk. He seemed to me strangely concentrated on my person.

"Tell her!" the grand inquisitor said. Meister smiled.

"The main difference between what you tell people and what I tell them I see in our understanding how we have ideas of the world…You say we are the cradle of life. It gets inside us through the senses and remains there like inside a storage room, a cradle of sorts, and hence that the world exists because in it we age, become an end that is closer and closer to what we are supposed to be in the end, and without which we couldn't ever become that. And I am trying to say that we bring a lot of stuff, if not all of it, with us at birth, and only then *elenxis* and *mayeusis,* which our life affords us, bring the stuff we already contain in our souls out into the worldly side of our being. Now, your approach lets us explain this world and its sad existence very easily. Mine not so. But then again, the Bible tells us that the world is not here to be explained, that you should trust. Believe, love, and trust. I have no doubt that you believe. None. I read your book, and I listened to you very carefully. Now how about trust? Does it make any difference? See? What, in your opinion, is the final reason for our being here?"

I felt, quite suddenly, a lot of sympathy for that man. He was here to try to understand; and as he stood there like that, taking my side in all this, as I felt about his position so far, he seemed to be a goodly mediator between me and William, who, cold and indifferent as he was, did not seem to have anything in common with what we both claimed to represent (unlike the naiveté of Cressonssart; this was wisdom speaking, right there feeling of superiority, which could only do damage to faith). He picked up after only a short while, without the other telling him to.

"You seem to be affected by what is here in Paris so popular lately, and that is Arabic by origin and with which the church demonstrates a decided position: no! That was some time ago Avicenna, very far away, beyond Outremer, and later much closer to us Averroes in Spanish Cordoba. I saw their texts most everywhere. It's like an epidemic in this town. I disagree that their interpretation is materialistic—well, at least doesn't have to be.

Matter might be interpreted as a particular case of something else we don't quite understand, and so the whole world might just be a specific idea of God beyond our understanding altogether, but the church already developed its position on their ontology and that of the Arabs, and I don't think it'll ever change that. Your medical ability and knowledge seem to confirm your affinity with Averroes and Maimonides, doesn't it? The grand inquisitor"—pointing at William—"writes about it right now in fact. He explains the reasons why, with all the appearances of being right it is hopeless, it kills our expectations, it weakens in the end, to say the least, our trust. Whatever in terms of ability you may prove to people, like you do in front of the churches. I saw you at Reims."

"I don't have any medical knowledge or ability," I said.

He didn't look surprised. "Of course that's what you would say. I expected that."

"Sir, I don't have any special ability! No, and one more time, no!"

"If someone touches a sick person, and that person that very moment becomes healthy, complete, what would you call it? And I, with these very eyes of mine, saw that happen, huh?"

William stood up then; I thought he, for some reason, had enough. He certainly knew how to be haughty, Supercilious, he looked at me, like I was at the bottom of a precipice. "I meant this thing here as a warning. Times are such that you might be apprehended without any warrant—well, without anything at all. Heresy is a direct attack on the king. And the final sentence would also be very easy to pronounce, and the preliminary sentence, which would put you in a dungeon, obtainable at once. Now! If I but wanted to. Don't you ever forget that! We shall see each other again, and you shall be asked to recant, which I would really advise you to do. Because if you don't, God, I wouldn't wanna be in your shoes, my child. We all have seen that many times, here, in this city, as elsewhere. Right? Have you?"

"Yes, I have seen time and time again what the church is capable of."

"Big mouth won't help you, you know? And inside that body is just one set of bones. And you have only one, this very body, with no replacement, got it? Only one!"

"I know that," I said.

"Good. Good-bye now. As said before, I shall see you again. Think about what was said today. Think about it intensely, and it may save you a lot of suffering. Don't forget. Ever!"

The door opened one more time, and the same servant entered, motioning both of us, Eckhart and me, into the other room. As soon, though, as we got there, he fell on his knees before me, crying and sobbing (the servant), begging me for the life of his daughter who was there in his house very sick. The doctors couldn't do a thing. The only daughter he had was dying right that very moment, and with all his connections here, as well as in the kingly court, he couldn't do a thing. I was standing there, in all the sumptuousness of that room (here, too, the walls were all in gold leaf over incredibly complex sculpting, the niches covered with high-class oil painting, in some of them huge mirrors framed in gold) and looking at the misery before me, and I will never know why I said in the end, "Your daughter lives. Go in piece!"

And he started kissing my shoes, which I then forbade him. Made him get up.

"Is his daughter okay?" Eckhart asked me already in the main hallway, with him gone.

I told him the truth. "I don't know," I said. "But so far it's been like that: I would say something, never actually knowing why, or what am I actually saying, more as if something or somebody was talking through me, and it would then turn out to be true. To my own amazement too." "Fascinating," he said, "how it was with our Lord. What do you think? There's that fragment in Luke, I think, where he doesn't know who touched him. That's quite like it, isn't it?"

"I don't know..." "I don't either."

"Sometimes I wish more than anything else that I could ask him and he could answer me."

"Same here! Oh yes, sir!"

"I don't think we are some kind of an exception as far as that goes, are we?"

"I guess not."

ZWEIFLER

saw, like through fog, that he bent over me, and I felt it again. I was trying to think about our Lord's torment the night before the Crucifixion and then the next day the nine hours on the cross, before he gave up the ghost. But the pain was unbearable no matter what I did. I heard my own voice of a dying raven, and the night was in onslaught, as it would suddenly stop (the guy's doing) in all those rare cases of silence. The question would come to me, in a low man's voice (abnormally low, reminding me of a screechy old machinery does at times, like a mill when the wind slows down and the old wheels, although still moving, are about to stop), a voice about our life. Are we sodomites? was the question. Hell no! I never, never ever, in my entire life, looked at another man as my sexual partner.

"No! It's a stinking lie!"

And I felt the same pain, and the night, only after a short while, came to darken what was hardly visible anyway. I wouldn't know how to describe it to someone else, the world of pain. I wouldn't know how define the time during which it takes place; how long, in other words, I have before the next question is asked. I have, at some point, given up hope. In the beginning, I thought someone was going to come and explain the absurdity of any of this. How could we spit on the cross, we, the defenders, the ones who dedicated our lives, every moment, all of them with no exception, to him and only to him? Which resulted first and foremost from our admiration of his accepting the torment, our unending admiration for his strength so different than ours. How could we trample on the cross? How could anyone be that stupid?

People like mysteries. Some believe even now we are devil-worshippers. Some repeat other kinds of nonsense because it gets attention, gathers together those who want to listen, allows the mystery to thicken, thus making it even more enjoyable.

The fact that I was suddenly reflecting on all that suggested to me that the torment paused for the time being; they didn't want us to die too fast. Nothing was clear anymore. The whole world was awash, sort of, no borders sharp, and yet I remembered that according to Saint Bernard a knight had double protection: that of his armor, which would allow him not to fear any bodily harm, as well as of his faith, which gave him power over demons and such. Oh, but times when Bernard was with us were definitely over. After the famous Friday the thirteenth, it was Clement, supposedly representing God on earth, and Philip, which was his representative for worldly affairs. And something was happening to us, which actually nobody understood. I am beginning to think that a base for existence of a state is misunderstanding (deliberate suppression of information by those who rule—for no other purpose than exercising control over the powerless, for proving to themselves that they are the masters; if consciousness is like a dog's nose, sniffing all the time, trying to make sure, they sure know how to spray pepper, how to punch and squeeze or otherwise disable the oversensitive nostrils). I wanted to stress (to howl like a wounded animal does): for no other purpose! None! To be in control, to feel that something depends on your viewpoint. There might be a lot of different purposes, but even if there's none, they'll do it anyway to satisfy that desire.

I tried to move. My legs were shackled to the end of the table I was laid on, and my hands, also shackled, at an angle, toward the other end. But then I felt the shackles loosening, and soon enough, I could move. Only to see the hell all around me: naked people hanging off the ceiling, at the wall there were crosses with human figures, emaciated, heads hanging down on their breasts; there was a guy with balls hanging down to his knees, obviously something done to them prior to my looking (I wouldn't wanna be in that guy's shoes, God); floor covered with blood, vomit and excrement; a girl, young, obviously poor, judging by her clothing, her hair unwashed for the longest time—she was the one who got me unshackled. I tried to talk, and my own voice got me scared. "Why did you do that? They'll kill you, they'll say you're a witch too!"

Her voice was like the murmur of a creek; it was in a strange discrepancy with her. She was small, kind of delicate, fragile bone, and this voice was like from the depth of the night; a shudder went down my spine.

"They are gone to eat," she answered me. "I'm here to clean. I am here, and I have enough. I want out. Out of here. Out!" She looked up at me, her eyes kind of watery blue. "I need help. Can you help me?"

"Me? How?"

The silence was a momentary interruption.

"Can you walk?" She was looking at me.

She helped me up, off that bench I was on. I was too heavy for her, obviously. But we both wanted out badly. They damaged so far my butt by trying to lift up my body off the bench on a steel spider hooked up to a chain hanging down from the ceiling, but now with a little care (a rag around my buttocks, dipped in something that seemed to have delivering properties, then pants and a shirt [that stuff was there too, right on a small wooden chair in the heads of the bench]), yes, I was able to make a few steps on my own in the end.

"Lean on me," she said. I thought vaguely she wouldn't tolerate any objections. "Now!"

We started. At the door she let me go, with my hand above my head, leaning against the stones. And then she opened it, sticking her head out of the room, looking into the darkness of the corridor. I didn't detect any movement there. Silence. Then she came back and put my arm with her both hands around her shoulder.

"Let's go!"

Outside we just kept on walking. I put my head on top of hers because there was a moment I wasn't quite aware of it wanted to fall down on my chest. Well, she didn't seem to mind. My butt was hurting me worse every minute, and I felt like lying down right there in the street. I was wondering why was there no supervision left, but then the thought came clearly to me that no one in that room, had they been loosened from their respective contraptions, was capable of moving anyhow. Had the little Simona (that was her name) not decided to end her professional carrier right then and there, choosing the least injured guy to help her doing precisely that, I too would still be on that bench (table?) awaiting more pain I was almost unable to bear with anymore (how long would it have taken before I would have signed my confession to whatever nonsense I would have been presented with?).

Moving slowly like that we got out of town, leaving behind us that fortress that now towered over everything like a nightmare without borders. And then after I had lain down on my belly, in the grass on the side of the road, and in that position I spent some time, resting. We kept on going until we got to the hut where a cripple known to Simona for several years lived; they knew each other from the distant past, when they both were yet almost children and he was abused and crippled by the same people (they found chicken bones and small bag of soot under his bed, which conformed the accusation his neighbors came up with). Today it was some kind of a communion in which he would get ready to give his life for her (and she for him), but it wasn't a relationship in the common sense—nobody knew about it these days, nobody remembered it, so nobody snooped. He gave us both to eat, and then as I was lying on my belly, he pulled my pants down, took off the rag Simona gave me yet back in the fortress, washed the wounds with some strong herbal solution that felt like fire directly applied onto my wounds, and in the end did the more proper dressing of it. Then I got my pants back. I felt that I had fever. I felt cold. I knew that everything was wrong with me. My body was damaged, and nobody might be able at that point to tell how badly. And I also knew that the only way to stay alive and, maybe at some point, come back to my full senses was now only patience.

The days were moving on slowly, like cold molasses; I'd spend time lying down, recovering, for most of the time sleeping. There was as it turned out no serious infection, which would threaten my life; so yes, it would from then on go rather fast. Simona would stay with me, and we'd talk a little bit if I wasn't asleep. Vidal (that was his name) would go out in the morning, and his main occupation as I understood what they were telling me, was begging (that was also the source of our sustenance for the time being); he'd come back in the evening bringing us the news from town, what leaked out about my disappearance among the other stories, and how they were looking for me all over the place, how the inquiry went since the day Simona and I got away.

"What do you think is the real cause of this whole chase?" "That," he'd say, "is simple to me. The king realized at some point that he was never gonna be able to pay off his debt to you, so he decided to destroy you. Declare you witches, the devil's servants, the worshippers of Lucifer. Finally, what did he do to Boniface? See, the world that's those who rule and the ruled. And it's all lies, meticulously maintained, repeated countless amount of times (as Nogaret once said, "See, a priest from Paris who held a sermon here, in our church, told us this thing from the pulpit"—that if a lie is repeated sufficient amount of times, even the liar himself will believe it, at some point, to be the truth) so the ruled wouldn't get the idea about the grand picture, whatever that might be. They think, after the big lie has been repeated sufficient amount of times as is necessary to create the faith, that their poor, miserable lives are what life in general is all about, that everything is normal, hence, and there is nothing to protest or even complain about (because it's always been like that and nothing ever changed). The base of our existence is lying, I'd say. The big lie is that we know something, that we have knowledge about anything: I about you or you about me, or both of us about life, what it is, and what it has a chance to be. That there might be somewhere life without envy, for instance, without competition, without falls pretense, where man wouldn't be a wolf to man, where man would mean more than just food for one another."

"Vidal?" I said then.

"Yes?"

"You seem to know things…How do you know any of that if you do what you do? And then tell me, what do you think about what did he need all those millions for? What did he buy for them?"

"Where do I know it from? I belong to the guild, our guild, beggars guild, and we get together and talk, and you wouldn't have any idea who might show up there, in a gathering like that. Now back to the king. His politics, I think. That costs a lot of money. Translating into reality something that came into being at first in your head, and only then once conceived you had to prove to yourself that you can translate that into reality for the others to see and envy you. Yes. That's death. Sickness. And that's also debt without end."

Right about then, Simona put on the table the now-cooked chicken Vidal had stolen in town a couple of hours ago, thus raising for me a question why did Vidal risk for stealing it the breaking of his bones on the wheel in front of the crowd. And Philip could break bones of those from whom he had stolen millions in front of an audience always of his choosing. Also in front of a crowd. I had a drumstick. And a bit of soup with sweet carrots and a little, shiny, round onion that made me laugh, now softened by cooking, that almost flew apart inside of my mouth.

"The almighty, all-knowing God cannot be challenged, right? Only the poor little Vidal will have to accept challenges, including those which include his most cruel death on that scaffold on the market of this town, to the incessant applause of its citizens. Now why is that?"

"Why?"

"You like rhetoric," Vidal said. "I do have a small problem with that."

"Do I like it? I'm not sure I do." "I think so."

I pushed my now-empty plate away from me.

At the moment of our departure for Paris, as we were saying good-bye to each other, he said, "You've got to remember and never forget…what kind of a place this is. You walk and your legs get tired, so you sit down on a tree stump or stone, whatever is there that you can use for resting a bit. And right there, a snake, a scorpion, or some other pleasure of this world is gonna bite you in the ass. If you don't die, you'll be very sick, okay? Don't forget that!"

The way to Paris was quiet. We traveled in part by foot and in part by whoever wanted to give us a ride (me and Simona, that is; she wanted to go there with me, and she couldn't be persuaded otherwise: Paris was something she wanted to see all her life). For a while it was, for instance, an oxen-driven cart moving like cold molasses; still better than walking—my butt, although incomparably better than on the first day, would still ache. Vidal told me that it might, injured this way, ache until my very last day, the worst being every weather change from sunny to rainy. Hopefully not! Be that as it may!

The way from Chinon to Paris is a long way, and when we finally got there, we both were very happy. Vidal gave us some money yet back in Chinon, not much because he didn't have much (the poor chap). But it was good for a couple of nights in a decent inn, where we could sleep in beds and eat good stuff in a restaurant. It was also possible to take a hot bath. In the evening, couple of days after that, I met an interesting fellow in the restaurant downstairs, by slightly helping him with the inn company that got a bit out of shape (usual—too much wine) and started making fun of him at first, only to brutally push him around in the end.

We sat down after it got quiet again and talked for a while. I didn't mean to pry but found out nevertheless that he was here because in the hotel he would usually find lodging while here in Paris, there were now too many people who already had paid and couldn't be thrown out. My man was a professor at the Paris University, teacher at the theology faculty. We sat there and spoke. He was of German origin and here in Paris only on invitation, living, if everything would go the way it was supposed to go in the house the university would offer him—as said before, now impossible for a few days, because of the flood, so to speak, of unexpected guests. We would sit there, drinking wine, and talk, which I enjoyed every day more and more. I told him briefly my life, not really hiding anything, including the arrest and torture as well as the fact that I came here as the member of the order, to which he expressed his major concern, fear that I would be apprehended again. He advised me to leave the country altogether, to which I said that I thought about it and just might do—that I hadn't anything decided as yet, but certainly not now. I'd like to get some more understanding of things here because it reflects so much on my own country. So I would like to sit right here for a while. Then he started, after a while of silence, telling me about his own life—and that right here, in Paris, he found something that meant a new form of life for him. Well, something at any rate he never knew so far. Feelings faced with which a human will means absolutely nothing, which before he would have never believed existed. He talked, and my curiosity grew. I asked him if he'd thought he'd leave some kind of a description of what was happening to him for the coming generations, and he said he so far never gave that a thought. I know how to write; that's what my thinking was at the moment, French as well as Latin. Father taught me. I and Father went together through most of the Golden Roman classics, some of which I knew by heart up to now. I don't know…

I see Simona less and less. Meister recommended her in a rich house where she takes care of the estate; her life changed, turned around, one could say a hundred percent, and she seems to be slightly different too. It seemed to me that she was worried that I might be discovered and, of course…Well, there's nothing to say. I owe her my life, there's no doubt about that. I'll always pray for her. And she has helped Vidal, her friend, giving him money he needed so much in order to go finally south, where according to her he always wanted to go.

Near the Notre Dame, on the other island, there are shops of a couple of copyists. I entered and bought a bunch of things. Since I didn't know much about this stuff, I asked for advice. Already advised, I bought parchment, a bottle of German ink, feathers, already precut; and thus equipped I went home. I told Meister in the evening that I just started my memoirs, that I'd like to tell most of his own story in them as I got to know, not so much mine. He was shaking his head for a longer time than usual. But he also smiled at me.

"Just don't let them get you!" was all he said, and I had a sip of the great wine we had there on the table. "Be careful!"

"I intend to live for yet a while," I told him.

"That's what I'd like to hear…That confirms that we are resilient species, and that type of resilience is very important to me."

"Now, aren't we?" I left my cup a bit up. "We are…yes, sir! We are that, no doubt!" And then I add, "You like rhetoric."

"Do I?"

"Yes, you do. And I have a small problem with that, and I think I know why."

"And why would it be, if I may ask?"

"That's one of the things I'll write about."

He kept on smiling, the cup of wine in his hand. The day was now toward the evening, and we started thinking about supper.

FATHER'S CHILDHOOD

remember a bunch of kids running down the street toward the river and then noisily getting into the water, splashing at each other, never stopping from shouting—a truly noisy little bunch. Jeez, I was one of them. Is it so long ago? Yes, if one takes a calendar in the hand, yes, it is. But when I look down my own memory, without any additional help, it seems so close I can touch it.

About two-thirds of the way to the river, there was a smithy, on the left side of the street, a place that I felt almost magically attracted to. I'd stand there, by the door, not daring to go any farther inside, and watch the miracle of the red hot iron changing shape. Into whatever those guys wanted it to change. One day an old man with long black- gray beard approached me. In his hand there was a pair of channel locks holding a spike, red hot, and he asked me if I would like to pick up a hammer and try to make something of the red hot spike he held in his hand. I nodded. He went a little back and I behind him, and as he put the spike on the anvil, I picked up the hammer and started hammering.

The spike was slowly turning into a dagger—well, a knife of some kind.

He started telling me about the steel that I was hammering, how it was made, in what type of fire, and why it would never be a great dagger, no matter what we did here on the anvil. Certain things are decided beforehand. Before you even start doing what you intend to do. I still remember his black beard with a lot of gray in that black, his eyes smiling all the time on me. Thinking about Vulcan I was reading about up in the monastery, I wasn't afraid, somehow that the temperamental god may do something bad to me down here. He was too good-hearted, too interested in what I was doing. I had a lot of questions. I remember that. I told him about the sword Father had, that you could use to cut steel spikes with, and Vulcan simply smiled. He seemed to know Father and the story of his swords. In a few days, I saw Vulcan in my house talking to Father. They were sitting at the table and smiling, both of them, drinking wine, and then with the Vulcan gone, I was told that I would be from now on in the smithy, that is in the afternoons and before noon in the monastery, slightly outside the town, where up to now I was trying to get the Latin declensions, conjugations, wording, proverbs, etc. I'd travel on horseback, and here he named the household guy who would be responsible for delivering me from one place to another. The monk was never my true friend; we never got close to each other, although I'd make a decent progress, and he spoke to my father about me rather highly. Vulcan wasn't my friend either. He was too big and too strong for that, but somehow, I'd preferred his company to that of the monk's.

In the backyard of the smithy there was a post, the height of the Vulcan more or less. He would take me there most every day and hand me the sword (a sword which was absolutely special for him, which was also his height, thereabouts, made for use with both hands and heavy like a penance in hell); and he would then, each and every time, tell me to take a swing at the post. At first the sword would just bounce back hardly leaving any marks on the wood. Then I was able to make precisely that: marks, a little deeper. He could—and he would prove it to me each time I requested such proof—take a slice of it, about one-inch thick. I would pick it up off the dirt and look at it with always the same admiration. And then a day came when I took a swing at the post, and I took a slice of it about one-inch thick, and then I picked it up off the dirt and was looking at it for a long time, with admiration that did not decrease. He kept silent, just smiling.

"How would you like," he said then, "to make a sword like this one? It's not easy. We'll be working very hard. We've never worked like that so far. It'll be days and days on end, of hammering, in different forms. Then polishing. Again a month or so. And then I give you the sword. It won't be for sale. What you say?"

Goes without saying I agreed like crazy. We started by building the oven. He put the bricks together as it would go. I would make the clay he would then glue them together. We were making the crucible together; he was showing me every detail of the preparation of the clay. The clay was then formed into a pipe about ten inches in diameter, and pieces looking a little like a sponge were put in there; that was the good steel—couldn't be turned into something less than we wanted to turn it into.

On top, glass, broken with a hammer to tiny pieces, then a bit of something he called borax. Two handfuls of a strange powder, grayish, about which he told me it was glass treated with the hammer. And then we closed it. A circle made of the same clay, dried in the sun, glued together with the body of the crucible, and baked with same clay I would make to glue together the bricks of the oven itself. The pieces of wood were introduced into the air channel, and fire was set. We pumped the bellows one after another, changing about half an hour. Day in, day out. Way into the second day, it was my turn at the bellows, after which he motioned me to stop. Here and there a blue flame would come out of the body of the oven as he started to disassemble it. The crucible was there, emitting a strange light—almost like itself had been made of light. That was when it started. He showed me forms necessary to hammer a sword, and he explained why this was gonna be worse than anything (how hard this steel was). We worked for about a month, the both of us. Toward the end of the day, he would invite me out into the backyard and try to repeat my success with the sword he had. I felt my body aching, my head far from clear; but I'd try, with sad results, until the day he would explain to me how one clears one's mind. A moment of prayer and concentration would do the trick. I was able to cut my slice again. All of a sudden.

"Oftentimes you don't have time to pray. You have to find it already fighting. Look for that one spot inside you. Focus on it. That's what you're looking for: asking God to help you to find it.

If you have proper tooling, which is what we are making right now, oh man, you can go far…" I won't forget him.

Then Birgit came. She was from a Swedish family; her father studied at the University of Paris, and that was, too, where I met her, during one of my numerous trips to Paris where Father would send me to learn. I married her. We left for Outremer where we heard about incredible possibilities. Before we left, we bought a dog, here in Avignon. The dog we bought because it was strange—had ears all the way to the floor and had a face that made me laugh. Essence of sadness. As far as I could be the judge of that, it was a very false creature too. A man like that would be called two-face. I never really liked it, but for Alva, it was a divine creature—sent to us straight from heaven.

MARGUERITE

Meister came to Paris, and as soon as he found me, we went to the old Sue, both of us in civil clothing, to have a good time and to talk. Kathrine, Sue's servant, brought us some good wine upstairs—no questions asked. That's the nature of the establishment, has always been.

At first it was the usual chitchat, but then Meister said something that gave me goose bumps—namely that he doesn't understand why William doesn't go for the kill yet. What's he waiting for? What he's got so far, which includes my confession to that Italian halfwit Guido de Collemezzo some years ago and the burning of my book (I had to be there, in Valancienne's main plaza, and watch my work as well as the investment of my life go up in smoke and that in front of a true crowd of local half-wits noisily applauding). But then there is also my admission that I had the book after that (I saved few copies, of course) and now delaying the whole thing as best I could, counting on more witnesses to appear on my side (like the three from the past, included Godfrey de Fontaines, who was a theologian and not a canon law expert like the Macaroni has been—I think this is a theological matter and not something to split hairs about like the lawyers do, this time William of Paris, also totally different from Godfrey). Meister shares my opinion that William, being as meticulous, thorough, solid and whatnot as he is, is at the same time a little too dull for this kind of matter. He's not sure, Meister, he doesn't understand, and yet there is something else for certain. What? well, who knows…Let's just pray that whatever it might be, it might also last. I'm in no hurry to that pyre precisely because I feel his hand. I'd like to be around a bit longer. Sit there, at the table, drink good wine, talk our doubts out.

My question to Meister then was if this situation might turn out to be really dangerous for me, if I might be turned over to the secular authorities for administering punishment, which of course would be death. It always is. And it turned out to be exactly what Meister was afraid of too; hell yes! If that something we don't understand (whatever it might really be that still holds him back) finally breaks down and he, William, follows the routine of the last period here—more and more of it lately, since he started already a while ago the Templars and the Jewish expulsion—oh my! One almost always follows one's own routines, and to do that, the turnover, that's just a few pieces of paper. And you know well, don't you, once you there, you're finished. That's the end of it, and nobody, not even God himself, might be able to do something. You're pronounced a heretic, according to the canon law, contumacious, for over a year, because it is a year and more already, and that qualifies you to be transferred to secular authorities.

We were silent for a while. I thought a little too long for that silence to be normal, and I turned my head to him and looked. From his left eye, which was to me, a teardrop was slowly traveling toward his mouth. Small, thin flow of brine.

"What is it?" I asked him. "Why are you crying?" "Just remembered somebody," he said.

"You remembered somebody, and that made you cry?"

"Yes! It's been long time ago, Margo. Different times. Less lies, more faith. And he was a great friend, you know? I still have something from him, a gift, and I wish he were alive today. I wish he could be here with us right now, and we could ask him what to do. He knew crowned heads as well. He was a great guy and really considered as such by most everybody in academic Europe."

"But you said it was a long time ago, right? Is he dead?" "Yes, that's what I meant. Yes, he is dead. And that world I still remember, just as I remember him, seems to have died with him, you know? Ours here is something else, I think it seems okay."

He turned to me now and pressed me against his chest. I felt his heartbeat. We were like that for quite a while—motionless, just breathing. And then he got on top of me, both of us joined together in a passionate kiss. And yet a moment later, we made love. Goodness…What a word! It's nothing like what I write about. Nothing. And yet what I write about becomes clearer after I am with him. It is an explanation of what love is—besides slowly dying when the object of it is not there. I think our daily life tells us nothing about love, and that's because love changes our daily life into something else.

He poured some wine then, and we had a sip each, feeling the wonderful taste in our mouths. I certainly don't want to sound blasphemous, but what came to my mind—the only thing that came to my mind, in fact—was, *Let him kiss me with the kisses of his mouth, for thy love is better than wine. Draw me, we will run after thee: the king has brought me into his chambers: we will be glad and rejoice in thee.* I knew I was wrong. I was just saying it, like my memory brought it up. It is like a spring unwinding a papyrus roll, although I know well it's only my memory, but I can't help it. His head is as the most fine gold, his locks are bushy and black as a raven, his eyes are as the eyes of doves by the rivers of waters, washed with milk, and fitly set. I begin to recite this time to him, at a regular level of my voice, just as we speak. His cheeks are as a bed of spices, as sweet flowers; his lips like lilies…

He looks at me, his eyes express everything that life has kept so far away from me. They are soft, tender; in his look is now the world I am after, have always been. He smiles and then recites, "I am my beloved's and my beloved is mine. Thou art beautiful, O my love, turn away thine eyes from me for they have overcome me. There are threescore queens, and fourscore concubines and virgins without numbers. My dove, my undefiled but one, she is the only one of her mother. The daughters saw her, and blessed her, yeah, the queens and the concubines, and they praised her."

He clears his throat, one time, strongly, and then says it again, looking at me, with the same tenderness, which make me feel strange—differently, somehow.

"Thy navel is like a round goblet, which wants not liquor. Thy belly is like a heap of wheat set about with lilies. Thy breasts are like two young roes that are twins. Thy neck is a tower of ivory."

I feel compelled to answer him and I do.

"Thou wert as my brother that sucked the breasts of my mother, when I should find thee without, I would kiss thee. Yeah, I should not be despised."

Then it's Paris again, the streets, la Seine. We walk along, talking, enjoying the day. Meister tells me he loves Paris, not as much as his little town in Thüringen, but it is lovely. And once he found himself here for the first time many, many years ago, it was a love at first sight. It was also here, in Paris, that he had met his friend he mentioned before and the remembrance of whom made him so sad. We stopped looking at the water.

His mouth moved like he wanted to say something. "You know…"

"Yes?"

"They'd say he knew how to make gold, you know?"

"Did he?"

"I never really believed that. Never! He was a fine theologian. He was a great connoisseur of Latin and Greek. Probably few other things I know nothing about—well, he had certain interest in alchemy as well, but I know nothing about his laboratory. I know nothing about his experimenting with other metals, no…He was more of a guy who'd look for the philosopher's stone in the sense of whatever potential is in us. In the process of living, which so often is going through fire, what can become of at least some of us, see? That's the way I see it."

"If he knew how to turn lead into gold, just hypothetically—okay, hear me out—would that make him less in your eyes? Is that what you're saying?"

"It would make him somebody else. Different than the guy I knew and respected. I don't know if you can relate to that."

"I think I can."

"There was a reason that I spotted you the very first moment I saw you. They say we are very much alike. Our beliefs are very much alike too. I heard not that long ago that I am actually a heretic as well and that we'll end up very much alike."

"At the stake?"

"I am much older and so have a chance to die before that actually happens. That's my chance. Margo?" He looked at me.

"Yes?"

"Whatever happens, we'll meet again. I know that. Do you know that?"

"Yes. Oh yes, my dear, I do believe that. Not even believe. It's a matter of knowing, you're right. See? I know that. I simply know that. I'm not afraid of dying because dying is just a passage from here to there. And we, you as well as I, haven't done anything down here to be separated. The moment of passage might be bad. In fact I think that's what's ahead of me before I find myself again. But, hell, what is it but just a brief moment in time, huh? A blink of an eye. And then I'm there, and with you again."

He put his arm around my shoulders. I saw he was moved; his eyes were watery.

"Take care of yourself," he said.

"Have you heard how he goes about getting the Jews out? About the consultations? How many people, experts, he got over here?"

"In your case it might be the same. There is that something that's holding him back, isn't there? We were just talking about it. When that is removed…"

The sun was reflecting in the water, in blinding little wavelets.

"I was just thinking about that."

"Don't stop."

"I won't."

He cleared his throat. "See, he is now under significant pressure himself in this first week of the month because of the growing momentum of the Templar defense. There were thirty-nine visits to thirty different places of detention in Paris, during which they got statements from over half a thousand of the Templar knights wishing to defend their order and their own innocence. See, every brother who joined in all those occasions claiming that their crimes had been fabricated and their confessions coerced is now offering an indictment of William and his attack on the order."

"Have you heard something, anything, about the Guiard fellow? What to make of him?"

"There is yet another one from Cressonssart, a certain Matthew. If he is related somehow to Guiard, I have no way of knowing. But he gave a solid defense, from what I was able to gather, of the Templars. There were eleven of them in the garden of the bishop and, for whatever reason, he, the Mathew fellow, was the one to represent all that army. And so he did. Quite firmly. Now as to Guiard. He was forced by the inquisitor to explain what function the angel of Philadelphia would have here today. You know that he claimed to be the angel of Philadelphia? The sixth in the revelation of John? That tells me one thing: they don't treat him too seriously. At least not quite. Is he not all there?

No! William talks to him, his statements notwithstanding. He talks to him still, probably as we speak right now. A mild case, hence. I've heard a little more but don't mean to bore you with things of no import. Is he going to help your case? I doubt that. Is he going to make it worse? He might, although, somehow, I don't think so either. How is his case going to end? I think they'll let him go. He seems scared to me. He'll go, sooner or later, for what William wants him to do. Most probably."

We stopped. Both of us were looking at the river where a huge barge was slowly going with the current. The sky was blue, the day was sunny, and somehow, I thought myself lucky—to be here, at the river, under this sky, with Meister…and not in some vaulted cellar, stinking mildew, cold and wet. I was wondering what caused this. Why would William treat me differently all along? Why? I felt lucky! Meister is with me now, under this deep, beautiful, blue sky (his proper name is Johannes, but I somehow prefer to call him like his pupils and other Dominican friars do: Meister). Here we are, and I consider myself truly lucky.

ZWEIFLER

The arrests started in the whole of Paris; my brothers are everywhere—churches, gardens, certainly regular prisons and whatever can be thought of as a potential prison too. In the garden of the Bishop of Paris there must be some thirty, maybe forty, of ours awaiting the trial as representatives of the give or take five hundred for which the inquisitor of Paris invited a whole bunch of theologians as experts during the proceedings. And they, the Templars, elected a delegation from among themselves (from those thirty) to represent their cause, which is, of course the trumped-up charges against them—spiting on the cross, homosexuality, and that kind of life they were supposedly forced by the order to participate in, total renouncement of Christ. Good God, us…

I hear a name of a certain Mathew de Cressonssart, who defends our cause, with I think three other guys, very energetically and very much to the point. I've heard that name before, and that's because of Meister and the Beguine woman he is friends with, now abandoned by everybody except Meister himself and precisely that guy. Only then I found out that it was yet another fellow, his name was Guiard; he just was from the same town as Cressonssart. That's also where the bishop is from, the one who destroyed the woman's life by burning her book, the woman Meister loves so much. They did the burning publicly in the main plaza of the town where she is from, Valanciènne in northeastern France, if I got the story right.

And I think I do (it was repeated to me several times by different sources, and each of those times I heard almost the same story, the differences negligible). And that wasn't all—she had to recant and promise, also publicly, she wouldn't copy her book and sell it in public, which disposition besides she violated almost right away. So much for Meister and his friend, at least for now. In what goes for ours since it started—the mock anti-Templar campaign—it has never so far been this intense. I think it really looks at times like we are winning, like finally, we regained our voice and are now shouting with such strength that it can be heard in entire France. At least that lying bastard—the inquisitor of Paris, William—gets for the first time a lot of water behind his collar. He doesn't really seem anymore as certain of his thing as he was before. At least in that sense we are winning here a little bit. Certainly, when I compare this to what they did to the grandmaster and some others—well, just a brief description gives me creeps. I've heard that he "confessed" to the accusations while nailed to an oak door, naked of course, with a hundred iron nails. Good Lord, I would confess to creating this world of ours or to destroying it, whatever they might want. And I am absolutely certain that it is not just me—anyone would. We are human and we can go only this far, and those bastards know that. All those tortures are based on that too. Have I confessed under torture back in Chinon? Ask me rather if I know or not that I did or didn't, and I'll have to tell you, if I'm to be frank, that I haven't got the faintest idea. All I really know is that in the end, I got out of it, thanks to Simona's help (who in turn was bribed by Alva). No more than that!

I run now all over the city, trying to find out as much as I can, and maybe help our cause a bit—that'd be great! Yesterday I was trying to enter la Sainte-Chapelle because I'd heard that part of the proceedings against us goes on in there (that is also the place where that Guiard fellow had had his vision: that he is the angel of Philadelphia. I was told he then twaddled some BS about the keys, which in the biblical version have a clearly defined function). Strange. Because he looks and moves, I'd say, normal, like any other. I am told they, the woman and he, don't see each other. I'm not sure about it right now, but so far she had not been arrested and Meister could see her anywhere they wanted to see each other in town. Even though she is the main character in this, he's got himself into it (I'm talking now about the Guiard fellow) because he wants to help her (it seems to me he really believes to be an angel, poor chap). Anyways, everybody wonders. Why is she treated so differently? She's never been tortured, for instance, and everybody wants to know why. What's stopping them? And the freedom of movement—as said before, she can go wherever she wants to.

Now, isn't that something?

From my running around, I slowly get the picture: this is not gonna be a process against this or that particular guy; this is a process against the order, and suspicions are of no importance. They know (*they* meaning our accusers), they know it's all made up and none of it is really true. The grand inquisitor of Paris, William, is no longer involved in these proceedings, and although the question of their guilt or innocence—most everybody in this country and in this town is thus far believing that the guilt has been in this case sucked out of someone's thumb and has no other origin—nevertheless that question is still bound to his reputation. Gilles Aycelin is now the guy, as I found out, who took over, and he seems to have assumed our guilt from before he even entered the process. Our defense, though strengthening itself as it does lately, seems to render it possible that they will have to exonerate the order. Then there's also the problem with the popes. I don't see quite how, but there is a relation, and I was told a significant one at that. Since the election of Clement V, the posthumous heresy trial of Boniface VIII seems a possibility, but now the pope agreed to hold formal hearings, from the beginning, whether or not Philip's opponent has been a heretic or not. What now has this got to do with the order is truly confusing to me. There are other names as well. There's more and more the more I talk to people, and I am afraid that I'll lose the perspective completely before I get to the bottom of it. William seems to have created a new habit in all these proceedings—that is consulting a lot of expert people. It started in the case of relapsed Jews, according to what I am told, that meant fifteen theologians in each and every case, making themselves acquainted with whatever available documentation (tones—fabricated or not, it's still documentation) and only then pronouncing, after weeks of reading, their final judgment. I've got then an abbreviated statement Guiard gave defending Marguerite (I've also seen her name spelled as Marguarette). I am not going to quote it here because it seems to me a statement of a deranged brain. It's all based on the scripture, but it only makes me reflect what cannot be based on the scripture (is there such a thing in this world?). It'll take any kind of nonsense and then, with a little legerdemain, with which some people just seem to be born, it can be presented to anyone of which the best proof is Guiard's present process.

Giscard is at the door with my dinner; I have to open for him. He is a young fellow who wants to get education, and serving and cleaning, and such he makes little money to pay his room and board. He learns Latin and Greek; this year he'll enter art's faculty because he wants to study theology. I talk to him sometimes, since we saw each other in Smyrna for the first time, and this is how I got these answers about his life. He also tells me gossip from the town, whatever he knows and I don't, like lately the stuff related to the Jews and Templars—what's happening in the city. So far, lamentably, I knew all he wanted to tell me. Can't recall a detail which would have been really new. None.

"Chicken today, broth with dumplings. Good stuff. I had some too."

"Good! Have you been, by any chance, to la Sainte-Chappelle today? Is it open to the public yet?"

"No, it's not. There is still the same thing going on. The Templars. Hearings. Defense presented and all that. Guards at the door and they won't let you in. I tried to argue and almost got arrested."

"How are the Templars in all that do you think?"

"Hard to tell. A lot of defense, I have to tell you this. But whatever I tell you is secondhand. People are not allowed inside to participate as regular public. It's just them and their accusers, and I'm talking not just la Sainte-Chapelle; it's everywhere the same. What I'm telling you is hearsay then. But people are praying for them. Civilians. Regular people, you know. Praying."

"People seem to have good thoughts?"

"Oh yes, sir! People don't like whatever the king does. That too. He isn't a popular fellow these days. And nobody really likes inquisition either, but you know that, don't you?"

"Yeah…I've heard this and that."

"Exactly!"

"Exactly!" I smiled. He actually made me laugh. Laughing, looking at him, I suddenly realized that he wasn't just a boy. He was a student at the University of Paris, to be theologian in the nearest future, and I suddenly realized that we get to know things about this world of ours in snatches only, single flashes which stupefy us, leave us with our hands hanging down and our mouths open. Is there anything we could know all the way from top to bottom right away? The Bible's answer to it is a clear no—our main household item is surprise, always and always anew. We were looking now at each other, and it wasn't the same picture for me that it has been a few moments ago; there was something new in it only I didn't know what.

"Giscard?"

"Yes?"

"How long have we known each other?"

"Years, I'd say. Years and then some. I'm not really sure. We've met in Smyrna, if memory serves." He looks at me, kind of helpless. "You know of the top of my head like that…I'd have to think a little."

"Sure, I understand."

"You want me to sit down and calculate?" "No, it's not worth it."

"As you wish."

"Listen," I said, "I'm not hungry. Would you like this soup and the meat—well, my dinner—Giscard?"

"You sure?"

"I think so. Take it!"

He did. I was hungry like a wolf. There is something wrong with my skin, I guess. Something seriously wrong. I'm standing still and it itches like hell, an itch which I shall never be able to scratch, I just thought, not smiling.

MARGUERITE

This time the carriage wasn't so elegant, and I didn't get to see him the same evening. I spent the night in a room reminding me of a church cellar, maybe then that's what it was, gothic room with very little light, high vaulted, and huge. I couldn't see the nother side of it. I could see the stones the walls were made of and the mortar between them, a bit clearer, and the cobwebs in the corners of the arches; no windows anywhere. I also found my bed then, all by myself, hay in a wooden frame—well, at least I thought it could be a bed. It was all damp, smelling mildew or something mildew-like. I couldn't sleep, I just lay down, my right hand under my head, and I thought, most of the night. And I thought still after the torch went out, and I found myself in a complete darkness. I thought about what was happening here in Paris as well as in other parts of the country, of which I knew from the people I managed to get in touch with, people coming to Paris from different regions of France. Gathering information this way is easy; a lot of people come to Paris for different reasons. And once here, they look around. Then they talk. If there is hearsay, they not only repeat it but also analyze it. Like most of us, they are trying to figure out what lies ahead, first and foremost for themselves. The night produces shadows that reflect whatever is evil to us, or what we think it is so. And it's only if we can dream, bring up desires that can disperse those shadows and make us await the sunup with a little less fear and anguish, the new day that wouldn't be about death.

The breakfast was a chicken drumstick with a piece of bread and a cup full of some kind of herbal tea. After that, nothing happened for the longest time. It must have been toward the afternoon that the door opened and the same two guys entered to pick me up. We were traveling up a thousand steps, inside a tower, the steps taking me up around some kind of a central column; then it was series of corridors and passages, until I finally was in—in what? I don't know. He was standing in the window, looking outside—not at me at all. The same brown habit on; the same face made of iron; same gray, short cropped hair; same steel-blue eyes when he finally decided to look at me.

"He prophesied!" he said. "Before he died he pronounced something that I call prophecy. The prophecy is a picture of the future, of what's it gonna be like in two hundred years or a thousand…I don't know, well, sometime ahead." He looked at me, or maybe he just looked with more intensity. I'm getting lost trying to describe that guy. "You don't know either now, do you? And what he said was that everything human was gonna die—art, religion, languages, all that would be dead then. For a while, one language would survive, one most primitive of all the languages on Earth, one based on *usus* with almost no grammar (they'll take *usus* for grammar; serious scientific sources will agree on that). Humanity would be then the most idiotic group of no religion, of no art or where art turned out to be only entertainment, a pastime—books would slowly be eaten by mildew on one side and dust on the other. Soon there would be no books at all. And nobody would be missing them. You know?"

"And that's the end?"

"Yes, according to him, that's the end." "Can we change that?"

"He didn't say."

"And you? What do you think?"

"I…" he said, not looking at me; he didn't move from the beginning, sitting in that gothic window, looking outside. Then I was hearing his voice again. "I think prophesies are given to us to change the future they warn us about. If not, then what the hell for? Would they be prophesies at all? Would they be then anything?"

We both were silent now. It was a long time in which we remained so. In fact my thought starts erring after a while. I leave this location for a certain period (Where am I? I don't think I have any idea. I am somewhere only because I can't be nowhere. But what is that somewhere: who the hell knows?)

He looks at me suddenly, or should I say that he looks at me and I suddenly realize that. Then I hear his voice coming to me like from far away.

"The annihilated soul gives license to the virtues and is no longer in servitude to them, because it does not have use for them but rather the virtues obey its command. That the soul annihilated in love of the Creator, without blame of conscience or remorse, can and ought to concede to nature whatever it seeks and desires. That such soul does not care about the consolations of God or his gifts and ought not to care and cannot, because such a soul has been completely focused on God, and thus its focus on God would then be impeded."

He clears his throat.

"You see what you're saying?" "What I'm saying?"

"And where it goes? Where it has to go?"

Then he picks up again. "Desert! That's what we recognize as left of this world at that point. And that's because your kind always thought you can, you have the right to say whatever you feel like saying, to publish whatever you feel like publishing, whatever of your lousy thoughts you feel like delivering to people. Fine! If you're alone, you might be right, although even then I'm not so sure. But no! You have to be listened to by thousands, right? Thousands!"

He nods. And then nods again.

"The first love can appropriately be called *cutting away* because it separates the soul from the dregs of temporal things. The second love is called *setting ablaze* because it inflames this same soul with the fire of divine love. The third can be called *wounding*, because with its sweetness it wounds the heart of the lover. The forth is called *binding*, because it immobilizes the lover. The fifth is called *boiling over*, because it rises up the one affected incessantly indefatigably so that he can only taste the divine gift. The sixth is called *languishing*, because it melts and dissolves the soul. The seventh is called *destroying*, because it leads the soul into an eclipse and annihilation of itself."

He looks at me now, longer, with a smile erring on his thin lips. He clears his throat again and passes his hand over his steely hair.

"Fifteen absolute top people in France have recognized you as a relapsed heretic."

Silence. Then he leaves his window niche and comes up to me.

"Any idea what the pyre feels like?" I don't answer him.

"Ever thought about it?" "Not really!"

I feel suddenly his hands on my shoulders. He holds me bent a little bit back, looking me in the eyes.

"I have a house in Italy, in Orvietto, I fell in love with already long time ago. Perfectly anonymous. Nobody, and I mean nobody, knows whose it is. I could just vanish from here hiding there. There are means in that house too. I could start a new life down there and so can you. Marguerite, you see, I have no reason to do it by myself. I have all my achievements right here, and I have access to reaches beyond your imagination, then why leave it just like that and go somewhere else?" He looks me in the eye, and I feel a delicate shake on my shoulders. "I had deposits here in Paris, in this currency Philippe had introduced some time ago, not a good locate, oh no, chéri, chéri a currency weak and shaky. But I have— having had the proper information about the Templars, what was gonna be happening here, in Paris as well as everywhere else—I withdrew all of it, and I have it now in solid gold. Not only a penny lost but even some made on top. We shall be happy down there. I thought about it, Marguerite. In fact I can't stop thinking about it."

"And you do it for both of us," I said, "Don't you?"

"Do I? I wish I did. Do I, Margot?"

"You have murdered a lot of people, you and your friends. Philip, and that pig down there, Clement you call him now, don't you? You three have tortured to death half of France, and what was left of them you burned at stake, of course defending faith, preserving the word of God, etc. And you talk about love? About new life? Starting all over? Oh, you will start all over all right. Just wait! You just wait, William!"

"I thought you had personally no reason to hate me! What have I done to you? I invited you here mainly to warn you…"

"It's not hatred, William. Justice speaks now through me. Voices of all those you murdered for no reason other than insolvency of your bosses. People are not completely stupid. Not yet anyway! Times you were just talking about are not here yet. We think, my dear fellow man. We do! And what we think about in this case is not pretty. Doesn't cost you much to have a scribe write you that Latin text you read on the plaza and then you hand over to civil authorities together with the fuel for the stake, hypocritically begging them for leniency. You know, and you know well, what their leniency is, don't you? Have they ever been lenient?"

He delicately shook me again.

"Marguerite, Orvietto is beautiful. Many would call my house in there a palace. It's full of art. Italian, but also Spanish, and ours. Philippe at this stage might not even be looking for me anymore. My disappearance might simply make him happy and will let it be, the whole thing. I think it's possible the way things are now. And you'd be everything to me for the rest of this life. Everything! Please!"

"You haven't understood a thing of this life. You think you can serve Satan and get away with it? You think the cross is just a Parisian trinket that can be sold to tourists at a great profit, because it cost next to nothing to make one? I assure you it's a lot more then that! A whole lot! Among those other things it means my life. And one more time: a whole lot of other lives. Dross to you."

I saw the beginnings of despair in his eyes, and his hands, still on my shoulders, were slowly becoming two steel lugs, as if he were trying to force me to accept his offer in this manner. I thought now I was beginning to feel a touch of pity.

"Margot, it is not the first time in our history that a group of stupid nincompoops has to die in order for a great idea to be realized. People in an average are a worthless mass, and nobody should worry about them. Nobody. There's no need for that. None! A measurement of what a man is should be and really is, with some exceptions, what he has understood, what is his learning. Most haven't understood a thing, not because we haven't given them opportunity to learn and to understand but because they are too lazy, born unchangeably too stupid to understand and learn anything. And as of right now there are too many of them anyway in this great world of ours, intelligent or stupid, and we have no use for such a crowd. One-tenth probably, thereabouts, you see, of what is out there today would be absolutely sufficient to do the work necessary for our world to move forward. Instead we have a lot of hungry mouths to feed, increasing the body of stupidity. Useless mouths, which should be eliminated anyway, at any rate. Done away with! If we, the ones who did what we all, not just us and not just them, what we all were supposed to do at some point, if hence we are to progress, get ever to the limits we have once marked for ourselves, this will have to happen. Get it! Have to! There's no way around that. None!"

I tried to free myself from his grip, without any effect. He was holding my shoulders, and I was standing, bent a little bit backward, as I spoke. "You're efficient, cautious, intelligent, and you will always know how to protect yourself. You'll always know how to build a rampart made out of necessary documentation around your *persona*, which will sufficiently cover your back in any possible situation. But I think you should understand one thing: it is here, here in this valley of tears, where we are only temporarily, all of us, William, no exception, to learn something, maybe to get some understanding, realization of who we actually are…see? And then, William? When you get there and you stand before him? Will you offer him a deal? Will you ask him to confess? Recant? What will you ask him then?"

He let go of my shoulders. Slowly, like he was suddenly twenty years older, he walked toward his window niche, where he just sat down, looking outside. There was such a silence in the room that I heard clearly my own blood in my temples. I felt now sorry for him. In a regular way. Clearly, time was passing by in an almost clearly perceivable manner too.

"William?"

He looked at me suddenly with the same steely eyes I saw before. I knew we both just had lost something, something very important—the most important thing for both of us. I suddenly knew that I was lost. My life.

He lifted up a small golden bell and rang. Two guys entered, and they took me back to where I came here from in the morning—the same infinite row of rooms, the same, unending steps leading to the center of the earth itself. My life was over. I felt sad suddenly.

It was the same night (must have been night—I don't have any windows in here, so I wouldn't know if it was day or night) a guy was let in, and he brought with him paper and ink and feathers, and I also had time to write. Whatever happened since I and Meister saw each other for the last time that he wouldn't know about—in as well as out. I sat down and started to write whatever I could remember. All of it. My eyes were full of tears, and I could imagine that so would be Meister's, while reading it. I wish he had a palace in Orvietto and a holding in gold, but I knew well he didn't. Meister lived of his professorship, of his books, of his church position. He didn't have any money; besides, who cares? Not him, not me, that's for certain. We live of whatever falls from on high, and I wouldn't wanna change that. And when the end comes… good Lord! Then it just comes; what can one do? I finished, or so I thought, and I gave the man the paper covered with my scribbles as he reached into his pocket and pulled out a small glass vial.

"Take it," he said, "before they put you up there. Up there you may not be able to take it anymore. Your hands will be tied, and you might not be able to move in any way at all. Best take it right now."

"Did our Lord have something like this before he was tortured and then crucified?"

"I don't know that. Haven't been there, see?" He looked at me a little longer. "And you don't either now, do you?"

"I believe," I said.

"Just take it, okay? At best right now as already said
once! Before they come and take you to Place de Grève."

"So that's where it's gonna be?"

"Yes," he said. "Right there."

Looking at the vial, I asked what it was, and he said, "Just something to facilitate the passage from here to there. Painless.

Last great gift of the chief inquisitor. Kneel down and ask if you're worth it."

Then he was gone, and I was alone again. Wiping off my eyes, I thought in this darkness, slightly bent back, my wiped eyes now dry and closed.

Oh, man, who are you? It's dark, I can't see my hand stretched, I am in the wooden frame, surrounded by dry hay. The only thing that smells nice in here—it smells a meadow, somewhere, under that mildew, which gets to one's nose first. Yes, somewhere down there I can feel the sun. I feel invincible, powerful, because of a small glass vial sent by my friend and lover-to-be—or rather not to be ever. I just rejected him, who isn't what, in my opinion, a human being should be and who is a cause of countless amount of deaths more painful than pain itself. And the vial is now inside my palm, and I have faith in goodness and forgiveness inside my heart. Come what may…I'll have strength and courage to welcome it. I will.

ALVA

Guy and Giscard, two people who sort of touched my life, both of them more or less at the same time—which is to say from the time of Smyrna all the way to Paris, which is to say all of it during an escape from places most dear to our hearts, with our tails tagged. Guy was big. Back in our land he'd carry equipment behind the knight. He never learned how to read and write in any language, and, as he claimed himself, never needed to—the best proof of which were we all: the ones who spoke a bunch of languages and in any of those could also write. We were all trying to escape. None of us, literate or not, could stay where we would love to stay. Literacy did not help. Illiteracy did not force us out of our world. Right?

Giscard was a thin fellow who never, in his entire life (most probably), carried a sword, wouldn't know how to hold a shield, wouldn't know how to put on armor of any kind. He had books. With us he spoke French, just like we did; with the Arabs Arabic, as far as I can tell, just like they did. Father tried him, to his satisfaction, in Latin. He even knew something where I was completely helpless and brother wasn't much better at, and that was Greek. Father knew some, and from him we found out that Guy read Averroes (which might turn out dangerous in Paris, well, in France; people reading Averroes would be considered, at present, heretics. Books in any form were confiscated and burned, and they themselves were interrogated and forced to recant while already crippled by the interrogation—even if they themselves would have no personal opinion in reference to the questions asked. (Back in Smyrna, when Giscard asked the question explicitly, Joseph Cartaphilus answered that he himself was only allowed to sigh. No talking. No explanations. Regardless of sales level, huh?)

I may have now and then in the beginning looked at Guy with sympathy, because he was a big, strong guy with a smiling face, and I may have done that without even being aware of doing it. But I already said how it ended up: by him grabbing my breast, like I was one of those girls serving him wine in the inn. Would it repeat itself? Most probably yes, if brother hadn't spotted it and did what he had done. Brother promised him that if he saw that again (that exactly or something of that nature), he would simply cut his head off. Saying it he seemed calm, his voice down, maybe even a bit lower than normal. Holding the hero perfectly immobilized. And that did it. No, after that, it never happened to me again.

Meanwhile, brother kept on warning me about any closer relationship between me and Giscard because of the above-given reasons. I would expose myself to those church people for whom, according to him, the church had the least significance and for whom the most important thing was the satisfying of their sadistic inclinations. I shouldn't get close to that if I don't have to, he would say. But listening to Giscard talking about Aristotle interpreted by Averroes seemed extremely interesting to me. Giscard would pose questions, like for instance the one how was it possible that Aristotle, being a pupil of Plato, turned out later on materialist, abandoning his master's idealism almost completely. Giscard would explain—and I loved to watch him do it—that if we assume the essence of matter to be only expression of cosmic existence, a being which is only a particular case of spiritual being, accessible to our language, created by our language, created by our love for things finished (in this case terminology), but whose expression our life is…

"See? Expression, nothing else. Nothing!"

"Expression?"

"Matter is the final frontier between the spirit and the stone, Alva. If the stone were only a part of your imagination, an important part of it would be missing: existence."

It was about then that somebody started knocking at the door, and I got up from where I was sitting to open.

It was Guy, trying to catch breath and telling us that they were coming. *They* were looking for Giscard; they knew all about his books, his intensions to study at the university. He, Guy, had no time to explain.

"Get out! Don't look back! Just get up and out!"

Giscard got to the window through which he got out, simply stepping over the windowsill onto a balcony that was going along the building, and down there was another balcony, just like this one going along the water, into which Giscard in the end jumped. I watched him get carried quickly away by the current of the river. Then I turned around, but Guy wasn't there any longer; in the door there was a tall guy in chain armor and a steep steel helmet, his shoulder seeming to be an ideal square. He introduced himself as inquisition guard and then asked about Giscard—details, his address, did he live right here—to which I started explaining our coming from Outremer and his getting attached to us in Smyrna, where we found ourselves in such and such circumstances after Acre fell, and then major happenings between Anatolia and Brundisium, the latter and Rome, then Avignon (here I omitted brother's arrest and his transfer to Chinon). Giscard was with us through all of the above. Now, do I interest myself in theological questions? My father was a Templar. They had documentation from Avignon concerning Dad. Fortunately, they had nothing concerning brother. All of the above they had found too chaotic to serve any purpose at all, and they wanted to fill that niche with information from me. And I think I did a good job answering in such a manner that at times I must have appear to them as a half-wit, to put it mildly. Or someone who really had no idea whatsoever what they were talking about. A housewife. A daughter of a rich parent who has no private interests, except to spend parental money on mad whims. That's where I was aiming, and I think I succeeded; that was exactly what they took me for. They were sitting there, one of them, exactly at the spot where Giscard was sitting only a short while before, and talking to me, more and more relaxed, though switching the conversation from the deadly serious of its beginning to joking and merrymaking right now, without even realizing the full extent of it. I could only be afraid that Giscard would suddenly come back. But he wasn't stupid, now, was he? Yet before they left and I had a chance to consult the whole thing with anyone, it crossed my mind that I was gonna have to change my own address as well. Almost anything could change their idea as to who I was. Most anything.

And then I was suddenly told that the grand inquisitor himself would like to make the acquaintance of me. Like right now! And I realized that it wouldn't be today that I'd get rid of them and be left alone. I had to follow, I had to accommodate their wishes, and what I wanted didn't matter in the least. Situation is unknown to me so far. Something my life surprised me with almost completely. I knew, of course, all along. I'm not completely stupid. That this was the time of danger, time of suffering for many people, for a whole lot of them baseless, directed against their innocence. I knew that! Yes. And yet when we were descending the stairs to get in the end into the vehicle awaiting us down in the street and getting in, I realized that it might be my last time to enter a vehicle… well, one of my last times for anything. I realized something I had no idea of before. Driving through the city was also different than anything I knew before. Colors, smells, noises, etc., were the same, yet there was something different in any of it. My own end was suddenly present, and I couldn't get around that. I never knew it would be like this. Life possible is the one we know absolutely nothing about (I'm not talking about when one closes one's eyes and imagines swimming in the Mediterranean, no!), life that is there at all times—your comrade, almost inseparable from yourself who's always there and is not coming, is not becoming actuality because you're not doing something you could be doing…

We entered the palace, and I was led through a net of corridors and chambers of incredible beauty. I always thought we weren't poor, but now I realized we also had no idea what rich meant. Shortly before we entered the chamber, which was our final destination, I saw a woman in monk's habit, tall and beautiful. I stopped for a moment, and they all stopped for me; there was something about her that I wouldn't know how to describe, something dictating patterns of behavior unknown to one, something out of the ordinary. Meeting her was almost like the rest of the day: unexpected, a little frightening in a sense, evoking the conviction that life didn't end here, that life was more than one could see or touch. She saw my reaction. She smiled and then approached me. I heard her voice.

"You can be scared, child, but never be afraid! You hear?" One of the guards behind her touched her back with just his fingers, motioning her to move, and so she did.

Before she turned around completely, she repeated, "Don't ever be afraid! Never!"

I was there, I was just there, left in my amazement and a foggy premonition that something incredibly important just had happened to me. A meeting of my life that I would never be able to forget. And then, as I was standing in front of the inquisitor, just a little bit later, looking into a pair of steely eyes (tall man, his gray hair was cropped shortly, he had on him a habit very much like the woman's I just had met, he also was a strong personality and yet totally different) I felt strangely okay. A frightening encounter now giving me no fright. I heard a very polite "Bon jour," and then the invitation to sit down. No, I didn't feel afraid. Not at all.

MEISTER

feel old. My presence is not really needed by anyone, and once that realization becomes a fact, one's life is also changed. We thrive on uniqueness, irreplaceability. And if that ceases to be the case (once you figure out that you could be replaced by just about anyone, and if there's a cause to take care of or contribute to, that very cause could only gain on your replacement), you're not the same now as you were yesterday. The sip of wine that just had been brought up here from the cellar is wonderfully cool, the bouquet perfectly ripe and full, and it makes me close my eyes. What we make is us too. That wine is part of my personality; somehow it is my effort throughout my life that now seems to be getting closer to a close. I spent months in here, helping them to perfect the recipe. It wasn't fruit; it was sugar content on one hand and type of yeast on the other. They needed me to do the degustation; they don't feel competent enough on that field, so it was my contribution, and the final effect was something that contained my doing as well. I feel sad.

My life is getting to a halt. I'm waiting for the outcome of Vienna, what those geniuses down there are going to conceive of—if I'm found a heretic, I don't want to go to the stake. I think in that case I'd seek asylum in the castle. The prince is an educated man. We've had our conversations, he accepted, and that not on one occasion, my recommendation as to what to read in order to think through the doubts he presented me with…Yeah, I would just vanish. And I also didn't feel like going to Vienna to defend my own case, to talk to a bunch of old people convinced that they ate all the reasons of the world. I don't have enough patience left for that anymore, if I had it at any point. If I went there, the outcome is easily predictable: I would explode at some point, simply because of my age, and I wouldn't come back here. They would make a pyre right there, in Vienna. I've seen enough of those processes, interrogations, etc., to know what kind of farce all of it is, no exceptions (in what aspect is the angel different, in that it has two legs, particularly the right one). That it's got nothing to do with any religion, faith, God…

The sip of cool wine brings me back here for a while.

Carla brings me huge steak with beans; these are good times. There's plenty supplies of just about everything. I put myself to eat. I enjoy every bit of it. I do. I say, *Thank you, Lord, for you wonderful, precious gifts*—not out loud. It's thinking that I consider the most sincere form of gratefulness. No church necessary—goes without saying, no special place, no long robe. There is nobody between God and me. It is me he has given something to, and it is my "thank you, Lord."

Carla comes then with a clay pitcher and pours more wine straight from the cellar into my jar on the table. I pour myself a fresh cup. I don't want it to warm up because then it loses its wonderful coolness (not coldness, mind you!).

It's all dross after what my eyes have seen. All of it just nonsensical after I have sought answers to my own experiences.

I've no idea why, but I slap Carla's huge bottom while she passes close enough to my table. She turns around, laughing, and gives me a kiss on the cheek, after which she presses my head to her belly in a sudden, instinctive caress. Then she lets me go. We smile at each other. Yet a moment later, she goes to her chores and I'm left alone at the table with my wine, with my memories, with my life I'm trying to question. I pick up the leather etui Albertus gave me so many years ago. I always have it with me. I pull out the parchments and look. I pass a while just looking, but then unchangeably, I begin to read, not quiet to myself—it's more like a whisper in which the past of the Latin Europe is encapsulated:

Tertia via est sumpta ex possibili et necessario, que talis est. Invenimus enim in rebus quedam que sunt possibilia esse et non esse, cum quedam inveniantur generari et corrumpi, et consequens possibilia esse et non esse.

Impossibile est autem Omnia que sunt, talia esse, quia quod possibile est non esse, quandoque non est. Si igitur Omnia sunt possibilia non esse, aliquando nihil fuit in rebus. Sed si hoc est verum, etiam nunc nihil esset, quia quod non est, non incipit esse nisi per aliquid quod est; si igitur nihil fuit ens, impossibile fuit quod aliquid inciperet esse, et sic modo nihil esst, quod patet esse falsum. Non ergo Omnia entia sunt possibilia, sed oportetr aliquid esse necessarium in rebus. Omne autem necessarium vel habet causam sue necessitates aliunde, vel non habet. Non est autem possibile quod procedatur in infinitum in necessariis que habent causam sue necesitatis, sicut nec in causis efficientibus, ut probatum est. Ergo necesse est ponere aliquid quod sit per se necessarium, non habens causam necessitates aliunde, sed quod est causa necessitates aliis, quod omnes dicunt Deum.

Who are we? We—me, her, Thomas, Albert...Who is Zweifler? Who is his sister Alva? Is there any answer to that, an answer which I would consider one, or just substitutions, which are no answers to anything? We tend to use the language as master key whenever we don't really understand something. We have ten, twenty words to express what's never understood and never shall be any closer to us. I remember suddenly the two of us, me and Albert, going along the Rhine, with the current, that went north, and then he gave me this etui, expressing true pain caused by the death of his beloved student. I have it now in my hand, so many years between the present and that past; who are we? The youngster ox bellowed, as foreseen, in such a manner that the whole of Europe heard him. In fact now, that he was dead, that bellowing of his did not quiet down at all. Who are we? Lord...?

This wine is truly excellent. Thank you, Lord!

ALVA

saw Guy walking down the street, I saw him entering the building, in which I knew the grand inquisitor resided. I had that suspicion already for a moment because it was hard to believe that they, the inquisition, would conceive of arresting someone like Giscard out of thin air; there must have been something that moved them. Well, here it was. I am trying to see him; I'd have a difficult time explaining what for (it's just that this type of piggy stuff is hardly believable by any standards, and when you already have something like a proof, you want to go all the way... maybe that's what it is); there must be some kind of a corridor with a post wherein Guy stops and in a slightly trembling voice reports (he himself terribly offended) a contumacious heretic. It starts. That terrible grinder starts turning, unbelievably slow; the first turn of those gigantic but rusty wheels seems to take forever, but then they go a little bit faster and faster, and then it is the other way around. To stop it seems pretty close to impossible. You know it's too late for anything. I thought now, clearly hearing the words, that as soon as I see brother, I shall tell him about this whole thing and then let him handle whatever his imagination prompts him to do.

I can imagine inside this building a place where there is a line standing, waiting to sell a brother human being; one will be able to see the results not here—hell no, on Place de Grève and wherever else those sick, sickly morbid spectacles take place. In some of those cases, money was involved, the delator would simply get paid, which would make things easy to understand; but there were plenty of cases in which no money or any reward for that matter was involved. They were bringing in the information only for the fact that they were listened to and no more.

Now I started walking toward the Rue Saint Jacques and the bridge because I wanted to get to the other side of the river; on Place de Grève there was a quartering scheduled, and the crowds must have been gathering there for quite a while. Some of them, to whom it was particularly important to have the full view, came there at daybreak and stood without any movement so as not to lose it. I crossed the bridge, got to the other side, and stopped at the natural border the crowd was representing. A murmur went over it. No direction. I always asked myself why would I come to see this, this…pitfall of humanity, what was my excuse? There was something inside me that was really crying, urging me to get the hell out of there, not to look—why?—and yet I'd stay, stay right there, with the rest, watch the sight and listen to the sounds only hell (if it existed anywhere else in this universe in which God had to die on the cross) could offer. I felt a slight trembling. And then the wagon appeared, and suddenly I felt that I would throw up. I got very sick.

It didn't look as they were fixing the victim on the sort of a wooden podium, built there especially for that occasion. I looked just briefly as they were fixing ropes around the arms and legs of the unfortunate and then those ropes were bound to steel bars pulled by huge horses. But before that the executioner poured something (couldn't see from where I was what was the liquid) into the wounds, and his voice got me shaking like a leaf and I threw up. A man standing close to me held me, protecting me from the complete fall. The spectacle out there lasted for hours more, but this time I didn't make it. I just turned around and walked away, back toward the bridge and across the river. I then walked very slowly toward our headquarters. There would be no talk about food, I'd just sit down amongst the people in the inn, and then later I'd go upstairs to try to sleep, which of course wouldn't work. I'd kneel down on the side of my bed and pray—to the virgin. I tried to explain my going there by the admiration I had for her to bear with the sight of her own son dying while she was standing there, propped by Mary Magdalene and St. John of the Cross. Were they helping him? I've no idea. But they were there, certainly ready to help, and maybe that readiness was what counted in the whole thing. Do we get a chance to ask him? We all shall find out as soon as we get there (that is if we ever get there). I thought about brother, remembering that tomorrow there was gonna be a breaking on the wheel on the same Place de Grève (as lately there was something of that nature most every day there, since the Templar thing and the expulsion of the Jews had started), and I knew I'd be there just like I was there today and so many days before today. I was holding my awkward huge Bible with wooden covers in black leather with both of my hands, praying to God for strength, that I may last at least to the end of that horror. And what if that was brother? How would I have behaved back in Avignon watching Father die? Hell, what if that was me? Do we have enough imagination (any of us) to ask that kind of question, the simple, simplistic, the simply stupid (don't ask for whom the bell tolls, it tolls for thee) what if it was me? Huh? What if ?

I could see the window as a gray rectangle when I decided to have some water; I had it in a clay pitcher at the side of the bed, and I poured some of it into a clay cup. Then I kept on praying.

I remained in the same set of clothes all night long. I didn't go to bed. I spent the night like that, on the side of it, like I just described, trying to talk to God—amongst the other things I wanted to relate to why would he allow the people to do stuff like that.

What for? Did he enjoy it by any chance?

It's got clearer outside. I went downstairs and had a piece of bread with a sip of wine, which I thought would keep me till the afternoon. And then I walked out—same itinerary: to the bridge and across the river, to Place de Grève. The victim was brought here in the same cart, or so it seemed to me. Four big strong men in masks over their faces took him down and put him on the wheel, which was right there, already prepared. Executioner lifted up a metal bar, took it above his head, and then let it fall onto the body of the unfortunate (careful—no vital organ could be damaged; he was supposed to live several hours). The voice of the victim made my skin crawl; it wasn't a human voice. As it then began to weaken, the tormenter hit him again and again. I had to listen to the essence of hell. I left there shortly after that. I went back "home," cursing my weakness, my inability to put up with life. Not that much later I found out that I wasn't the only one; moreover I also found out that this kind of weakness was rather typical, and that improved matters a little bit. I thought I felt less ashamed. Embarrassed by my own life. Yes, much less.

I slept some two hours, which gave me some rest. As I was then sitting in the inn, waiting for my breakfast, through the entrance door I saw (at first outside and then walking right in) my favorite at this point: Guy. He spotted me right away too and started moving toward my table as if nothing had ever happened between us that should stop him now from such an action.

"Bonjour, Alva! How are you doing? By any chance, have you seen what was happening today on the Grève? I was too late, had something else to do, huh?"

"I feel lousy," I told him. "Sick. I need to go upstairs and lie down. I doubt if I might be any good today. Maybe not even tomorrow…"

I didn't want him offended because I knew what he was capable of. Giscard avoided death by a friggin hair's thickness. Huh?

"And what about monsieur your brother?" "What about him?"

"Well, where is he? Why isn't he with you here? What kind of a business can possibly be more urgent than this?" "I don't know," I just said. "No idea! He's somewhere in town. Loitering about. This is Paris. There's always something to do, to watch, Jeez…"

I couldn't tell if he had bought it or not. His mug wasn't clear to me. But there was also no vengeance on it, and that was exactly what I was after. For at least as long as I really don't know where brother is. It's easier to lie if one knows facts are almost answering the lie. I was pretty sure he knew that too.

ZWEIFLER

haven't seen Alva for a while, practically from the day I found this job through the guy I met at Grève—they were looking for somebody, man or woman, to clean the room where the interrogations were conducted. Same things were done to people that were once done to me at Chinon, and my idea was to repay the kindness (or whatever it had been in my case—I know vaguely that it was Alva who bribed Simona to get me out, but I never tried to find out all the details; I know I would have done the same thing, had the situation been reversed: she in and I out). I knew all along that I had one shot, just one: seek situation where I'd be left alone with the subjects to interrogation, unlock their restraining devices respectively, whatever it might have been in any given case, and then just open the door and let them out. Some of them were passed anything (in order for an escape like that to succeed, the guy thus liberated would have to still be able to walk, and most of them in that room were not anymore); still I thought if I could save one life, just one, I would repay sufficiently what had been done to me—one life! But I was never left alone with the victims.

Serge, the guy who helped me with getting the job, and then yet another fellow, one of the executioners—a guy from the north seashore town whose name I have forgotten—both of them were there at all times. I had to wait was my theory. Thanks to which I saw things…One time they took me to another prison to do the same thing I'm doing here, and I saw the lion: until then I saw only pictures, paintings of the legendary Master de Molay; but then that day, I saw him right there. If it was him, I can't have any degree of certainty; he looked at the end of his strength, emaciated, smaller than I would ever have imagined, his skin sort of transparent, his long beard glued with crusted dark blood. He didn't look at me. I guess he didn't look at anything in particular anymore. I felt such sadness, right there (I wasn't doing anything at the moment, so nobody noticed anything), right there, on that floor…

He dedicated his life to create his image—to be, in other words, who he was, unquestionably, unchangeably: a picture of defender, right hand of God. And what was I looking at now? And that only because of a bunch of stinking lies. The worst part of it was, probably, the fact that everybody knew that should his innocence be once and forever proven beyond a shadow of a doubt, there wouldn't be one person truly surprised anywhere in the world. He confessed, I was told, to his homosexuality, to spitting on Christ's image and trying to trample it into the ground, he to whom that image was the dearest of all things in existence. Oh God, he confessed while he was nailed to an oak door with a hundred steel nails. And yet something appeared and that right here, in prison— which gave me a little hope—the conversation here, whenever it is possible to talk, bring news about what is going on in all that chaos out there. Lately appeared talks about the apocalypse, which also before—long before at that—played certain role in all this; and yet that role had never been properly understood. Apocalypse deals with Jerusalem, and the latter has an instrumental role in the revelation of John.

For people from outside of Paris, the trial of Guiard de Cressonessart might have been a lot more important than that of Marguerite Porete, because of that fellow's concept of the angel of Philadelphia and the latter's role in the end (Antichrist's coming and all the entourage of the latter). Just about this time in Paris appears a very important and extremely controversial figure of Arnau de Vilanova, a silhouette pouring out treatises and letters and an ocean of comments, a feisty fellow who would never be silenced, and he contributes to that understanding of these matters considerably. Does any of this change the fact that the Templars are being crushed in the way they are? Certainly not! Then why am I mentioning this variation on the subject at all? Well…it pushes all of it back into the frame of a spiritual conflict and that from the shallowness of the former version in which a stupid, presumptuous child is trying to get out of a situation, into which it's got itself, and there's no stopping it…Viewed this way it is less hopeless. There seemed more humanity present in any of this. At least I see it that way. For a moment, I also saw the other giant with whom de Molay associated himself in that famous standing up and denying the lies they were forced to "confess" to Geoffroy de Charnay. I lowered my head, although not requested by anyone in there (I don't think anyone was paying me any attention anyway). However often or however rare I might be coming to Paris lately, I always go to that little island, Ile aux Juifs, to say a prayer for those great people. Then I came back to my original prison, where my plans of liberating a prisoner or prisoners (whatever I might be able to do) revived again.

Days are passing, and the only way to do it, I can see, is to stun the two somehow; and the only thing I'm afraid of is that not having had much practice, I may simply kill them unnecessarily. There are stone benches throughout the room, which is really huge. Each of those stone benches is now occupied by one of the interrogated ones, the latter being fastened to the stone by means of chains and locks. I stun the two guys. I do it, after certain amount of time spent imagining things, one by one. It goes easier than I anticipated because they have no suspicions—I've been here with them for a while. The first one, closer to the entrance, I hit him over the head with a mallet he used to break bones. I did it in one quick movement of my hand while the other was looking toward the wall, his hand in a sack where he had his lunch. His hand was still in it when I hit him with the same hammer over his head, still directed toward the wall. He went down right there, on the hay. Just in case they regain consciousness too quickly, I tied their hands with a rope, of which there was aplenty in the room. Then I went opening restraining contraptions of those I had already chosen; people were moving only very slowly, their members now truly numb, but they managed. Only five could move in such a manner that it wouldn't be hopeless, so I let those out, telling them where to go. I thought just letting them out wouldn't do; they had to get help outside the prison as well. For now, I had some clothing prepared for them in the aforementioned room, clothing I had rented especially for this purpose. Some food too. I paid a carriage, which was supposed to come in front of the building at a set hour. All went good. They'd go east until they'd cross the Rhine, and then it would be Meister who'd take care of them. That's where they were supposed to go and tell him who had sent them. I wish I could tell Meister about it all somehow ahead of time—before they get there, that is—but there is no way to do that. He will get the message from them, whenever they manage to get there. I'm sure he'll do whatever he can to accommodate their needs.

Then we just sit and wait for the night to come (the coach was supposed to come with the dark); we'll start then. For now they were asking me details; they wanted to know everything that I knew about the present situation here in France. Is there any chance to return to Outremer? I told them about the first version—strictly financial—and then about the second version with the de Villanova fellow, Cressonssart, and apocalyptic implications, the Angel of Philadelphia, which evoked their great interest. One of them, giant, but not thinking too quickly, wanted to know why not all of them—why did I make a selection and what was it based on—and to this Vadim answered instead of me: he was a knight, a guy of great education, philosopher, as far as could be established in this short time (one more time the past turned out more vivid than the present—presently, I had not a foggiest idea where Vadim might have been).

"To escape, my dear, you need to walk, don't you? He was watching them—well, us—in there, and so he knew who could and who could not meet the requirements. Seems obvious to me."

The giant was looking at me, so I nodded. He sighed. "Poor chaps…love it the way it is!"

"Yeah!" Vadim confirmed. "Poor chaps."

MARGUERITE

They came obviously to wake me up and found me on my knees, praying, the night all around me solid like cobwebs. A while ago I had the sudden vision of the pyre and couldn't put myself together; I shook and tears were falling from my eyes, and I would not be in position to tell what was frightening in that. The fear of physical pain? Hard to imagine when the fire already starts licking your body, and what was the realization that this is my last day here, on Earth. Then one tries to imagine the other side where one is going. Suddenly, it is not heaven; one suddenly remembers little things that now are not so little and on that scale may take quite a place…

I drank some water (I had some, they brought me a cup full of water) and after that, I was a little bit better. Was I? I haven't been tortured, so my body was in its usual condition. I could walk if I had to, or sit down. God, suddenly all of it mattered. I can't stop thinking, like a band were rolling and rolling in my head, just can't stop. Everything seemed to be different that day, and I remember a conversation with one of the women in here, condemned to death, who talked to me the day before, saying that it didn't matter to her: the worst shit was over. Hell, she was certain that it could only get better. Wow! I wish I had that certainty. In fact they had to help me up; my legs were trembling like a jelly or something. I had the impression they weren't mine at all.

I'm better now. As the cart passes along the streets, people don't even look at us. There doesn't seem to be any interest at all; burning witches became an everyday occurrence. And then I see the crowd of the Place de Grève. This is a lot different: they are here to watch; they are not just a passant, quickly moving to their destination inhabitants of the city. These here are at their destination; they have arrived, and they behaved respectively. The pyre is there, already built. I don't think it's impressive; in fact I've seen peasants up north where I am from building bonfires bigger than that. And there is no scarcity of wood around here, as far as I know. And I see them, the inquisition functionaries, colorful mix—there is a few bishops in red; a cardinal, whoever might he be, in purple; monks in brown habits. I don't know them, except for William. He has the same brown habit on when I saw him in back then as we spoke, the first and then the second time so differently; his hair hasn't changed at all. I can't see from this distance his eyes, but I think they must be the same. Eyes don't change, they say; eyes are the mirror of the soul, indication that there is a soul in some cases.

And then the cart I'm on stops and the clerk begins to talk, and he talks about all those things that happened so far, that I have been warned. Yet back in Valancaciène, where Bishop de Collemezzo publically burned my book and forbid to copy it, I, of course, did not react—not only not properly but not at all, spreading the heresy all over as if nothing had ever happened, preaching its pestiferous contents in front of the churches leading people into heresy, for which reason I am now where I am. I listen to the voice of the clerk reading the sentence for some reason only too carefully:

"Therefore, after diligent deliberation concerning all the aforestated matters and having received the counsel of many persons expert in both laws, having God and the sacred gospel before our eyes, with the assent and counsel of the reverend father and lord, Lord William, by the grace of God bishop of Paris, we condemn you by sentence, Marguerite, not only as one elapsed into heresy but as one relapsed, and we relinquish you to secular justice, asking it that short of death and mutilation of the body it act mercifully with you, as far as canonical sanctions permit." He had to clear his throat. "And we condemn, by sentence, the said book as heretical and erroneous, as containing errors and heresies by the judgment and counsel of the masters of theology residing in Paris, and now we want it to be exterminated and burned, and strictly order that each person having the said book, under pain of excommunication, is required to turn it over without fraud to us or to the prior of the Preaching Brothers of Paris, our commissioner, before the next feast of the Apostles Peter and Paul."

Then I listen to the secular sentence. I have to swallow William's sainthood mentioned. I'd have a hell of a problem to tell how many more times before the secular sentence is finally pronounced. I'm standing on the blessed cart, my hands bound behind me and then to a post right in the middle of the surface the cart creates, so now they undo my bounds and hand me down a lot like a puppet to the ones already on the ground, where from I'm lifted up onto the pyre and tied up again to the stake, which is right in the middle of it. The secular judge gives the sign to set the fire to the wood under my feet. And then I see him—suddenly, unexpectedly. The life I already said good-bye to touches me again with its full power. Johannes…Meister, the only man I knew. The only man I loved. He looks at me from the crowd; he is now one of them, even though he lived together with William in the same Dominican house in Paris as he was still regent master. I think I see tears falling down his cheeks, but that might just be an illusion. The distance is really far too great. He looks at me, and that was an intense look. I don't know how to describe it; just don't know…The fire climbs quickly up. I keep looking at him, trying to understand my past. My life.

ALVA

I am slowly running out of money, so time has come to cash one of the checks papa left me in a wooden box yet in Avignon, before he was taken by the guards. And it was brother, not long ago who pointed to me our contact here in Paris. He had foreseen (obviously) what was gonna happen to the rest of the brotherhood, although I think after what had happened in Avignon, it wouldn't take another Isaiah to predict that. Brother had also his share of our earthly possessions and most probably was using the same contact to get money or gold he needed to move around, sleep, and eat in the city. That was, according to him, one of the greatest inventions of the brotherhood: a traveler to the holy land did not have to have the money or gold with them, thus being protected from the pirates and bandits of all kinds with which the Mediterranean teamed at all times. A piece of parchment made in Europe (anywhere) was as good as gold. All one had to do was go to one of the exchange points pertaining to the knights, and there that piece of parchment would have been exchanged to gold or local money at the actual rate. The transaction itself wasn't expensive, but it was over time, considering how many wanted to do that—very lucrative.

With the time it became the main source of income for the brotherhood. Brother told me that the knights were the richest union of that kind in the whole world. Plans were made to organize a line from Brundisium to Acre and then a coach to Jerusalem, all of it at fixed dates and times, which facilitates traveling enormously, giving it the steadiness so far unknown. Goes without saying what Philip the Fair was doing could only mean one thing: destruction of any of that and returning the status quo to what it was a hundred years before.

I just recalled, entering the Parisian fish market, a story from a totally different place and different time, told me by my brother not that long ago about the defense of one of the English castles defended by only twenty people against an army of a thousand—the story with the bitter comment the king trying to sack the castle made about the battle: how was it possible that thousand men armed to the teeth could fail so miserably against twenty. The answer was given by one of the leading knights on the attacking side: "The twenty defenders, Your Highness, were Knights Templar..." I'm walking now among the tables covered with fish of different kind (fish with scales and those scraped naked and white) tables with lobsters and shrimp, still alive and moving the pincers—all of it emanating an odor of the sea, which is so far away from here.

I'm in Paris. And suddenly I feel a hand on my shoulder, big and heavy. That hand turns me around with no effort, and I'm standing in front of a very tall man with the chest wide as Notre Dame's western facade, with a head up there somewhere, but I rather hear than see the smile in his voice when he greets me; in that voice there is kindness and some sort of invitation—to do what? Do I know him? Have I ever met him somewhere? Hell no! By the same token I like him, I have the impression that my answer to the above questions should be in the affirmative: yes, I have met him (not the slightest idea where or what is it all about). All I truly know is Father's story about him. They met in Jerusalem and fought together at Acre. This guy also came to France, just as Father did, except he had foreseen more things and faster than father did. He decided to vanish before he came to Avignon, and only a little later father had received a piece of writing from him, from Paris: that he didn't trust the system anymore, that there was something monstrous going on. The past, our past, is wounded and dying; and if fatheror someone related to him somehow needed something, one never knows, he could be contacted in Paris, in the fish market. His brother was a matelot on the Seine, on a barge going all the way north with the city's products. No talk about Outremer, Templars, or anything related to our past. One more time: we are dying and that should be one thing to consider in all seriousness. The prince of this world (who is finally already judged, as we were told by our Lord) wants us dead, and be that as it may, he is the main force here with which we have no chance playing whatever kind of game. So let's die, even if we don't. Okay?

I was now standing in front of him, feeling amazingly well, as if father came back from some forgotten swamp of the death to see me.

"You are Alva, right? Your dad sure knew how to describe people..."

"Julius?" I managed. "Yes."

"I've got..."

"I know what you've got, dear. I promised your dad I'll honor it, no matter what the situation might be."

"Thanks."

"Come to Rue Lepic, after midnight. You want all of it?

In gold, francs, gems? What?"

"Not all of it, no. Whatever you consider I might need to move around for a couple of months. And I got nothing left. Whatever he left me is gone now!"

"After midnight. Rue Lepic, remember!" "I will. Rue Lepic, after midnight!"

And then he just wasn't there. As huge as he was, he just vanished. He was now (I think) a short guy, about my size, behind a fish table covered with fish scraped white, who said, smiling, "Wonderful bass, ma'am. Give it a shot!"

The fish looked really fresh so I gave it a shot. "This much, yes, sir, I still had left. Yes, siree!"

There was a long way until midnight. I was trying to find something to do. I thought about my brother, where might he be right now. What is he doing? Is he okay?

I put a bucket with water on the fire and got it to almost boiling, after which I took a bath. That was easy because there was nobody in the house with me, except my mate. She, at my request, scrubbed my back with a hard brush we bought together a couple of days ago on the market on the other side of the river. Then I took a nap. It is hard to believe how time may stretch if we are waiting for something important. The moment I woke up, it was only six o'clock. I had to do a lot of things until midnight. But then it finally was midnight, and I walk out of the house and directed my steps toward Rue Lepic. When I got there, I started walking along the dark houses, in that empty street, with a few stars up there on the sky made of black velvet, between the roofs above me. And then he was there too.

"Don't turn around!"

I didn't.

"This is it. Take the box. There you have some money, which is the amount I think should be sufficient for you, for reasonable period of time. If it isn't, come back, just as you did today. I'll give you more.'

"Thanks!"

"This is only because you didn't tell me how much you want. This should hold you over for some time, I'm sure. You just like your father. Just like him…"

I didn't see him. He was all this time slightly behind me so that I could only hear his voice.

"Go now! We are watched. Now too." "To see you," I said.

"Yes. I'll see you. I'm sure."

"Good night!"

I was alone, on an empty dark street, with my bodings and something I couldn't explain even if I wanted to; the man reminded me of father, of our home in Outremer, my childhood. All of a sudden I was playing with my brother, chasing a chicken with him and our dog, who was killed so hideously in the end by the Mamelukes. I felt like shouting, but also like laughing—both; life seemed to me strange and not really making any sense. None at all. What did he say? That we are watched? Whom am I watched by? And what for? Even now?

There was a stone step, just one, leading to a door.

Up above it there was an awning under which there was darkness now (which, as the saying goes, could be sliced with a knife), and I stepped under it, which hid me from anyone watching me from farther up the street. It didn't take long till I saw a guy, indifferent, looking the other way, and yet moving quickly in the direction I would have taken if I had kept on walking. Did his presence there have something to do with me? Or was it accidental? I'll never know. Fighting with my thoughts, trying to clarify my feelings, I slowly started walking toward the river. The night seemed to me to get denser. A little oil lamp at the door I was just approaching made the impression on me… well, I'd say it was the sun. The more intense the darkness, the more outstanding whatever the light source. I'll have to tell that to brother. Let's see!

MEISTER

did that when I was in Paris those so-and-so many years ago, teaching there for the first time, all puffed up with pride (God knows how proud I was having received the same position Albert the Great once had…). I stood there, with the day far spent and waited for her like a street prowler would have. I grabbed her and turned her around, toward me, and started kissing her all over her face; and to my greatest surprise, I saw that she was kissing me back. And that was right then and there that we got truly together. I felt the inside of her mouth with my tongue, eyes closed, and hers was in my mouth, our hands around our backs, touching and probing…

I've never seen a woman this beautiful before. She was my size, give or take. I remember now just as I remembered it then, in that *ruette*, in the dark, kissing like two kids crazed with love that came too early in life. I remember her in flashes, standing and preaching, talking in that voice, I'd say as unique as the rest of her was, about God and his love for us, I saw only her; the whole crowd wasn't there. Was it morning or evening? I had no idea whatsoever. I was stunned by her beauty, that's just about all I could say. At some point of her preaching, I noticed that she had noticed me too. I was not the first best of the street people standing there, no. She was clearly looking at me. I wasn't sure at the moment what did I see in her eyes, who I was to her, in other words. But I knew and I was quite certain that she had picked me out of the whole plaza somehow. I knew that I would wait for her and that I would try to start a conversation, which would have been easy, considering what she was talking about right there, in front of the church. (A copy of her book had been given to me, if memory serves, by William of Paris himself; we lived at the time in the same building, and he, being familiar with my work, thought hers was similar to mine beyond belief. And I think that might have been the true reason of his approaching me with her book; finally in her last days he would have hired fifteen greatest theologians of our times to continue the proceedings). And so, instead of trying to start a conversation about theology as I had planned for it to go, I just grabbed her like a rapist, and she not only didn't mind but seemed to really appreciate it. We were standing there and kissing like crazy, and I didn't think about my swollen lips, my tongue bitten up, my hands getting numb; behind my back the beguinage building making big black windows stare at the stump of a stone wall we were hiding behind. And we looked then, with the onslaught of the night, for a certain woman she knew from the holy confession (absolution had to be given the woman periodically, and Margot was milder and easier to convince that this was the last time and that it won't happen again; the woman had her den a few paces from there). The woman was to show us *un toit pour s'aimer.*

Love, goodness…yes, I was in love. At my age…And what it is, I think, the best expression had been given by our footman in the building, whose name was Paul, when he said, "And when I touch you, I feel happy inside." I still think that's it; it certainly goes for certain kinds of love. In the darkness of the night or then, after the sun was already up and a new day had started with the noisy street outside. If I can touch your skin. If I can feel your touch on mine. If I can see your eyes, wet of tears held back, your mouth, slightly open, seeking next breath, silent.

What revives in the memory are our steps in the old wooden staircase, each answered with a sound reminding one of a cry of helplessness—old wood does that. I see her then taking off the habit, under which she has close to nothing, and I too take my clothes off. After which we fall together like hungry falcons on their prey. In my whole life of so-and-so many years, I knew nothing more intense; nothing I'd like to say—cry out loud—last! Don't be over, you're so beautiful! And both of us catching breath, trying to think what actually had happened—*What is it?*—and that life only rarely takes you so completely by surprise. And such surprise! One that leaves you stranded, creating a need of going back to your beginnings, childhood, youth, the forming of your character. Who then are you? Who is she?

I looked sideways, furtively, and I caught her look seeking my face. We both smiled at each other.

"Are you embarrassed?" I heard her voice then.

"Not yet," I answered. "I guess I just haven't gotten so far yet. What I'm trying to do right now is try to figure out who actually I am. Where do I come from. See?"

"D'you have a name for this?"

"I can sense it coming. Didn't form yet in my mind, but is close. I'm almost there. You?"

"Yes." "What is it?"

"Can't speak for you, see?" "What is it for you then?

She was looking at me with intensity that would almost scare me, prolonging the moment, sighing.

"Yes?"

"It's love, Johannes. I love you! That's what love is!"

I remember myself trying to think; my eyes on the ceiling, at some point white, now dark gray, like fear that was surrounding me on all sides.

"Young people have some kind of a future. They make plans. Love takes them where they didn't even suspect they'd be some day. But what about us, Margot? Where is it taking us? Is it taking us anywhere?"

She put her hand around my chest. Her head on my shoulder so that her mouth was close to my ear.

"Here, you are the rector of the University of Paris. In your country, you're a big guy too. You are known, everywhere up here, Johannes. I think the only way for us would be a place where nobody knows anything about either one of us. Southern Italy? Outremer maybe? There's but one question in all this, the way I see it. Is it worth it to you? To leave behind the life as you've known it so far, life of great success, and face the new, abandon and failure, as it approaches at an accelerated pace?"

I knew she was looking at me. Waiting. And at that moment, I thought the answer was simple, so simple in fact, that I did not see the necessity of answering at all. *Sure, let's go. Let's drop it. Things here aren't worth much. They might be, oh, yes, they might be worth everything to someone who never had them, but we did, both of us, we've had it all. Our life here was full up to the brim. It shouldn't be difficult then.*

I turned to her and we kissed; still kissing, having my tongue inside her mouth, I got on top of her and we started making love, passionately again, in a way which would make me forget myself, the place we were at—well, everything. We'd just do it till it was over, and we'd lie down on our backs again, recovering our strength.

He gives to each, passes suddenly through my head, according to what is best for them and most suitable. If we are to make new clothes for someone, then we must make them according to their dimensions, and those which will fit one will not fit another. We measure everyone to see what fits them. So too God gives everyone the best thing of all according to his knowledge of what is most suitable for them. Indeed, whoever trusts him in this entirely receives and possesses in the least of things (viewed from the outside a sheer poverty lacking even the basics) as much as they do in the greatest degree (kings, palace, and everything that comes with it).

We were looking at each other, and she was smiling.

Somebody seemed to be dictating this to me, and I seemed to myself to be only listening to my own voice, as if it wasn't me who was speaking:

"If God wished to give me what he gave St. Paul, then I would receive it gladly, if this were his will. But since he does not wish to give it to me, for he wills that only very few people should attain to such knowledge in this life as Paul, if he does not give it to me, then he is still as precious to me and I'm as grateful to him and I'm just as content that he should withhold it from me as I am that he should give it to me."

"That's love too, Johannes," she said. "Unlimited trust."

And then, "Are you answering my question?"

"Yes," I said. "That might just be the best answer I could possibly come up with."

"Let's work out the details then."

"Now?"

"Not necessarily. No." "Next time?"

"Yes. Okay. Next time. Or whenever."

"I may not have sufficient time for whenever," she said. I don't think at that moment I understood what she meant by that. I knew, of course, about the prosecution. I knew how they hated her for her success with people, how people were buying her book, coming to see her and listen what she had to say—all the bad rap from church's side notwithstanding. I knew all that. And yet when she said that "I may not have sufficient time," I don't think I had any idea what that meant.

We ordered some food (very good roasted pork, a bunch of potatoes, and some vegetables), and we were eating them, after which we've had some wine, and we had a little chat. What would we do. We would have to vanish, no doubt there. Preaching, wherever, would sooner or later bring the church people on her track, and at that point, I was beginning to feel the Franciscan-Dominican differences as well. The, by then, clear tendency to eliminate everything not orthodox within the Catholic church (the Albigensian crusade, the Beguines in Paris and elsewhere, the Beghards, and above all the incredible cruelty with the Jews and the Templars) was well known to me. I asked her what she thought about that all, and she said it was the world entering something bigger than we—I and her—could even conceive of. The world is something we know really nothing about; it's there, in its place, held there so that it would cradle our lives, giving us a chance to become what we are meant to become: after birth from a woman's womb, we enter the bosom of the world to pass another gestation necessary to be born in heaven. It is, according to her, somewhere between hell and heaven, our place down here, and yet in our times it slowly inclines toward hell, as if the forces holding it for us there got tired or bored—anyway, it isn't what it used to be. Oh no! It'll be more and more difficult for us to get out and go home, to retain what the faith was preserving so far so good. No, now it's different. The yesterday's world is over.

She put down her empty glass on her nightstand and then turned back to me. We made love again. Each time we do it is like losing one's self in something so much bigger than one that I'm beginning to thank for that experience too. I never thought something like that was possible at all; with all the thinking I have done throughout my life about love, I don't think I had a real idea of what it is. Toward the end of my life—yeah, only then—it's been given to me in this form, and I think about it as finding me worth it, Good Lord, finally, in this very end I was found worthy of this experience. Thank you, Sire!

The bed Sue had given us is great—soft and silent, guarantying that our experiences shall forever remain ours only. The wine reminds me of the one in Carla's cellar, in Thüringen, cold cut meat left us to quicken our strengths, doesn't fall far behind those in my own land. I liked Paris from the day one.

SMYRNA

GISCARD

Smyrna is a big city and there are a lot of places to go to. And yet to some of those places we go more frequently than to others, as if our steps were suddenly directed by something inside us we are not quite aware of. And so there was a library, right at the corner of St. Swiller's Street, so named after his martyrdom already had taken place so-and-so many years ago. The king's people came with armors and swords, and after a sword had been plunged inside his huge round belly, about a barrel of heavy red wine from Cyprus spouted out of it and stained the street stone pavement in a way that turned out permanent. Up to the very now—yes, sir—there's a stain one can see quite clearly. And if one happens to see it, which means to be there, there's right there an unexpected source of a story: how did that happen, where did the stain come from? The book dealer, Joseph Cartaphilus, owner (I think) of the library, will appear at your side and start telling you about the past of the spot in such a colorful language that no one would have any doubts about his own eyewitness status. I like entering the store, its smell of ancient parchment in scrolls, some cut into rectangles sawed together and framed wonderfully with wood and leather, pressed with gold leaf...He sells pictures too. By artists I never heard of, some of them so-so, and some I'd truly like to own but could so far never afford. I'd discussed art with both actually, mother as well as father, when they were still alive. Now there's nobody, not just to discuss art, but to do anything. They partook in an expedition Far

East, near the China wall, in those deserts where there are things slightly different than here. And there it was too that a sandstorm first, unexpected and unusually strong, surprised them in the middle of that nowhere and then an earthquake coming with such a strength that it seemed miracle to see two stones left on top of each other. The guy came back, and that's how I know the details. They did not. Their graves are there, in those sands, made with friendly hands, now most probably naked; nobody would bring any flowers.

Over here our house was left untouched, heirloom to me in the future, now empty, with only Grandma inside. We didn't bother each other, Grandma being a very lonely person, keeping to herself most of the time. It was Father, long before all this had happened, who introduced me to Cartaphilus at the same time telling me the story of his name. I still remember father, lowering his voice down to almost a whisper, telling me how an Armenian bishop visited England and how is the purport of his conversation, if rendered correctly in the historia major, begun by Roger of Wendover and completed by Mathius Parisius, noted in there, how the conversations took place in St. Albans, through Henry Spigurnelj—in French, the boy being French, native of Antioch and servant to the bishop. And if the replies of the Eastern Prelate were rightly rendered, his tendency to the marvelous was sufficiently strong. Father was interested in this type of story, and obviously, for Joseph it was sheer delight—deserving lowered voice, down to whisper, eyes half closed, ignoring anyone if there was anyone inside at the time: how he was asked, for instance, whether he had seen Noah's Ark said to be still preserved on an Armenian mountain…We talked today about a papyrus, written in Greek, a copy obviously, not certain though, copy of what… But his conviction would grow with the reading that it might be Aristotle, a fragment of metaphysics—well, he'll know soon. It's precious considering how much nonsense he bumped into lately, to the point of truly wrecked nerves. I said good-bye to him and left. Marching down, I directed myself to the water, for now toward the port, but I changed that quickly for the open long beaches with wavelets rushing onto the sand, affording one the sense of infinity.

Light breeze on one's face, a delicate taste of salt in one's mouth, marching at a steady pace along the waterline, one slowly would gain the impression that something like this cannot possibly end—not ever; that one shall march like that till the end of the time. Feeling good. Feeling certainty, steadiness of life.

The sun was already high on the firmament when I changed the direction, back to the port. I think now it must have been under the influence of the far sight of a ship with the French flag, if I could be the judge of that at that distance, maneuvering to enter the port's waters. I didn't speed up, just kept on going, all the time at the same pace. And there they were: the ship already moored, half of the crew or probably even more than that already gone to town. And there was a group of young people, French, which wasn't atypical (was it the First Crusade, its influence in these parts?). The ship was moored to the wide shore paved with stones upon which lots and lots of carts were moving forth and back. I approached the group, and we started talking; they had no accent, and I asked about it, and the middle-aged gentleman answered that they were French. They defended Outremer as long as there was something to defend, and after Acre was just another beautiful memory, they packed up whatever they considered worthy and left. I was told how they sailed on the open sea for days before they found the ship. They told me how the ship picked them up, in the end letting go the small boat, until it disappeared in foams. There's a woman with them who they call Alva, who made on me an incredible impression: a beautiful woman, and then there is in her face something that I don't think I know how to call or describe, maybe this: if there should be a group of some twenty thirty people I'm dead sure I would be able to pick her up and that independently from the conditions, meaning after a journey one is covered with dirt and dust, one should be able to change clothes, etc.… And I stayed there, even offered to go to town and get some food for them, because I felt incredibly well sitting not far from her, hearing her talk and laugh…I think this is the first time in my life something like that happened to me. They are all good people, forthcoming, friendly; they are wonderfully educated too. We tried languages. Her father started that, and it turned out that we could switch from, to, and back, all of us in the same manner. She is French, but she spoke with me Arabic like she was an Arabian woman, no accent whatsoever. Her brother calls himself Zweifler—that's actually what his father invented for him. I didn't manage to find out what his real name was, even though I tried. One has to have a name, don't they? God bless it! On the shore, people were dancing, and Greek music seemed too loud to me; it bothered me in listening to her voice, but I knew well that if I went over and ask to keep it down, I would just be ridiculous and nobody would pay me any mind. I am not good for that kind of affair, which definitely involves looks. So I stayed where I was and did nothing. It made one feel even worse.

Two big guys were then carrying along the cobblestoned shore a fish hanging on a long piece of wood, sharp on one side, like a pale; the fish seemed gigantic, seemed to me to have no end—well, what do I know about fish. I didn't even know its name and didn't dare to ask. Those people were working hard…

The sun was setting slowly, and we started talking about the night. I invited them to my empty house (in the meantime, I told them the story of my family and the fact that right now I was almost all by myself in a big house); but they didn't want to go: too far, it's already getting dark, seriously dark, and all they need in the end is something to lean on, like, Zweifler said, "that crate there with the boxes on top of it, see? I'll put my back against it, close my eyes, and I'll be sound asleep in few minutes' length. Thank be to God for that." He smiled at me. "That's health." His father smiled too. Yes. I bloody agree. That's health. What else?

I sat there too. At first I closed my eyes and tried to fall asleep; discipline is everything, my father used to say. But I could close my eyes or open them, whatever, and sleep did not find me worthy. I gave that up. I always dreamed about theology somewhere in Europe; Paris would be beyond dreams, of course. University of Paris was the best in the world. Every child knew that, here and elsewhere—every child. And now these guys were going to France. A bunch of very nice guys, and they invited me with them, and wasn't I a lucky skunk? To see the world like that? They do not depart tomorrow, so I'll have to go back home and do the final preparation, do the final accounting with Cartaphilus. Finally, I have something to be grateful to him for; he started me on my way to the church, to the robe… Yes, it was he.

And then I'll come back here. I'm probably gonna have to have a cart or something of that nature; my stuff, books in particular, won't fit into nothing else. And then I should be shown my place aboard. What if I am refused? I didn't like that captain. Now, did I?

Hell, I, then, shall buy the scow and fire him with bad references…huh? I'll think about it, damn it! But even without much thinking, that's exactly what I'm gonna do!

And then it was another day, and I told them I had to go to get my stuff because I'm taking them up on the invitation. I'll pitch in, of course; they shouldn't think of me as a burden, no. I do have my resources; they were left to me by my father, and I might even be of help on the journey. One more time I was assured that I was welcome aboard, to my great pleasure, I must say. I thanked them.

ZWEIFLER

I found simple work on a barge going to Seine's estuary with certain products characteristic of the Parisian region, and when we go back, that's the shellfish which fills the barge's body. Nobody here knew anything about my past, except Julius, of course. All I am to them is a strong young man, certainly willing to work. I am quite fast at doing whatever the job requires—for the most part that's carrying stuff from the barge onto the shore or the other way around, depending upon where we are. Going north, we use the sail; if the weather is propitious it is the sail only. Going the other way around, the same, aided by six pairs of rows. Now that's hard work, at which I'm really good, which is also to say much appreciated by the people the barge belongs to. I don't care all that much about the payment, and that's because I live still on my old sources—only now I am very careful: to get to my own money I only slowly steal like a thief, on my way using all the possible tricks of the trade. So far it had worked out, and I don't think anybody has any suspicions as to who I am.

I haven't contacted Alva or the young guy Giscard at all, although last couple of weeks I spent in Paris because of a little accident in the river estuary: I was carrying a basket with lobster from the shore into the barge, and one of them—a huge monster, more like a dream gone bad—cut my finger so badly that right there and then it looked like it was gonna fall off. Goes without saying I couldn't do much physical work with one of my fingers held in place by the gauze. The lobster was thrown into the boiling water alive, and I ate it to the accompaniment of the hearty laughter of my companions. I love lobster's meat, and this one was quite a bit of a creature sizewise, considering the region (I was told by them, people who owned the barge, that France, the north in particular, isn't the best territory in the world for that—whatever else is, or might be, I have no idea. The lobster living in the Mediterranean is tasty but has no pincers; the best is all the way north, in the Arctic). And so, having found out that my favorite food is the lobster, surprise to me as well, they'd afford me some of it most every day, did I do some work or not. We'd sit on the barge in the evening, once the day was up, and cook some of it and eat, drinking also wine and singing (they did—I don't sing but love to listen). And then when morning came, we would start the journey to the estuary, little town there—goodness, a few hours' journey—to see people, who liked us just as we liked them, and do with them the business, which sustained all of us. Few hours; journey into the day, in the delicate fog, the banks hardly visible, sort of mixing with the air above water, air, which closer to the sun, would unveil the latter's presence to us as a mysterious red disc with no borders. The villages would pass by, quite fast. I never learned their names, although they seemed mystery too. There was incredible amount of them on both sides of the river, such that one day I asked if there was anyone who'd know their names, but there was no one, at least not amongst us aboard.

The river was really curvaceous, going from east to west and then the other way around, like somebody were paying for that. I know one thing from that time: I was beginning to learn the river (which isn't easy at all: the where is what, sand dune, shallows, deeps, eddy currents and whirls and twirls, and how to navigate among them; if it sounds like nothing, you try it! Only then you'll know!).

There's a village about halfway between Paris and the estuary where I've seen what was to be so ominous: the water there forms—jeez—like a marshland, with bays covered with wicker and such, and from the main stream of the river I could see the woman taking a bath. The water wasn't deep, and I saw her breasts as well as the black triangle under her belly. Her hands moved slowly in the blackish water, like she was observing something in there, trying to exert a delicate influence moving her hands like that. And then she looked up at me, smiling. I asked them guys to stop—please—if we could, and we did. And there she was, in a white garment on the shore. She had a round white cheese she held out for me. I sat down on the sand beside her. She broke off a morsel and gave it to me—white, wet, soft, marvelous, marvelously tasty.

We were sitting there, on that sand, till she asked me when I would be back. I told her I'd be there the day after the day that was coming. We'd be going from Paris to the estuary. Then we kissed. Her lips were wet and soft, marvelously tasty too. I touched her breast under the white garment—also soft and full of consequences. I didn't mind any. I knew, I just knew, I would come back and love her and give her and myself what I knew so little of in this life, and what this life in the end was supposed to be all about. The boys in the barge didn't push. I was sitting there, on that sand with her, until the day was almost over, with her head on my lap.

And then she said, "I'll see you soon?"

She knew I had to go.

"The day after tomorrow. We'll be making another pass again. Yes, I'll see you then." "And then?"

"And then we'll see…"

She laughed, and her laugh was like pearls dancing on a mahogany board. I just knew something very important has happened. The day after tomorrow we just picked her up. The only parent was her mother—little, tiny, dried out—who we just took with us, and I didn't think she knew who we were and where she was going at all; I didn't pay her any mind. I thought and thought about what was I going to do now, and I think leaving Paris altogether might just be the best idea I've had ever so far. Question was to where?

The owner of the barge thought we should stay right there, without any changes, until something more sensible would pop up. Fine. Like what? And then we saw it: an English ship going from there, from the estuary, all the way down to Gibraltar, to get then onto the Mediterranean, east, to Italy. One of the ports on the schedule was Brundisium, which sounded great to me. Just great. I had no doubt that was my more sensible thing—the setup that I was waiting for, somehow, all this time that I was waiting for it without knowing about it at all. At this point, the question was Alva. What's with her? And then there was that boy; his name was—goodness, Giscard now, wasn't it? He had problems in Paris because of Averroes's books, found where he lived, in his quarters. Alva could be really obstinate. I knew that. If she wanted him to go with us, he would go with us, period. There's never so far been a point in trying to convince her about something she didn't want to be convinced about. I knew that since Outremer. Nothing changed in that department. And I guess nothing ever will. Nothing.

GISCARD

It started some forty years ago; it was long before my birth, Aquinas was still alive. He even wrote a small treatise, if memory serves. *Contra Averroistas (leave this alone, please)* he called it, and it was accepted as has ever been everything else from seiner feather. A short time when he was a suspect in the bosom of the church and Albertus Magnus himself had to defend the greatness—oh, but he did, and how at that? More than successfully, and the memory remains unstained; the oxen bellows all over the world! Doesn't God have the right to create ones for honor and others for dishonor? And to those whom he loves he gives crosses now, doesn't he? Now I remember my father (may he rest in peace!), like through a dense fog, repeating that and then reflecting and then repeating it again, after which he pronounced the final comment— that's exactly the kind of love to keep up one's ass…I've been trying to understand any of it ever since, and all I do is that so human: *errare*. I feel lost and I don't see my way. No, siree!

I wrote a little treatise too, for Alva, since she is the only woman I know who knows how to read (she also knows, give or take, who Aristotle once was). But then, after she was already through, I asked her what her thoughts were, and she complained to me about the fish she had bought that day on the market and that it hasn't been quite fresh… Only a drop of briny dew floating down my cheek toward my dried-up lips, as the local song I like to listen to goes. Why do they sell fish, here in Paris, that isn't quite fresh if it isn't only a day from the Seine's estuary where you can have every blessed thing that lives in the channel? Oh, she knew well. Her brother would go every week on a barge until he found his wife somewhere halfway there—God bless it! I wrote about Plato believing that we bring everything from heaven, and then about Aristotle for whom it is the world we live in that starts a world to live in us—goodness. But that's also where the problem starts: if the world is only the content of our perception, then how do we know that there is a world out there, somewhere, how would we know that? And there is quite a few of thinking people whose problem that is, as well, precisely that. How do I know there is anything beside me in existence? Sounds awkward, but as I was trying to explain to Alva, it's a very serious problem in our thinking if you're ready to accept all the consequences logic brings into our thinking, as long as we are ready to apply it to the task.

Her concern was the stinking fish.

And then there is this very basic question: what we'll do next, what do they plan to do? Stay here in Paris, trying to arrange our lives in such a manner that we would just be French, or maybe move somewhere inside this country to become French, or maybe travel back to Outremer…I tried to talk to Alva's brother, but he just patted my shoulder without saying anything; I've no idea, none whatsoever.

Here in Paris might be difficult if not impossible altogether for me because of my interests. (I mentioned Averroes and some of his writings I'm in possession of. In the beginning it seemed to me not so deadly; it maybe not quite innocuous as it seems to me now.) I rent a small room from a tailor, and they've been here so far time and time again; the king's guards—sons of bitches—took my stuff as if it were theirs. No, decidedly, I couldn't stay here now, could I? I gotta move! To where? Well, that seems to be the question from the very beginning. Since we crossed the border of France. To where? For a moment I thought about that place nobody ever heard of, where Alva's brother found his wife; I don't have any ambitions as to where I might have been or be from. That place would be just fine for me. But Alva's brother didn't like the idea. Hell no! We shall move all together; and I, Giscard, will stay with them, wherever we decide to go, to the very end. Finally, I wasn't born in France either; I only came here with them now, didn't I? He felt obliged to recall some of our past, which we seemed to be inclined to forget. Why do we always forget our past? Do we want to, is that deliberate, or does it just happen? I mentioned Chartres, place we all liked and traveled to, to see the church in building, which united so many people, transcending petty quarrels and bringing about the fruit that all of Europe would seem to enjoy more and more.

Alva as well as her brother was serious, deliberating within themselves. It took a while. It did. It seemed to me part of what it seemed to be for the whole country: a giant trying to get rid of something or maybe to call something into being, something that wasn't there and only now would appear—in all the pains of birth. The entire France seemed to answer to that description. Templars. Jews. The Papacy. Cathars. Beguins. Beghars. The Albigensian crusade. Something was in the making, and we, willy-nilly, were a part of it, a part which isn't there to understand, certainly not to explain. A part which one just lives through, wondering.

I'd like to be able to say more, to explain, but I'm who am. Yes, of course, I have my interests. I read whatever I can, but is that enough to measure up to what's happening around us? Is it? No, I don't think so. One feels too small—one's preparation inadequate, to say the least.

Trying to think about it all, I feel like I am sufficient to go to the fish market and get something fresh and edible for all of us here. No more than that. Talking about Chartres—right here in Paris, the church has been built, which doesn't seem to be less than Chartres, and I've heard about Reims and Amiens…Now, what would that mean, if it means anything? Does it mean something? Is God gonna come to see us again? How are we doing? Are we something that is worth his worry, or should he maybe forget, let us choke on our own crap, staying wherever he is in that better part (it's got to be better)? Not moving at all? Alva asked me time and time again about the university: how was it. I remember her and I see, suddenly, the old man talking. I hear Joseph's voice, which carry well inside this room of stone, every word pronounced perfectly. Yes, it is the main room of the library, where we used to talk the most. In what goes for the academy, there's a question everybody asks: how was it possible for Plato to produce a student so different from himself—he, Plato, pointing to heavens as to the source of everything whereas Aristotle's claim was that it is the earth and our moving over it that creates us, and that seems to be a claim opposite to the first one. And that, once started, starts me also. Now is it really? I'm trying to be as articulate as I only can be. Plato seems to skip the first part of the process—we come back here full of ideas, and how they got there is unimportant (not for us to know anyway). And the other guy seems to be fascinated by precisely that: how did we get those ideas? Have they been given to us directly, like written by a hand that can't be seen but is there, or rather, the gift is something else, common to all, final product differentiated by each individual soul, which is also the final form of the body? So we have two opposites: the world, out there, unknown, and the body that transfers from unknown to known, individually everything there is, including itself.

Plato destroys wrong ideas or ideas gone wrong through teaching (Socrates), and in Aristotle, it is the transfer of the world the inside of which does the job. So the world is the teacher. Or rather, the living in the world means *elenxis* (that too, for all that goes wrong, but also the effort to keep it right) as well as *mayeusis* (here as the final stage, the meticulous care for details), both individual differentiated by each of the souls of any given individual.

She keeps nodding.

He looked toward the small window showing a small garden with a monument of a poet in the middle. The poet's hand is on his heart, his head lifted up to heavens. The day is cloudy, the rain is about to start.

"Now and then"—he picks up then and his voice has never so far had this strength, this naturalness—"the world stops teaching right things. It deteriorates. It's we, the people, who make it degenerate, and something has to be done to get it back in the right tracks: wars, revolutions, uprisings, religious movements. Well, we sense it. We know, somehow, that the absorption process has been disturbed and is changing. We usually feel, then, abandoned, cheated, sad. Some die. So many in fact that we seem to accept death as basis for our existence, and we begin to speak of "the gift of death." Maybe some night, the starry sky far up there above you, you yourself feeling small, confronted with all the beauty and power. Or maybe not, when you're deep asleep, and from somewhere other than whatever you might be dreaming, a sound comes, a sigh, like a tortured body finally got a break. And you'll know that's it: there is something new out there, something so far unknown, which will slowly give the world back its gift of changing you in agreement according with which you came here to complete the gestation before you might be born somewhere else—now a true you, uplifted and complete, capable of complying with the requirements of the new reality you've always dreamed of. The one never reachable since you came out of your mother's womb—now yours for good."

I see him, Joseph Cartaphilus—an old man and yet a man—one hundred percent, noble, beautiful face in a frame of silvery hair: he wore a light beard and his hair was little longer. I see him standing there, behind his pulpit, yet a moment longer, concentrating, maybe seeking the right words. He too left Paris. Went to his country where he was born, supposedly very beautiful, at least according to him. He would, rarely, say something to that effect—a delicate comparison between this town and the one of his youth. They started to bother him too—with the suspicion of heresy. He wasn't accused openly, not yet anyway, but things were on their way. He was Dominican at that time and his accusers Franciscan, so it wouldn't take a lot of imagination to figure out how the whole thing was gonna end. He sighs now, quite loudly.

It's like the other old man Zweifler was talking about, and quite a bit at that.

He didn't wait, to my great regret. I haven't listened to him. Never got to know him personally, but Zweifler knew him precisely on that basis. One time Zweifler showed me some papers he had in great esteem, present from the old man—Thomas Aquinas had written in his time as five proofs of the existence of God, and then they were copied by Albertus Magnus, personal friend of our great old man just as he was for Thomas Aquinas, on a piece of very expensive parchment, in beautiful style, first-class calligraphy…

Here I leave Alva for a moment (with the impression that she still ponders the lack of freshness of the fish she just had gotten) and devote a bit of my time to her brother. Zweifler mentioned his old man's relationship to Porete.

Nobody knew much about it, but what fascinated Zweifler was the fact that the old man stood there, right there, at the pyre on the Place de Grève, and watched her die that horrible, horrifying death, and that didn't change his faith in the least. I'm trying and trying, and I fail to even imagine somebody I may love, slowly roasted in front of a crowd, still producing that shout, which curdles one's blood (it can last quite some time, so long sometimes one wouldn't believe). And yet a bit later, when the strength leaves one and it becomes just a prolonged, seemingly endless moan (life is still there, I've seen it), after which I would kneel down and thank God for whatever I might be thinking was worth thanking for. There are differences between us that are irreconcilable. I'm not him, and he shall never be in anything like me. Anyway when the heresy crap started, he didn't wait (the old man, Zweifler's friend)—he went right east, back to where he was from. To those unending greens, woods of no limits, great stone houses, fortified with wooden beams in a characteristic pattern, in which the stone is embellished by wood and wood's sense in the whole construction gets deeper then when it lies around just piled up. He showed us a picture of his own house in his Thüringen.

I wish I could say more about any of the above, but I'm saying what I'm saying, for whatever it's worth, and may thank be to God for even this. I wouldn't wanna be boring to anyone, and the more details I pile up here, it seems to me the more chances I have to be precisely that: boring. Stop! No more!

MEISTER

That day I ate a few streets away from the river, where I don't do eat all that often, and this time I did it because I felt like having beef prepared in the manner they do it—supposedly the manner requested personally by William of Paris. He, William, and I, we live in the same building, but I haven't met him in person for the longest time—as they say, some things are just meant to be and some are not. This time when I entered the, eatery he was there, sitting at the massive oak table all alone, all majestic; and seeing me enter the room, he greeted me with a hand movement, motioning me also to approach and sit there with him. I obliged. He started explaining how his beef was prepared and that for years on end by now, and that I'd be welcome to it, would I feel like it. He also motioned the owner to bring another plate and another cup for the wine, which happened in an instant. I thanked him. He started talking politics of the day right away, which is something I always try to avoid for as long as I can: I disagree with most everything that's happening. I just didn't know how to tell him that. And so he talked about the Cathars in southern parts of France, about Albi and Carcassonne, pays Languedoc in general. His knowledge of the time is truly impressive, and listening to him, I can't help the impression that he must be involved emotionally, somehow, in the history of the region. When talking about Montségur and its siege, he expresses sheer admiration.

Taking a sip of excellent wine, he talks about the treasure they managed to take out with them (and just how, in the hell, if you were there, you can hardly imagine taking with you anything getting down that precipice, any blessed thing!), and that's why he himself, William, is inclined to think it must have been something spiritual, rather holy, text of some kind—for instance, a reliquary, piece of bone or parchment not relating to riches of this world at all. It's then Queribus and Peyrepertuse, Montaillou…

We sit there, drinking wine and eating excellent beef made according to his own recipe (marinated for a week or so in a mixture of best wines and spices before cooking, a very little cooking), and time's a-flyin'. It truly is. He might not be the most sympathetic person to me, although I don't blame him for things that happened in the past because of his caution before any kind of final pronouncement, that going incredibly easy with his subjects, hiring serious people in vast amounts to deliberate before anything impossible to undo would be declared. It's like a sticking of a dagger in your belly then: Marguerite… And again the same thing: he hired fifteen people, fifteen top theologians, guys of truly highest rank, deliberating whatever was available at the moment for an amount of time that today seems ridiculous (he didn't hire me, did not even extend an invitation, because he knew beforehand I'd refuse). Was it his fault? Could he have done something to save her? I wish she could be here, with us. But by the same token, she is now where she always wanted to be, and the perspective of joining our company at this table most probably wouldn't be so tempting to her right now, would it?

I was trying to recall the meadow I saw her on in a dream, full of flowers, where I wanted to approach her but for some reason couldn't move. And she saw me and saw my efforts and smiled at me, and she seemed more beautiful to me there than when she was still alive down here with us—and suddenly it is the cart she stood on, chained, I hear the wooden wheels' ominous clunk on the stone pavement, and I jump. Like through fog, I see William on the other side of the table, jumping too; he looked at me like I were totally crazy and that made him simply afraid of me, of what I might do. And she smiled, mildly, her face forgiving; my lips are praying—we both, William as well as I, just sit down, still looking at each other. I strongly suspect he knows what I'm thinking and doesn't feel good about it. I apologize. Another night, I saw her on the same meadow—or maybe it wasn't the same, just very much like that one—and I didn't recognize her at first. I remember the expression of my astonishment with the beauty surrounding me, that expression ending in my whisper: "Oh, so the mother of God is here too…" Only then I recognized Marguerite, and she addressed her beautiful smile to me.

All of it must have taken a split second while both of us—I as well as William—were sitting there at the table and eating the excellent food he ordered, rinsing it down with the even more excellent Rhine wine, whose soul reminded me so much of home, of the time of my youth, when life is still hope for the future and one doesn't know yet that a major part of that life will play itself out on the ashes of that hope, and that regardless of how far you got in this life (when others will say that you made it, you scored great, etc.,), any of it just doesn't matter.

His gray eyes are looking at me carefully. He holds his cup halfway between his mouth and his snow-white napkin on the table. Some strange expression is erring on his lips. unexpressed.

"Johannes…" he says then, waiting yet, obviously uncertain.

"Yes?"

"You wanted to ask me something, I was told…" "By whom?"

"That's of no importance. Just tell me what it is?"

Now we were looking at each other with the same tenseness.

"The Templars…" I said. "You have met—well, spoken with de Molay, have you?"

"Yes," he just said.

"Who is he?"

"I wish you told me," he said. He didn't smile. "I don't really know."

"Any chance I could talk to him?" "Would you like to?"

"Yes," I said. "Very much so."

He cleared his throat. "Done then. When?" I took a deeper breath. "Now?"

"Sure. Let's finish. Wash a little. And I order the carriage, huh?" He was looking at me. "We go?"

"Whenever you ready!" "Okay."

On our way, we were talking about de Molay's arrest and then examination under torture in the building of the Sorbonne, which took place on basically two days: twenty- fourth and then twenty-fifth of September. He confessed and was taken to a dungeon, dank and mildewed, because the University of Paris did not have space to accommodate him—that first and second, he had to be punished for what he confessed to. From that dungeon he was then taken to yet another one, probably worse, and so on.

"Do you believe his confession under torture to be true?"

I asked.

There was a moment after that of prolonged silence.

"I don't know," he said then. "In the beginning I believed, like probably everyone else. But after he recanted…See, Johannes, he is over seventy years old. He's been over seven years in different prisons, under torture in the worst case, undernourished, and constantly plagued by his arthritis, which gets worse every day in the mildest version of his predicament, and yet none of that seems to be able to really break him. I think even the devil begins to doubt himself. So that's basically what I am telling you: I don't know. Maybe, maybe not. Nobody knows at this point. Nobody!" Then the carriage stops. We get out and enter the building where William is obviously well known, the signs of reverence surround us from every side. We walk through long corridors and descend steps, which don't seem to have an end. The building from the street never looked that big—vast majority of it seemed to be subterranean. Doors would open and close with the characteristic sound of metal bars, reminding one (as if anyone could ever forget that) where one is: that life as one knows it is left far behind in some kind of the night, possibly without end. And if the night doesn't end, does my life end, ever—question appears—or will I err in here like the Greeks described it, telling us about Orpheus in the aftermath? Theseus? Aeneas?

And then I see him: he has a white shirt on, covering what's left of his body, skin and bones mostly, his face at first getting one scared. Also for the most part bones, as kull with burning eyes, long white hair on both sides of his head, bald on top, and the white beard that reaches his breast.

"My God…"

He looks at me. Silent. And then that bonehead turns into a smile I shall never be able to forget.

"Scary, isn't it?" his voice resound one more time as the iron door behind us did a moment ago. "Yes, it must be… See, I haven't spoken for a long time. All I know now is shout and howl of a wolf. I'm asked a question and even before I start answering, something gets broken in me. Or burnt. Or something like that. The world sheds its skin, you see? Time for that has come, and we are the ones to pay. And so we do, dearly. We just stand there and dish out whatever we got, brother…"

"You know me?"

"You bet I do. Just as you know me. You're just another miser, exactly like me, only you haven't gotten this far yet. You don't quite know it. You still believe in goodness."

"You don't?"

"Oh, I do. I do! But not in here! No, siree! In here, there is none!"

"Are we in hell?"

"No, sir! Not yet…" "What's the difference?"

He smiles again, and it is a smile that makes me take a step back, even though there's a fence of steel bars between us.

"From where I stand still, the eye I see God with is the same eye with which God sees me…"

"I wrote that…" I couldn't help. "Some time ago."

"You seem to have a true perception of what this world is, Meister Eckhart. You can only hope it's not gonna go all the way. You can only hope, like we all do. All we have is hope. And to the very end, we hope then that our hope is not just hoping. One more illusion. That there is something to it, that is actually more substantial than hoping. And all that we have to do is remember his words: that every hair on our heads has already been counted, so only the question—the last one, the true last one—remains: what then are we doing here?"

"Is there an answer to that?"

"Mine is biblical. Our suffering teaches the devil something he couldn't get in any other way. We're here so one day he might be restored in heaven. That's the true love."

"And us?"

"Meister, don't you remember that it is a bad thing to give what is for children to the whelps? Only now and then something falls to the ground..."

I had my head lowered. I didn't dare to look at him, let alone to say something trivial. I usually don't give a-flyin' if I am considered wise or stupid; but here, in front of him, I cared, suddenly not to be completely stupid. After some time I looked at him.

"I'll be praying for you, Maître Jacques..." "That'll help."

All this time William stood back in the shadow, silent. Now de Molay lifted up his hand as best he could, pain written all over his face, not exactly, and yet sort of pointing at him through the dirty linen of his shirt.

"Be careful with that one! That's the type of servant you wanna be very careful with. He does the job he's been entrusted, but you still wanna be very careful!"

I have the feeling, suddenly, of misinterpreted friendship. Misplaced. All I know is that it starts here but that it also ends here; I can't do for him anything. I simply can't do a thing no matter what. Not a thing!

And then we are back in the carriage surrounded by thickening night. I feel my body too tight, squeezing me inside (whatever that means). I feel inadequate, childish; I feel cheated, exposed to mockery.

"Good night, Maître Jacques. I pray. And I won't stop.

I won't!"

"I can't even pray. But thanks!"

I remember. And I know I shall never be able to forget. William looks out the door window. Still looking the same way, he says at some point, "He's right as to one thing: we all serve something we know nothing about. It's fear makes us fawn, but we know nothing about goodness we talk so much about. Nothing!"

"What makes you say that?"

"I stood there and couldn't do nothing. There was a woman I loved. The only one I ever loved, right there, in front of me, burning, and those flames were burning my insides as well, and I couldn't even show that I had feelings of any kind…Now what would you call that?"

He looks at me, waiting. I cleared my throat.

"He said it," I said. "The world is shedding its skin… Something is in the making, William. Something is. Something terrible. A true hope killer—what shows the naked truth, you know? Thundering? Deafening! It'll make us crawl!"

"We don't know what it is." "We don't."

Then we are in front of our house. We get out of the carriage and say good night to each other, with the feeling, though, that something of extreme importance has just happened. Something that none of us shall ever be able to forget.

And then I sit in my room; the fire is quite alive in the chimney. The servant I have had to be wakened for doing it, but then he took care of the fire, and so I now have the warmth emanating out of it. I sit; I am not sleepy yet. After a short while I reach for the leather etui given to me such a long time ago that it seems like something I have driven into me with a hammer. It is also a face of a friend from long ago. His death separates him from this present by several years.

I admire, then, his calligraphy I'm not certain for which time. It is beautiful.

Quarta via sumitur ex gradibus qui in rebus inveniantur. Invenitur enim in rebus aliquid magis et minus bonum, et verum, et nobile, et sic de aliis hujus modi. Sed magis et minus dicuntur de diversis secundum quod appropinquant diversi mode ad aliquid quod maxime est, sicut magis calidum est, quod magis appropinquat maxime calido. Est igitur aliquid quod est verissimum, et optimum, et nobilissimum, et per consequens maxime ens, nam que sunt maxime vera, sunt maxime entia, ut dicitur II Metaphys. Quod autem dicitur maxime tale in aliquo genere, est causa omnium que sunt illius generis, sicut ignis, qui est maxime calidus, est causa omnium calidorum, ut in eodem libro dicitur. Ergo est aliquid quod omnibus entibus est causa esse, et bonitatis, et cujuslibet perfectionis, et hoc dicimus Deum.

I think each time I decide to open the etui and look at the sumptuousness of the super expensive parchment that doesn't age, at the golden shade of the ink, I shall only be able to admire it. Feel the pain of loss. It was Köln where he gave it to me. We were walking along the Rhine. And then he died. And I couldn't be there. I was too far away. Just as his pupil before him did, filling everything with a taste of sadness.

ALVA

Brother asked me to take care of Gabrielle's mother—he found us a lodging a bit larger and more comfortable for that purpose. At first I wasn't necessarily in love with the idea; why should that be me? Can't he hire a woman who would do whatever needs to be done, if anything? But then after a while that I had the opportunity to get myself acquainted with her and see that she really needed nothing or close to nothing, I changed my mind. That's fine; I accept—don't mind anyway. To go out and look at things was my idea because she didn't want to look at anything. Her custom was to just sit there, her eyes on the wall—physically on the wall, whatever she might have ever been looking at with her spirit's eye. She reminded me of my dog that the Mamelukes killed yet back in Outremer. It was a bitch; she'd sleep all day long, without bothering anybody. I would fill her bowl once a day with rice mixed with small pieces of meat. She had also another bowl for water and that was all she needed. I remember her, and suddenly my eyes filled with tears—maybe first and foremost because her death served only to joke of our faith and that by very bad people. I'm not sure. Or was there any other purpose I didn't grasp? But then I also liked her, liked to pet her now and then, feel her short coat, see how she liked it too, her body trembling slightly.

Being in every day with Gabrielle's mom provided similar experience, and so the sympathy we had for each other grew unhampered by things usual when two people live under the same roof. Brother asked me to take care of her because he'd take Gabrielle with him on the barge and that was an environment unsuitable for the old woman, whichever way we tried to look at it. I had to see Julius one more time, and one more time it was a very positive experience. And it was he who told me that our situation did not seem to him regulated properly, as a *provisorium* certainly, as a permanent fix—though no, not by a long shot. We've gotta do something, make some kind of a more permanent decision, which would satisfy better our preparation—the fact that we both knew how to read and write and that in a couple of languages. The work he, brother, was doing—good Lord, what's that got to do with his former life? He wanted to know. All of it is hogwash is what I'm gonna use here then, goes without saying. He gave me the money, too, which temporarily would solve our problems, moving us a level or two up in terms of what we could afford. But it was not the long-term solution, we all thought about. Whenever we got together, we would talk about our past, about the Outremer, and I saw the nostalgia in everything that was his. But we also asked whomever we could about the Outremer, and the news we were getting didn't seem encouraging at all: starvation, poverty such that we had no idea of. One would have to be a Turk, if in the north, or Egyptian Mameluke, if south. The rest would suffer. There were changes amongst the crowned heads, but those did not implicate almost any changes in the situation of the Europeans. French was rare as a language. If we go there, we would have to use Arabic.

Granma called me, asking about the water. The clay pitcher on the table was empty, and I went out to get her a fresh pitcherful from the outside well. We have a good well here: deep and clean; the water is cold and fresh no matter what the weather. I stood there then and watched her drink. She put the cup down and smiled at me. I smiled back. I asked her if she wanted to have something to eat, but she said no. She felt full. When the hell did she eat? And what was it? I couldn't recall. And then there was knocking at the door, which turned out to be Julius. (Talk about the wolf!) He sits down, right in the middle of our salon, and then asks me what's new. We are back to our conversation about stability, about our travel to somewhere, about which we know nothing yet. The giant just sits there and talks. I offered him some wine, but he turned it down.

"Alva? It won't stop. I know you people wait for some of it to blow over, and then, like everything else, it too—the rest, that is—should be over some day, no doubt about it.

The world will be back to what it always was, and there is no need to worry, right?"

"Right," I said.

"No!" He was right there. "No! It won't! See, there are things about Templars that are in nothing like what you already know. Is it true, or is it just another piece of humbug? Doesn't matter, it won't stop. The persecution you've seen so far is gonna keep going until one of us—get it, just friggin' bloody one—is still alive. There is a lot of fairy-tale stuff. A lot of hidden-treasure type of thing. And there is also a little bit of a reason, if you will, based on which those tales are whispered around…"

"Like what?"

"The fleet in La Rochelle, for instance. Templars had a whole fleet there, in the port, whatever else might have been on those ships—the fact that they left the port and literally vanished, and that just in time, see, right when the persecution started, okay? That by itself was a source of fairy tales. How did they know? How did anyone know? Okay? Here a lot of people get arrested, tortured, and burnt alive, on the other hand there's that group—rich, undoubtedly—a group of filthy rich too, who takes off, vanishes, as if for them the king made an exception. Huh? Why?"

Then he looks at me, although I have my doubts (dictated by the expression his eyes had assumed) if he can see me at all.

"There's a lot of things they say about the southern stuff. Carcassonne. Montségur. Rennes-le-Château. Facts. Whatever little gets through to us. Take the story of the cathedral in Chartres. How many strange things there, see? I guess, what I am trying to say is that the knowledge wasn't divided evenly. There were people, and there were people. And I'm beginning to think that whatever they say might really be true in same cases. That there is not one single political body in this world within which there would not be another, smaller perhaps, nevertheless a body, too, using the rest of it for their own purposes, without that rest being even aware of that. Only then later, shit comes out, and you don't know what to make of it because you're unprepared, stunned, sort of. Everybody is talking about you and yours, so you try to defend, but doing so, you're not sure at all that the defense you are presenting is in any way adequate."

The old woman motioned me to get her more water, so I had to excuse myself and go. When I came back, Julius was still here, and we continued our conversation from before I'd left.

"She doesn't talk at all?" He wanted to know.

I petted her white hair while she was having her cup of water, not looking at anyone of us. Her hair was such that I had the impression of touching her skull as if there was no hair on it.

"She speaks perfect French, and we have our conversations whenever she feels like having one. It's just that she is very quiet. She loves silence more than anything else. I don't know how far her realization of where life would go, as there is no way to tell at this junction, but I think that living long enough this life of ours just teaches you silence. It looks to me like the older you get, the more you appreciate silence, and she is the best proof of that."

"I feel my life as a mystery," Julius said. "You've done a lot of reading for a girl, I know. In fact you're the only girl I know who knows how to read. And?"

"And what?"

"Didn't your books teach you that life is a mystery and that forgetting that means to say that life is whatever you say that it is and then some—that 'some' meaning the whole universe? See, when I was at Chartres, they were explaining to me the sacred geometry—that man is the picture of the universe, that constructing a building representing man's proportions they were building the stony representation of God who is, as Bernard once said—your father knew him, see, I know that from your brother, yet before he'd left France for Outremer, he and Bernard were close friends for a while—he said that God is the width, the length, the height, and the depth. Ever heard that? You must have... in this house..."

"My books and my father taught me that everything is God and that I should be aware of everything. That life isn't about sleeping. It is about being alive. And that towards the end you realize, if you have lived properly, actively as you should, that nothing here can possibly be yours and your life is about trying to become part of this here theater, which can never happen. That is silence, Julius. We haven't got much to say."

"I wish," he said. "I never encountered a girl like you. Well—" He looked now embarrassed. "I'm sorry, Alva, I didn't mean..."

"What do you mean by 'girl like me,' what is that?"

"I said I was sorry..."

"Tell me!"

"I love to talk with you, Alva, you know? It's always a treat. See, when one soul can see itself in the other's eyes, that's what's worth living, I'd say. I can go to bed with a whore for almost nothing, and it means almost nothing too. It's like going to the bathroom. This touching what is untouchable—that is the kind of togetherness I would kill for."

"Would you, really?"

"Alva, I know I am older...well, much older than you. But do you think that there might be a chance here for me? Am I ridiculous?"

"You're not. Just do it the way that is considered normal, can you?" I was feeling strange too, to say the least. I'd have never expected that, not so sudden anyway. I thought about him, certainly. He was a good-looking guy, as opposite to what he just said; he wasn't anywhere near being old, just his temples were beginning to turn gray, which gave him so much more interesting expression. And he was huge, which is what I like in man (Father was like that and brother is now). I knew he was intelligent, but I didn't know he read, which would open yet another horizon at this point.

I looked at him.

"Shall I kneel now, Julius?"

He did. His face was now slightly above mine. I kissed his front, standing on my toes. And then he grabbed me (yet a little stronger and that would have been the end of this unusual story; he truly had strength of a bear, that's not just a matter of saying).

Holding me like that, he was now telling me that he had always loved me, from the very beginning, from the moment he saw me the first time. Yet before we met in the halls, I wasn't aware of him looking at me. They were together with brother who was showing me to him, somewhere along the river. He supposedly asked only if I was married, and brother's answer to that was a growl: "Don't you forget it's my sister!"

He asked in the end, "Will you marry me?"

And I said yes to that. I also told him I couldn't stay in France. We shall all move to somewhere else at some point. He agreed with me.

"Would you consider Outremer?"

"With you," he said, "I'd consider hell itself. Yes, love! I would!"

"We'll talk about that one of these days."

"That's gonna mean all of us. Your brother, Giscard." He looked up at me, smiling. "I know you like the boy. In fact I wasn't sure about him." And Julius laughed now out loud. "He's so much younger. And well educated. He was one of my problems, Alva. Now I can tell you: a damn serious one! "He's also one thing I don't want him to be, which besides you just named boy, see? I couldn't marry a boy, no matter how much I might like him."

"He was still kneeling in front of me and we kissed for the first time.

The old lady, smiling, motioned me toward her. When I followed her motion, she kissed me too on the forehead. "Is he a good man?" I asked, and she nodded in the affirmative.

The light outside was beginning to die. The day was over.

Julius was still on his knees.

GISCARD

The wedding was supposed to be in that village Gabrielle was originally from, where Zweifler found her the first time around. Now the question for me was, have I ever really thought that she would be my wife, at some point in the future? Did I really think that? Well, maybe now and then it occurred to me. She always treated me well. This much is true. By the same token, her being good to me was always more of what a sister would be like. Not a wife. Not a lover. Not even in a stage that would develop—you know, things are what they are and then they are something else. No, here it wasn't like that either. And yet when they made it known—I mean that Julius and Alva would marry, which is always like saying in a way that they will die—I felt that small ball of pain somewhere in my belly, and I couldn't find a place for myself. Julius is a man with whom I certainly can't compete. He's a giant, physically speaking, of immense strength but also isn't a lummox as far as education goes. He read a lot. He's a good-looking. Even, I'd say, exceptionally good-looking. Goodness…

We went there in the barge Zweifler works on and traveling with which he's found Gabrielle. The village is so small that is not even on the map. It's few hundreds of steps away from the river, few thatched hats, with very few people in them. For the wedding, the arrangements were extremely simple: just one long table made up of shorter tables put together and covered with white cloth. A plain cloth awning above it, in case it rains, was carried by a few bars. Food was prepared by the women, mainly Gabrielle and Alva, but they certainly had a lot of help from the village. Zweifler took a lot of stuff from Paris, and when they were unloading the barge with Julius, they suddenly found out that most everything was already set, and the local people welcomed them both as family. There was a blind musician who would sing the popular songs of the troubadours of that time, who was now rehearsing, and the music wandered over the fields far and wide. And both of them, both the lucky men who were about to change their social status, were standing there, sort of stupefied...

The day of the wedding, a priest came from the nearest hamlet, where there was a church, and it was he who married them: a double wedding in one day.

Alva's outfit was very simple: a loosely fitted gown, reaching the floor, tight sleeves, and narrow belt, over which she had a cyclas, sleeveless surcoat, one almost identical worn by Julius. But colors were perfectly matched, all of it fresh, freshly washed, giving the impression of spring—should I maybe say renewal? At first she also wore the barbette, which she then took off as the day was getting warmer. Her head without covering, her beautiful blond hair let loosely far down her shoulders, emanating all around her its natural beauty (the northern nations have that kind of hair and her mother as far as I could remember was Swedish). Yes, both couples, clod in the same manner with the same modesty but also the same freshness, gave us all the impression of something we also all, with no exception, have been waiting for a long time. Something different than the world we've known so far: abandonment and cheat, all which has so far been bloody and merciless to the degree as to making us forget that there might be something else altogether.

Gabrielle's hair was different than Alva's: black as a raven and shining, reflecting light like a mirror. When they all answered yes and have been declared married, something seemed to have appeared around us, which filled us with hope—I'm not really certain as to what the wording should be. Something good anyway. As then later, we spoke at the table, relaxed, resting; we all had the same feeling: we wanted to stay there, in that small, tiny village, without going back to Paris. Same us, the family, as the barge people, who finally never had any problems in the capital. I think it was just the lifestyle. What we all had to see, were forced to watch in the streets and plazas, all the propaganda flooding our lives incessantly, in every day, even the lives of those who were not interested at all in any of that.

Yeah…this here was definitely different than anything we knew; and it wasn't just the talking about it—we all felt like something extremely important happened to all of us. The priest didn't have to say anything, and he wouldn't have been blamed if he had said nothing at all. But having joined both couples in the matrimonial knot, he made a lengthy speech. And it was not just an occasional twaddle, no—he managed to draw our attention to what he was actually saying: that what is most important in our lives is the live of the other (not mine, for instance, for me but life of the guy next to me), and he was saying it in such a manner that it was difficult not to listen to him. Hell, we don't see in our lives any of what he was saying. None of that! What we do see, every step of the way, is taking care as carefully as one can manage of one's own butt—why should I care about that guy there? Screw him! What's he to me? Who's gonna take care of me? Of my business? My stuff ?

People I consider important?

Our world: I'm here to take care of myself!

Right then and there it began to dawn on me that precisely that, his sermon, might be what I was looking for all along: a common denominator. If one lives like that, the world certainly would be different than what it is now. Come to think of it, it is almost exactly what our Lord told us about ourselves.

Julius motioned me with his cup, and I had a sip of wine. He came over and hugged me, and after him it was Zweifler, the latter probably aware to some extent that Alva wasn't to me just anybody and that, hence, this couldn't possibly be my time. He kept hugging me, and we remained like that a goodly while, until I started feeling a little uncomfortable. Then he let me go.

"You still so young!" I've heard.

"I know," I managed.

"The time always comes, Giscard, you may not know that yet, but believe you me! It'll come! It always does!"

I nodded this time but didn't answer.

The musician was singing for a while (he had sung before) but then put his instrument aside and started eating. Now he picked it up again.

> Ciax qui vienent plus que le pas
> Molt se merveille et dist: par m'ame
> Voir se dist ma mere, ma dame,
> Qui me dist que deable sont
> Plus estrée que rien del mont
> Et si dist por moi enseignier
> Por aus doit on seignier

That too sounded important. Even very important. It has been then one of those moments when we realize something we were never aware of before; we don't yet know what it is, but the idea of something new, something bigger than one, begins to loom ahead. Looking at them, I suddenly knew that we are not what we think we are or that we might be most anything, not even having much of an idea at present as to what it might be, and it is only our life that will get us there. We may never get that idea. Or we may get it very shortly—it only depends of how we live and if we are worth the answer. For Lent, we went to Chartres, and it was there that I was listening to something very much like what I just thought; it was the sermon during the Lent mass, pronounced by a huge, fat priest, talking about upliftment and completeness, talking about the necessity of looking at the spires of the cathedral, not staying down, crushed, trampled into the ground. No, it's getting up each time one falls, with no exception.

He, the priest, thought that could be the meaning of the spires; well, that could be the meaning of the cathedral? Don't be puny, you're God's creation. Be immense, knock those clouds up there so they wouldn't be so conceited looking at you from so up high…

ZWEIFLER

We spent few more days in the village, enjoying ourselves, eating and drinking—although a couple of times the idea of abandoning our present position surfaced, making us a little more serious, a little more silent, contemplative. We get like that, all of us, no exception, whenever long journey appears in front of us—clearly yes, it will happen. And then it was the minstrel again, playing his instrument and singing; he knew a lot by Chretien, which he was now reproducing. And having a rather pleasant voice, he was a rather pleasant fragment of the festivities, something we would remember for a time a little longer.

When we finally restarted the travel toward the estuary, Giscard didn't want to go with us. He wanted to stay in the village. I thought it must have been one of the nicest moments in his life. Anyway, there seemed to be something special in the whole ceremony, which dictated for him that kind of behavior. Life is more complicated than at times we might think it is was my reflection. I already mentioned somewhere else the travel to the estuary: slowly moving back landscape, the beginnings of each new day, unforgettable because of the colors, of the reality surrounding us, painted only by colors, close to each other—like sort of colored fog, covering the objects out there, making of simple everyday things a huge mystery stretching beyond the borders of the known to where we have no more ideas.

Gabrielle stayed in the village with her mother, and so did Alva. They will still have the extension of the festivities. There were plenty of food left and plenty of drink. The minstrel didn't move to anywhere—I just said something truly true: extension of the wedding party. Even though it's a new day, new promise. The priest from that village, which had a church, did not manage to get sober yet, and so was for a while trying to get married the servant girl with the minstrel. And only the present ones held him back, trying to explain where he was and what was it all about. Then he fell asleep right there, at the table, snoring aloud.

Getting on the barge, I had a regret that I had to go and so couldn't see the rest of it. It would have been so damn colorful. It is so rare in our lives as we know it to get a color into scenes unveiling before our eyes, so much so that when something like I just described occurs, it truly is regrettable to let go of it and go.

In the estuary, we unloaded the barge, which today was half-empty anyway, and we took a new load, mainly lobster—it looks a bit scary when one looks on the bottom of the barge how the monsters move there, crawling over one another. Well, I find it very much some kind of a fairy-tale like. Wouldn't want to have my leg or hand in there. Lobster is something I love as food, but looking at it like this, on the bottom of the boat, always gives me creeps. They are fresh; they mean good payment in Paris. We have guys there who sell them from the table, by pound, and it's the experience that teaches us they'll probably go in one, all these I'm looking at now, at the most in two days. And that means good income for all of us. The barge certainly doesn't mean a waste of time. The bottom is built separated from one another, drawer-like compartments, holding water so the fishery can be held in them all the way back to Paris—it's fortunate that we deliver them, hence, absolutely fresh. They do bring the expected top payment.

Today there is almost no wind, which means we have to row like crazy to make any progress. Seine looks like it has no current, but that's not true; and we learn that truth in such a manner that, well, I don't get any more blisters. But that only because my hands are now sheer callus, and when I first started, I had to stop after a couple of hours because it was water with blood that was coming out of my hands and I had them swathed in a towel. At some point it was over. No more bleeding. Muscles in the body also got used to the pounding; they don't cause you anymore pain—it's just work, job, not a cross anymore. You do it like you do the rest of the stuff that has to be done, and there is nothing out of the ordinary in what you're doing. Just one more way of earning your room and board.

In the village, Gabrielle hangs herself on my neck. and it isn't unpleasant—would have been not that long ago. Julius brings meat in a clay pot, steaming slightly, smelling heaven—I think when one works, one doesn't realize that one is hungry; it's only when food appears…He has boiled potatoes in another pot. We were eating like wolfs, hungry animals, carnivores. Then I just sat there with a glass of wine in my hand, my eyes half-closed, and it felt good.

Twice that evening I had to go to the barge to pour some freshwater into the drawers with lobster and sole—it's not saltwater of the sea, but it's still water, fresh, with a lot of air in it. Besides, I add a handful of salt to each drawer. It works. We bring to Paris live stuff. And that's all we care about, because it's what we work for, our livelihood. I reflect on our situation: Julius gives Alva money, which means there's still some left of our fortune Father left us. I don't dare to ask him how much, what can we afford, and what we can't. He will at some point tell me that unasked, and right now we really don't need it. In fact it was a surprise that Alva made that request. She could have addressed me if she felt like she needed money. Or maybe she just wanted to know how it was gonna work. Women don't have that much patience. Well, maybe. She's got it. Now she knows. She does. We stay overnight under the sky. The weather is clement; we don't need a roof. And it's the night, such night, that teaches one what a night is and that a roof, enclosed space, could only destroy it. This is the way it feels good. It is what it is supposed to be. Unspoiled. Undiminished. Our way of celebrating life.

After that already all of us were going to Paris. And again those are the shores slowly moving backward, objects not sharp, rendered like they are by the fog. The ladies get incessant warning about what's in the "drawers" on the bottom of the boat and to please careful with their extremities if they have to walk, for whatever reason, only over the planks. The water is quiet, so the boat moves quietly too, and there's almost no danger of slipping off. But then again you never know now, do you? And then after yet a while, the houses on the shores get denser. There's obviously more and more of the human settlements in the green on both sides, and we know we made it one more time to Paris. The dock for the barge is deep in the city, and from there we need transportation to get where we want to get, but any of that part are already small potatoes.

We are home; for now this is our home, this old capital—in fact so old that nobody knows anything about its beginnings. And today it's difficult to talk about France; half of the world lives in this city, and you can hear the languages from just about anywhere in the world. People are coming for the university; the magic of learning is this powerful, working like a magnet, renewing the population of the city. How many live here? There is no way to really know that with any reasonable degree of accuracy. There is a way to make an estimate, and that is what'll have to satisfy the curiosity at this time. And that's all we have. But we know that it fluctuates in every day's time, knew people come from literally everywhere in Europe, and some of those who were already here depart. It lives its own life. Right now, in getting the cart that will take us to places where we live, I think we can hear its breathing: the giant sets out for the night. I take a steel bucket and one more time add water in the drawers. The moon has its double in the river, crystal clear, calling…The hoofs of the horse give us a rhythm that prepares us for the night too. I think about the travel we'll have to undertake at some point. Do we really have to? I think it is something close to that. There'll be no going around it; we all seem to agree. And then it's our street and our house. The cart stops. One last time I look at the stars up there—renewal; the air smells fresh. There is a joy in any of that, I think to myself. I know I'll have a hell of a hard time to fall asleep—because it's also a lot of pity to leave this and go somewhere else…

GABRIELLE

know he got this lodging now after we got married. It's the whole story in a building; our main room has a window looking out to the river. I can see barges like the one he works on pass by, but it is too big, simply. I told him that. I'm not used to something like this, in the village, we had, with Mama, a house that was only one room, and small at that, and we got used to it—goes without saying too. This here is a palace; suddenly, I moved a couple of classes up, and I am not too happy about it. He wouldn't tell me how much he has to pay for it either, but I would imagine it must be a fortune. All I've got from him was that I shouldn't worry; it's his business now and none of mine.

To the left I can see the cathedral's towers (one of the things that really got me after we had already arrived and he took me to the church to show me what a church really is). It is an experience not necessarily religious but certainly spiritual. I suddenly remembered my conversations with our priest in the village from years and years ago when I told him I wanted to be a nun, would like at least to try. His objection to that was my mother.

"What's gonna happen to her, huh? When you go to a nunnery?"

I asked him if he knew how to read, and he said yes, he did. He wasn't exactly a university professor, but he could read. Could he teach me?

"Well, it's not all that easy. But yes, we may give it a shot." And we did. I don't want to brag, but I know how to get through a fragment I'm interested in. He had few pages with drawings of Outremer, wonderfully colorful, with a lot of gold—the text in a golden ink—and I learned those by heart.

Ever since it was my dream to go there and see it all for myself. People did so much more in this world than I have seen so far. And it's all worth seeing. And now I am here, in Paris, of which I didn't dream even last month, before we left the village. La Notre Dame was something that took my breath. Standing inside and looking up at the vault, letting my eyes go up the western façade, all of it made me tremble, which was to his satisfaction, as I noticed at some point. I asked him about it and he told me that it is of extreme importance to share things; only then does life—the proper feeling—come to the surface. Doesn't it?

"You can't show Notre Dame to your goat now, can you?

Sure you can! Certainly but what is the goat's reaction to it gonna be, huh? And yours is what mine has been."

We were walking together, holding hands. The day was nice, not too hot; breathing was quite easy.

"This way I know you're my kind. We live in the same—give or take—world. And that is the most important thing to me. The sharing."

I love those walks with him while we talk. Things that died long time ago suddenly were revived, one is here and then the next minute somewhere else, and all that is submerged in sympathy and friendship. I thought suddenly that I neglect mother now. These days that we are here, my schedule has changed, changing also my habits and priorities. I stood up now quickly and turned around to go to mother's room. She slept. Covered nicely all the way up to the chin, she slept. I went over to the bed. Her right hand was out, as if holding the cover. I touched it. Her hand was ice-cold. I touched her front—same thing. I had to sit down because my knees gave me a strange feeling, forcing me to thinking about falling down. Then I lay beside her. We were like that for a while as I suddenly realized that my hand was on top of her, on her breast. That breast I sucked not all that long ago—her nipple, now ice-cold, then dispensing milk into my mouth. God…

Then it's childhood, just about exactly as I heard that it happens: we are on the shore of the river, playing in the sand. mother comes to tell us that our dinner is ready—yes, she wants us to come home. I'm fighting with Giselle, we always fight, somehow. mother comes and puts things right. I see her standing there: who started and what the problem was. Church: singing, a small organ timidly accompanying our song. We sing we want Mary, mother of God, to have mercy on us, and I have tears in my eyes, which I try to dry with my sleeve. I feel her hand on top of my head—is it the same occasion or another one? It doesn't matter anymore; she is there with us, always, we shall never get lost. Never. And now she is here, on her bed. She is cold. She is obviously not there anymore. In my memory she was, warm, talking, smiling; obviously there was something that now isn't here anymore, so where is it?

Later on the day I see Julius, and I tell him about her.

He says he'll take care of that. And he does. He gets the casket, and it is also he who finds the right people to pay for the place where the grave shall be dug, the guy who will physically do the digging. And when everything is already prepared, he marches at my side as if we knew each other all our lives.

I felt like I never felt so far in my whole life. When the casket has been lowered and the first fistful of dirt had to be thrown on top, I couldn't do it. They asked me and I flatly refused, choking on my own tears. Nobody called it hysteria though. And it was Julius again who obliged; he took a shovel and threw the first load. And then the grave was filled, and the priest intoned the sung prayer, and whoever knew how joined in. I stood there and just cried. For the first time I realized that I wasn't gonna see her ever again. She wasn't here with us anymore; she was somewhere else, whatever that might mean. Somewhere else. Goodness… Somewhere…

Even though she never needed anything, lately she was just sitting there. If anyone looked at her she would smile, I don't remember her asking for anything in a long time, and yet she too had to go. I think there are at least two ways of looking at it. One: we all have to go somewhere, that's our destiny, our way, and there's simply no way around that, period. And two: going from here we go to a place which is a lot better to be than this here, valley of tears, hence leaving here means liberation from the yoke of the body. That's what our priest would always say: liberation from a pillory our body is to us, end of chastisement. We've got it and now is finished; we can go wherever we go—again his own expression: we are free to be born from the womb of the earth into the heavenly life…

ALVA

'm not laughing at her, but when we came, didn't she hide like a savage? I had no understanding for that, and it was brother who spoke about the little tiny place where she had used to live, far away from the main part of the world. Wasn't that so? She was excusing herself then, explaining that she got scared, she didn't know what to make of the noise—heck, too many people...

From in between the lines I fished out that there was yet someone else in there in the meantime, and part of the fear caused by our visit was actually leftovers from that time. Yes, there were king's people in wire armors and helmets looking for Giscard and his books. They didn't find him. But what if he had been there, eating dinner, for instance, or some such, huh? What if ?

We had the conference right there, the family reunion about staying or going. I was, goes without saying, for going. I had dreams lately about Outremer, more and more clear, my nostalgia was getting more and more intense. I even had an explicit dream about our dog with her huge ears hanging over the gate with the idiotic inscription above her: "In hoc signo vinces."

Is there any difference between that wild middle of nowhere and the most civilized place on earth? Are we the people any different here and there?

I repeated time and time again, I remember that clearly, that they cannot come here, to our place, looking for whoever pleases them. Giscard, in this particular case, entered, stirred everything, and, because he was not there, packed up his texts (for which he had paid everything he ever had) and just took them away...

And then the true nightmare remains: what if he was there? What if they had found him? We wouldn't know him anymore, like father in Avignon, like brother and so many others, guilty only of belonging to a group of people who did not please the king (who in turn did not please anybody I know of).

Brother drew my attention to the fact that their outfits this time were slightly different and so they did not represent directly the king; they were Pope's; goodness, they were pope's hence representing exact same danger as the others. In exact same manner had he been found by them, he would have disappeared as people did in all those other cases we knew of before and were able only to find the leftovers of the pyres outside towns, still smoking and stinking that horrible death. (Did they ever do anything which would endanger the blessed king or his crony? Most of us would agree that it wasn't the case. And like in any case of this nature, it would be difficult if not impossible altogether to prove it beyond a shadow of a doubt in the court of law.) Isn't it enough to look at those cases that are accessible to the public, during which the defense struggles against the prosecution for long days, after which everybody is dissatisfied and two people are close to impossible to find who would agree on the outcome's plausibility? And those are usually not cases based on the questions if and how God exists. I guess these are questions about legitimacy of the whole judicial system—what it is really in its nature—and whose business it represents at any time. Why does anybody want to be a king? Forgive me the naiveté of this question, but isn't there something to it? You see the absolute mediocrity reigning and finding itself well beyond the circumference of the abovementioned judicial system, as very much opposite to that, using that system to bury great people in public whilst nobody can do a thing about it, even though most people feel the big cheat or that something is simply wrong. I've heard, "This cannot be right." You read things because they tell you to read things, where you find out that the law is something you bring with you from somewhere else only to violate it down here. The most of that rape does not happen in the streets—no, it happens in the courtrooms, covered with distinguished togas and wigs, sticks its head (which at some point becomes clearly a head) out of solemn quotations the biggest minds have suggested to quote on the occasion, and then, when those minds ran out of quotations, the guilty party burns or is quartered or yet some other form of entertainment is invented ad hoc or brought up from the past as a friendly reminder, and the crowd applauds like crazy. And even through those applauding crowds one can hear the shout of the one being murdered in order to uphold the law.

Then Julius entered the room, which meant that the barge made it back to Paris a whole day earlier than they had planned. His cheeks were pale; he was obviously concerned. Must have spoken with somebody before getting home from the dock.

"Are you okay?"

"Yes," I answered him as peacefully as I only could; he seemed at the verge. "What did you expect?"

"Frankly," he said and I saw that the tension on his face was receding, "I didn't know what to expect. Giselle was at the dock, and she told me about the Pope's knights coming in here to seek Giscard, then breaking his door and going through his stuff. Now that's bad, that's something which gets one's blood to boil—mine at least. What rights do they have to do that? And the crap of God's rights that's something good for them and nobody else, wouldn't you say?"

"Julius, please, calm down. Thank God nothing happened. Giscard wasn't even here."

"Precisely! What now if he had been? You think there's nothing to worry about?"

"I now as well as you do that there is. And yet I will tell you one more time: take it easy! Your reaction is exactly what they want. That's war of attrition, Julius. As long as you react the way you just did, they win, period."

He was nodding. His face still all tense.

"When we first came here and that crap started, everyone of us expected some kind of a culmination and then assuagement, the whole thing petering off, didn't we now? I know I did. And? It didn't change at all. Not at all! They still come to wherever you live and do whatever pleases them, like turn your quarters into a pig stall at any time, day or night, whenever their respective leaders find fit. And there is not even the lousiest apology for such a state of affairs." He looked at me, and I knew he was pretty shook up. "When Giselle told me the story, I was seriously afraid that something may have happened we won't be able to make up for. You know?"

"Like what?"

"Do you have something screwy with your head? Where the hell is you father? And that your brother is here that's not because times are so good, but because you managed to get him out, right? For a bloody hell of a lot of money, right again?"

He sat at the table. His huge back to me now. "Would you like to eat something?"

"Yeah," he said. "Whatever…"

But I know it's not "whatever" shellfish. No, he'd rather something that they take from here to the estuary. Like beef?

I put some hay in the stove; it's a very good stove, I use the flintlock to make sparks, and once the fire catches, I add small pieces of dry wood, watching it grow. Then it's branches and finally trunks cut in pieces with an ax. I put butter they take from here to the estuary—very good, clean butter. I watch it melt and then start ready for frying, making the sound informing me about it, and then I just put a piece of beef, big and truly beautiful, and watch it fry. The steak is about an inch thick and that edge, sizzling, looks like it was about to come alive and get off the cast-iron frying pan to follow the smell it is spreading, which gives me appetite even though yet a moment ago I hadn't even thought about eating. Then I turn it over. And after that one more time. In the end I take the meat with a fork. which seem to me to be too big for this particular task, put it on the plate. and put it then in front of him on the table. Beside the plate I set down a clay bottle of Rhine he likes. and I watch him eat. I find strange pleasure in watching him eat—that wonderful appetite of a giant. I wish I could do more for him, but for now, this is what he requires. Nothing more. Which means almost a disappointment.

Eating, his mouth full, he starts talking—about the same thing: we have to make a decision. That is something that cannot be delayed anymore. We'll have to speed up everything. We'll have to decide how we wanted to handle the details of the journey, the first, the most difficult part of it: from here to the estuary.

He pours himself a glass of Rhine looking at me, waiting. I know what he is waiting for is some way of making sure that I have understood our predicament and that, hence, I know that we have no time to spare, not a second to waste. Things have to be decided right now and then the plans seen through until we are somewhere else where none of us shall be taken away like that and killed according to somebody's liking. I nod. He knows that I have realized where we are. He knows I agree with him about the time we have left. He knows I agree with him. He knows I do.

ZWEIFLER

The day is gray at this time as we got to the Île aux Juifs in our small boat I took from the barge. During our travels north, we hauled it behind us on a piece of rope. We came—and that is Alva, Gabrielle, Julius, Giscard, and me. We came from the shore, crossing the gap between the islet shore and the shore of the river. And to our surprise, we found quite a few people already on the island, however they got the message—it wasn't easy for us to find out; how others did there's no record. The pyre's already built; a scaffold was over it, making sure that the burning of the bodies wouldn't be too fast. Alva asked me, bending over to me and whispering in my ear, who were all those people, but I simply had to tell her I didn't recognize anyone. (If Eckhart were here, well, that would be another story, but he had to flee from Paris because of the same persecution; he had the same chances of ending up on that scaffold as they had and only because he wasn't a Templar and, throughout his stay in Paris, never actually got too close to them. He had he the ability to move and so he chose to travel to the other side of the Rhine and then disappeared there, just like a bear disappears in the woods. The last I had from him was from Strasbourg, where he was teaching at the university and taking care of the Dominican house there. He was a big guy of some kind for that order.)

It's the Prévôt de Paris who today pronounces the sentence, stressing that the relapsed heretic does not need a hearing and the sentence can be carried out without any further ado. Today. In fact right here, right now. We can't see that, but the boat with the condemned is already here. I see a bit later: they are led slowly toward the pyre by the king's people in the wire armors, which seems kind of strange since they had not been delivered to the lay authorities yet. I don't know if there's any others as well, but I see just those two, and I tell Alva and then Gabrielle—all of it in a whisper, of course—that the old guy in front is Jacques de Molay himself, and the one slightly behind is Geoffroy de Charnay, his friend, also a grandmaster. It looks bad how they led this old, emaciated man, not looking like the stories about him and his worrier exploits at all. On the contrary, he looks like he's had it, like whatever he might have been doing all his life; the only thing he thinks of right now is rest. Looking at them, I am deep in thoughts; I'm trying to figure out what man's life is. What are we here for? I'm pretty sure not one person from among all these who gathered here can help them in any way. They are beyond help. Well, our help. But where the hell is God?

I suddenly remember an incunabulum in the Bible Eckhart showed me once; one of the prophets (Ezekiel? Or was it Isaiah?), one of the super important guys in there, enclosed inside a tree trunk, and two other guys outside that enclosure sawing the tree with an iron saw in two with him inside. Why? Who the hell was the king he supposedly offended as compared to God? Unless they have (the guy who manages this brothel of ours and the one up high, huh?) some kind of a pact of no intervention...The better the servant, the more pissed off the prince of this world, and so the worse his death. Huh?

Up on the scaffold they are bound back-to-back, I see de Molay is saying something to one of the executioners, and I can't see if he gets any answer. Shortly after that, everybody gets down except the two up there. There's a little delay, caused by God only knows what, after which the fire is started. I watch the Templars—their faces, their incredible composure. The pain must be indescribable. I burnt myself time and again dealing with the stove, and the burn, as little as it was each of those times, was painful enough. And here I was watching the whole man's body being licked by the slow flames, and that man's face didn't change in any significant way. The same would go to the other fellow. And yet a little bit later, it is the voice of de Molay, not particularly powerful but audible enough to deliver the words: that it'll be God himself who will avenge the two innocent man dying today for no other reason than greed and a savage will to power, that their oppressors shall depart out of this world in only one year's time, after which he repeats that the only thing they—himself, that is—as well as his friend here, Godfroy de Charnay, might and probably should be accused of was their lying to save their own lives under torture, thus betraying the order. The rest of it is true in no measure. It's all been admitted under pain that couldn't be resisted any longer, and for that, he asks God's forgiveness. Which as he knows shall be granted him. Executioners clod in black, in black hoods with only eyes visible, add wood—fresh, clear pieces of chopped wood, well dried that catch the fire in no time. One of them moves the pieces already in fire using a long stick, thus sending teams of sparks, gay, joking, laughing up toward the faces of the Templars, and I see de Molay's bird going quickly, as if with a haste, up in flames (after this, he can't possibly be seeing anything; the flame, quite sizable, must have destroyed his eyes, boiling the fluid inside the eyeballs). His initial request to leave his hands unbound must have been granted him, which I didn't see back then with any reasonable degree of certainty, but I see him now making the clear sign of the cross on his chest, now that the darkness enveloped him and the light has no more access to the former servant—as far as I know a good servant—such that the absence of the tree halves from the Eckhart's Bible enclosing the body being delivered as an offering seems to be questionable, to put it mildly. Well, every bit of this seems at this moment questionable to me. I feel like shouting— like producing a shout, long, deafening…I don't have voice for this. However intense I might try, it wouldn't be deafening. I know that. Even in an unattempted protest, we have a fair chance to be simply ridiculous. A horse neighing in protest because the driver smacked his ass with a whip.

Watching it seems to be enough. As if it took all my energy.

I stood there, Gabrielle beside me on my right and Alva on the other side with Julius at her elbow, Giscard behind him, Julius holding her carefully, of which I had the impression as if he's afraid of letting her go, even for the shortest moment. Up there they both died with the same peaceful look, de Molay first and the Charnay shortly after that, both of them unafraid of pain and death, as if suddenly liberated from the yoke of the body—from the here and now, from the sick nonsense, sicker and sicker, to the point of deformity. People were waiting for the fire to subside, which took a surprisingly long time, to gather the ashes into whatever they had—clay pitchers for the most part. Those were the ashes of true martyrs. Toward the end, the king and the pope departed with their respective corteges. We too went slowly toward the boat moored at the shore of the islet to a tree stump. Rowing to were the barge was moored, we talked about the journey that was ahead of us, a journey that would take many months with the weather not quite propitious. But we saw no reason to delay, considering also what we just witnessed. One way or another we had to go, get away from Paris. Start a new life somewhere where people didn't die like what we just saw. We had to. Had to. No way around that. Just had to.

There's always a moment arriving of a certainty beyond doubt, and such a moment has just arrived; none of us needed any more convincing. Yes, we are going. To the place we know from the past, and that is also human, isn't it? And where else shall we go? I know, I've known already for some time, that whatever we do, there's a chance for ridicule—that is the destiny of one born a woman. That's the way it is, and there's no point in protesting.

ALVA

After we made it to the estuary (actually it is a village just about like where Gabrielle is from, with which brother developed commercial relations—since brother started working on the barge, things started changing; the boys to whom the barge belongs would say they had lots of luck lately), we still had to wait almost three days for the ship. The barge couldn't stay; they left for Paris, and we, Gabrielle, brother, I, and Julius with Giscard had to spend couple of days in that village, already in the channel. And then on the third day, we finally saw the ship. Brother and Julius took care of the commercial side of the whole thing and we bordered—all of us. I won't forget the takeoff—things getting smaller and smaller behind us and we ourselves more and more lonely in that bluish vastness. From the deck of a ship one can't see it is only the channel which on the map (particularly if it is the map of the whole Europe) looks like a little creek or something like that. Until the French coast simply continues straight west, which the ship followed, I had the feeling that I still am in France—to some extent, that is—but then the shore made a sharp turn south and the ship did not follow. We went along the string of the bow, straight, or almost straight, toward the northern end of the Spanish coastline then, once spotted, around it, south, until we saw Portugal's coast—way out there, just a line, like drawn with a coal on a piece of parchment. One interruption in that line, evoking discussions amongst the crew (shall we or shall we not try to land, get the fresh water and some provisions) was Coimbra with its citadel on the hill, high enough for us to see quite clearly in this weather. We had good weather, I was told, considering the time of the year and regions we were crossing. I'm aware of the fact that when I write about it, it seems to be close to nothing; time shrinks, we are here, and then we are there while in reality we are talking about long days, without accommodations we got in the meantime used to. We did not enter the port of Coimbra in the end, which was based on our very limited knowledge of the relations France may have with Portugal. Sitting here, my back against a huge roll of rope, the sea wind trying to make me forget that I have a nice brass comb, I remember our first few days in Paris, in that huge house that brother found in that city that didn't seem to have an end, with the help of someone I know nothing of—how cold and hostile it seemed to be, and then slowly how it became a home too, until the last days came and we had to pack and kiss it good-bye. I had tears in my eyes. The streets all around us having become so familiar that every stone also seemed a part of that family, especially the people one gets to know, like your butcher—gay short guy, laughing nonstop—then the guy I used to buy fish from, always telling me what's new, interested in anything I could tell him, and yet another selling bread, and so on and on…Hell, that's a lot of people one gets to know over time. And they know me. They become family once lost and now one gets it resurrected in this shape.

A seagull just sat down on the railing, his round eye lustrating every movement I make. It rests for yet a while, and then just picks up where it had left off, for some reason against the wind. I see him struggle, almost not moving at all, just hanging there along the line the ship moves along, just opposite direction. Then it dives, and I lose sight of it. It's only that wind now, playing with my hair to its own sad tune, and the sea, empty all around, that looks like molten lead. I feel the body of the ship trembling slightly, as if of expectation.

The days pass by almost unnoticed, becoming a strange body we all agree is past but strangely homogenous, like there was no difference—the same colorless, tasteless body without smell all along. And then it's the Hercules pole. I've heard about it before. But now I could see it. Majestically emerging from the fog, reaching the sky above us, causing us (well, me) to feel grotesquely small. Somehow we were all expecting something to happen (that something out of the ordinary would suddenly appear, somebody would speak with us maybe, some superbeing from under the water would board the ship against anything normal—from the later conversations we all had that expectation at the moment, more or less conscious, more or less shaped up in our minds as one more facet of the morning's silent fog). Goes without saying nothing such had happened. The giant was slowly moving backward on our left side, until it simply disappeared and there was just water all around us. In my prayers I had to thank for the weather—all the way so far from the French coast to here we have had a relatively good weather. No stronger winds, few days when a little bit of clouds appeared, but for the most part the sky above us has been clear. I remember very well our travel to Smyrna and then to Brundisium, how terribly sick I was; there were moments that I thought about dying. All of that time I couldn't even think of eating; I slept in snatches, still remember having fallen asleep while standing, and it was a miracle that I didn't fall and break something in my body… Well, I just had a pretty good breakfast, and last night I slept uninterrupted till morning. Few more days and we see land again. This time we have to land because our provisions are touching their end—no chance to make it all the way to Brundisium. We buy some food in a small village (I was given the name of it, but don't remember anymore; never heard of it before anyway). And from this moment on we had the view of the land most of the time, all the way to Brundisium, which I remember from the last time I was here amazingly well. I feel excited and I have the impression that brother shares my excitement, that there's hope in this, some sort of expectation that doesn't have any logical base: we all know, and know well, that we are going to a land devastated by war, a land of which nothing is still in our hands. What's left of our home? Maybe nothing. Carbonized stumps smelling smog. Leftovers of the mason's work, whatever didn't crack and fall down. Goodness… But I was born here. This is my land! Like it or not. My true home, people around speak a language that I can at least understand, and I know that should we decide to stay, in a few years our French will be the problem.

We leave Brundisium on Monday, the weather still being as good as it has been so far. Again, it is the same monotony of the sea travel, infinite shades of blue, omnipresent seagulls and their shrill, at times truly piercing squawks. Rarer voices of people—our voices; I tell brother about my memoirs. He laughs, sort of—no, not maliciously, it's a laugh of someone who had tried and failed; but he is still around, ready to try one more time, without asking why should it be any better this time. He'll try. He'll find out. He won't leave his post, I know that, as long as it will be humanly possible to keep it. We are talking, brother and I. Like we haven't for the longest time. I assure him of my support. Yes, I'll be there with him till the end, whatever that might be.

FATHER (YOUTH)

We were just a couple—young man with a pregnant woman—and the dog, the latter affectionate, but tending to present a fight about authority in the family, which I would never have anticipated while buying it. It doesn't reflect (poor thing doesn't know how to think in that sense). It is only a dog, it just won't take orders from nobody. And I think that's the way things are going to be because I don't have a heart to beat the crap out of it each time I say something to it and it pretends not to hear me. Is that an ego trip? A guy who knows about dogs told me it is, at least one could call it that. It's not exactly what's happening in case of a human being, but yes, in the end, it is an ego trip. Is everything an ego trip? Is life an ego trip? We are here to think. To reflect. What for? Haven't found out yet.

I think. The best thing then would be to get rid of the ego, now wouldn't it? But then again, who would I be without my ego? It would be someone else, not the bloody me, now wouldn't I? I think it's a hell of a problem, and thinking back about the beguine woman and her book that so pissed off the authorities in France, I tend to agree with the latter: I want to be me. Me! As best I know myself. On the other side as well. Better. Not so prone to anger, not so vindictive, but nevertheless I'd like to be an entity capable of saying *me*, and knowing what that means too.

From Rome we went to Venice and then aboard a commerce knaur, under the open sky, to Brundisium. Our backs to the plank nailed to the mast, I felt Birgid beside me, and I don't think I could describe how she felt, even to me, describe the feelings the sight of her would evoke in my heart: how unique and how fragile, how much of a cause for bottomless, immeasurable fear wandering down my spine. Fear that I would lose her. Fear that something would happen that cannot be undone later, which will make her disappear. Above us there was the sky, black, full of night stars, and there was that immensity we couldn't see in the darkness of the night, all around us, and I felt lucky having been given her but also scared that I might not be able to hold on to her. Our luggage took half of the deck (we took some furniture with us), and at our feet there was the funny dog with incredible ears, sleeping. Does anyone know how dogs sleep—their breath even, undoubtedly that of a sleeping creature, and then, all of a sudden, opening their eyes (or just one) and looking at you, checking, examining. I felt very strongly the uncertainty of change not yet realized and yet actual, so far that we were part of it irrevocably (there was no way back, no changing our minds)—every fiber of our bodies could feel (and did) that from that point on we could only go forward. It's a long trip—whichever way you slice it. I knew we both felt the same.

It must have been somewhere south of Sicily that the storm started—from the beginning of the strength absolutely unusual, mixing the sky with the sea, making the boat behave in such a manner that we both instinctively sought ropes to tie our bodies up to the mast, because staying inside untied wasn't easy, and at times simply impossible, the boat being tossed several feet up and then coming down, all of it with the hellish accompaniment of all the instruments at the devil's disposal. I saw the face of the matelot before me, eyes wide open, shouting words and sentences now impossible to hear, leaving that face in a silence and separation of death. Now and then we would get the wider picture when the lightning decided to bridge the gap between the sea and the sky, showing the sick, pale omnipresence of foam covering the waters, the same paleness reflected in the clouds above. With the lightning over, the darkness was absolute. Lamp that was nailed to the mast, has been ripped off and ended somewhere outside, in the water, and nobody tried to compensate for the loss. There was simply no point. Not that much later a lightning hit the mast, leaving only a smoking stump shorter than the height of a man. The knar seemed to be built incredibly strongly, because now, taking all this punishment, it was still in one piece, with us in it. I wouldn't be able to tell how much later I heard a sound from the back, which reminded me of a shout produced by a man dying under torture, and I thought it must have been our rudder; there was nothing else on the poop. It dawned on me that at that point we had no control over anything anymore: no mast and no rudder. We, the people, were inside a shell, tossed and kicked around by a particularly malicious kid, like sometimes can be seen, when kids play in some obscure backyard without any parental supervision (no parent would like to see that kind of expression on his kid's face—we simply have to).

At the crack of dawn the knar was empty, except for us, the living, hanging on to it for dear life, to whatever was available with whatever we've got left in terms of physical strength. Our furniture was gone. The rest of the cargo was out of the boat too, leaving us with the strange impression of boldness whenever looking at deck. Most of us were sick, throwing up right there, wherever we were. And then suddenly, in all that hopelessness, somebody cried out, "Land!" and it seemed to be true. In that emaciated light of the dawn, there, right there, we saw something that seemed to be different than the sea and which probably was a piece of land. The weakening strength of the storm was pushing us toward that piece of land, and shortly those of us who had a little bit more experience with this area informed the rest that it seemed to be Cyprus. Its western side called Paphos. As said above, things we had with us were gone for good, but the main part of our earthly possessions was what I had in my belt: a cheque issued to me yet back in France, in a house of the Knights Templar, a piece of parchment with a huge wax seal I have obtained in their house after depositing my gold, which represented the status of our family at that time.

First thing I checked after boarding and having had warm food and great Greek wine from Cyprus—well, first thing was naturally the belt; it wasn't damaged. Whenever we'd get to Haifa, perhaps even Jerusalem might turn out necessary for that, I wouldn't know, would be to present the cheque from France at a local Templars' house and get my gold back. I thought maybe not all of it at once. Perhaps I should save a little for the future? I have no idea (just hope) how the sword business would go. Yes, a partial cashing of the cheque might be advisable. By all means. And that's what I'm gonna do!

It took us a few days to recover, after which we bordered a boat going to Acre, back then in full bloom. I had (not at the moment, not anymore, that is) drawings of the city, castles and temples, streets and ramparts—certainly a source of pride for Outremer.

So far I've only heard about it—stories, told me by people who knew something about it, who had been there, for instance, for one reason or another, but also from reading. The Bible would be the good example here, but also other sources which I managed to lay my hand upon now and then, here and there. And here again was I reminded that everything I had written was now gone. Except the certificate issued by the Templars in Europe. Thank be for that.

ZWEIFLER

We approached Cyprus from the Paphos side. And now I am in the town I've already been in long time ago. I was still almost a boy back then…We were sitting with Alva yesterday and talking about our past, and at some point, I said that in a few days we'll leave Cyprus going east to our childhood…Goodness…And how'd she feel about it? She said she was nervous, afraid that we might not be able to stay in the country this far destroyed by war. I know that we can stay and survive anywhere there are other people. I know I can.

For the few days the ship would stay here, on the island.

We rented an inn room, more comfortable then the ship's deck and not too expensive, big enough to accommodate all five of us, each and every one having only his or her bed and a small table with a candlestick on it on the side of the bed; a maid would bring a huge pitcher of fresh water brought down here from the mountains in cisterns hauled by horses to wash off the sleep of the night in the morning, and then also our breakfast would be brought up here, which we would eat at the huge wooden common table in the middle of the room. After breakfast we would go out. Sometimes to the port, to see ships, masts poking the sky, and the unforgettable view of the Paphos castle, which if I'm not mistaken remembers the birthday of our Lord (but I'm not sure of that, and it's most probably wrong). It's very old anyway; I think anyone would agree to that. If you walk along this coast, it is a presence that would be difficult to dismiss. It's there while you watch it, and it, sort of, watches you back, a little heavily.

Julius and I were walking along the port entrance into the harbor on that day a little bit windy, talking about when we finally get there, Julius knows the territory (well, used to know while living in these parts) and even past Jerusalem to the south. There was constant presence of a few of them, the Templars, on the roads to Beersheba, protecting the Christian pilgrims willing to make themselves acquainted with that part of the scripture.He told me that there had been hardly one day he would remember now without fighting. You could lose your life over a true trifle simply because the mugger thought there was a chance it could be sold in town for a coin. I had to, searching my memory carefully, tell him almost the same about my region. Walking and talking we agreed that what's ahead now doesn't seem to be any worse, and that life shall mean for us fighting, almost on constant bases. And then, I believe, it was Alva who said that fighting is life and that it is anywhere (the fight itself might be different, she explained, in other parts, but it's still fight). If you had to duck constantly, hide yourself, mask you presence with something else—what was that? And what was life of Giscard in Paris? And that only because he wanted to be a priest in the future. A priest who got himself acquainted with all sorts of priestly thought. Because he could read and speak Latin and Greek, because he could speak and, of course, understand Arabic, like most of us, being at the same time more curious than any of us. And isn't jumping out of a back window into the river in order to save his own life a fight as well? Getting your books for which you had spent a fortune (whatever it is to you) confiscated, whereby you know well, that the confiscating people are analphabets, completely unable to read. See, she was there, calm but decided, ready to defend her point. What unnerves one the most is the nonsense of it. There is clearly more sense to her in a fact of the highway robbery, where the bandit expects some kind of a gain, right? But what is the expectation of the state when it robs expensive manuscripts nobody shall ever even look at? Not that is a robbery, which doesn't make any sense whichever way you slice it. Is church a state? That can only be answered by what it does to you. How is your conscience affected? To some people yes, it is. To some it isn't.

I see Alva pray; she's kneeling, her lips are moving, she obviously is addressing God, and it is something big, something tremendously important. She whispers in such a manner that I can hear it. I watch carefully: "Give us our daily bread and do not throw any more logs under our feet, any more stumbling blocks, while we are trying to walk falling every single step on our faces, thanking thee for everything, loving." Was that before or after the earthquake? First hit came like in the afternoon, relatively early. I'm sure we were still outside, taking the same stroll. Thunder, deafening. Not stopping. Continuous. The earth feels like it is alive, like one is standing on a dog who is trying to work himself from under one's feet. I still can see, already on my belly (the dog seems to have gotten out) the wall of water hitting the boats moored in the basin, turning them into separate slivers. A boathouse that was in front of me suddenly wasn't there, turned into a pile of rubble by one single movement of the dirt it was standing upon. I think it is dust which make sun disappear; it gets almost dark. And then it is silence again, with the view of the town completely changed: rubble, everywhere rubble. And only slowly we get the idea that the background to it all is human shout. Howling.

"Give us tonight our daily bread, and stop throwing stumbling blocks under our feet while we try to remain upright against all the odds. Lord, you want to be loved, not hated. While hatred swims in with our tears, there are so many of them that it is really sufficient to swim in them, cursing."

I ran to see how Alva was, but she seemed to be all right.

No damage done, just awfully scared, like everything else there. Everything alive. The Paphos castle was now a mound, irregularity of the terrain—like there'd never even been a castle, or anything for that matter. And a question crossed my mind where was it exactly that Aphrodite stepped on to the dry land in here, leaving the foamy waters.

Alva was still praying. So was Julius, just a few steps away from her, right there, on top of what was left from the old pier. Looking at it, willy-nilly, I was thinking how long will it take now to remove the traces of the disaster and bring the city to its former shape; years perhaps? And I knew, right away, that it will never be a true problem, that nobody will even give the situation a thought. They'll put themselves to it, with all the energy they can still gather, and sooner than anyone could have thought, the town—all the towns affected—will be in the shape from the past, unaffected or maybe even better in some cases. It will exceed the petty quarrels, discrepancies of opinions, differences in views, and a new town will quickly grow from under the ground that once moved. We knew that.

GISCARD

wonder, looking at the destruction all around, *What am I doing in this? Damn it, right in the middle of it, in fact.* I already thought danger was left behind. France was the danger. *And here we go again, Lord…*

I got out of what was left of our inn into the street, again, into what was left of it (most everything I could remember now trashed), the sidewalk hard to walk along, filled with the leftovers of the houses. And now also the wind made appearance, wind of the strength I won't forget, lifting up tones of dust, blinding. The world I was surrounded by now reminded me of Aristotle's analysis of the chaos, which for the time being (and not really clearly expressed) Anaxagoras imagined as possibly primary and why it could not be: that nature doesn't allow things to get mixed up and therefore it is absurd to imagine that in the beginning all things were mixed up because if they were mixed at some point; they must have once existed in unmixed form. On this view, accidents and modifications could be separated from substances. If nothing had been separated, nothing could also be asserted with any measure of truth of the substance that then existed, which I saw just a few steps down the former street where the Greek butcher was trying to get pieces of meat out of the rubble his former stand was now all mixed up with. I wouldn't be able to tell which pieces were which—beef mixed altogether with pork, and both of those mixed with the dust still in the air and dirt now everywhere. Meat, pieces of wood, and stone. Glass and splinters. Water in the basin seemed mixed with something that must have been in the beginning, then unmixed, and now because of that substance it just looked dirty, killing the feeling that one should perhaps plunge into it and get the dust off. No—hell, I wouldn't wanna swim in that soup. I couldn't get over the fact that the Paphos Castle, once such an impressive, overwhelming presence, was now simply not around, reduced down to a small mound of rubble. I stood there for quite a while and looked, and looked, and fought my thoughts, the thoughts that kept on crossing my mind about us, our lives, God, his goodness, and what we actually believed in—thoughts which I as a Christian didn't like.

I wouldn't be able to tell how much time had passed since the first hit and the moment the second one started. All of a sudden I was in the water fighting for my own life. The water looked like there was terrible storm of some kind around us; water crowned with white, blinding foam, and the fight wasn't easy to the point where I thought that this was the end of the tether. But then I was all of a sudden returned to this side; I was kneeling, surrounded by some more rubble, so it seemed, on what was left of the pier, the dust and dirt now washed off. And a thought came, over time more and more clear, more and more terrible—menacing thought that there was no place to escape to was getting more and more ripe in my head. At some point what I really felt, I think, was fear, the animal fear of dying—that type, right here, inevitably, unavoidably; a fear that I've just been doomed to and I myself had absolutely nothing to say anymore (or that I could say whatever I wanted to absolutely no avail). Nobody would listen to my puny voice (or maybe they would, if it weren't for that roar all around me now, thundering and unstoppable, mighty and invincible, compared to which my voice was simply nonexistent).

Lord, have mercy on us. Do not treat us the way you treat the heathens because we are your servants—certainly not the best, certainly of little faith, all the time ready to flee, and yet we then almost always come back and try again. And even if we fail again, doesn't that speak for us and not against us? Our strength is only what you, Sir, have given us at the point of giving, and if we lose the battle time and again, should that be viewed as our fault? And what about our love? Doesn't that count at all? Please…

Several days had to pass by before we were able to embark again; we helped to fix the ship, and in those tasks, Alva's brother and Julius, because of their animal strength and gigantic stature, truly exceled. Helping with the boat, we were watching how the town was rising from ashes, and one couldn't help the reflections about the resilience of the species we were. Looking at that ocean of destruction surrounding us from all sides, one just couldn't help thinking that if you really wanted to eliminate a human from the game, no matter how important or how unimportant it might seem, one had to kill. No other way, not really. Is that the explanation why so many untimely and unjust deaths all around? All the stakes I have seen back in France, all the torture and persecution—is that the big why? And just what is the game? And whatever it is, who wants to win it so badly? I talked to Alva's brother because I thought once, and still do, that he had now and then also reflected on this. He's answer disappointed me though: "What do we know, Giscard? We are like gnats. Today there is a whole cloud of us and tomorrow not even the memory." Answering me, he didn't even put down a cedar beam he had been carrying on his shoulder. Just stopped for a short moment to say what I quoted a moment ago and then moved on toward the crew rebuilding the ship—well, from where I stood building an altogether new ship, bigger, stronger, with a lot more cargo space. But that is the normal influence of any disaster.

What we came in was a typical northern trade cog, clinker built, with steep sides and flat bottom; the boat they were building now was a round bottom, carvel-built vessel, a lot faster, although still using single mast and a square rig. It shifted from the side rudder the old one had to the stern rudder. There was a guy in the port (considered a visionary, sailing vessel expert at any rate) who was trying to convince William, the owner, to build since we already decided to use the old material in this manner, just supplementing the new wood and generally starting the whole thing anew to build, hence, a two-masted Latino sails equipped vessel. But the idea seemed too extravagant and they—William himself, that is, as well as his chief adviser from England—didn't want to go toward something they would consider experimental at the time. The seamen are always very conventional people, willing to deal only with stuff that has been proven in countless cases of long trips as positive. Here it came out as probably nowhere else. I don't know anything about sailing, but looking at his drawings (the whole tables, tops of which were especially prepared plaster surface on which he'd draw), I thought there was something to it all and that we were losing a lot by not taking his advice. But who would listen to me?

The last day the ship would sail to Smyrna, leaving the five of us—me, that is; Alva and her husband, Julius; her brother and his wife, Gabrielle—in what was left of Acre. A new chapter of our personal history would begin that day.

I felt someone's very strong hand on my throat. Looking at me, one could easily think that my main occupation was swallowing; I couldn't stop. Does this shape of things facilitate sailing or it makes it more difficult, I couldn't tell. Once it restarts, we'll know something more certain about that…

ALVA

efore we get to Acre, a new and fully unexpected situation develops: We can't go into the port. A whole lot of Mameluke's ships are on the water, and they not so much block the entrance as from time to time they get on board of a ship about to enter the port to conduct inspection, which makes it for us at this junction a forbidden territory. A quick debate ensues. Part of the load on board is for Smyrna (which is the final ship's destination anyway), so the captain goes for a sharp north turn, leaving Acre to the right as if that never had been our goal.

It's gonna be a long time, quite unforeseen. And then we enter the old port.

I'm here for the second time. Smyrna is for me what Father intended it to be: something unforgettable—not a city, one more in the Western world, with more or less tradition from the past; houses concentrated at one point where certain amount of people live over a longer period calling themselves inhabitants of this city. Hell no! Smyrna is a place where everything mixes with everything else—there is a present (I am here now, huh?), but there is also a past as alive as I am, whose blood I can hear pulsate in the arteries of life as I know it.

I'm now in a narrow street the houses on which must go back so many years that a comparison with Paris, for instance, may seem only—I'd say—strange. I hear a laugh: Paris is not in the league. As are so many other centers of our European culture. I clear my throat. Shockingly many. I am here at the cradle. The world is young, doesn't know yet how to speak, and it has to be changed; its voice takes a longer getting used to—oh yes, more effort, more patience than it usually does. Everything around seems virgin, including air we breathe, and although many a thing may seem laughable (as is usual case with life anywhere, now isn't it?), we suddenly prefer to preserve our seriousness.

There's a couple ahead of me walking in the same direction, a little slower than me. I'll pass them in a moment, in a brief nick of time, but seeing the smoke, we all stop. Right up ahead a thick black smoke rising quickly up toward the sky is like a command for everybody in this ancient street to stop at once. Now I'm trying to deliberately speed up my pace to get the couple ahead to do some questioning, but they suddenly (seeing my intentions) speed it up too and so does an old guy on the other side of the street, so that I am left with a youngster in the door on my side, who remains immobile, as if deliberately waiting for me. As I approach him, he says (serious, not a trace of a smile on his face), "You think it's a fire, right? One of those old houses, dried up in this sun like pepper is burning, now wouldn't you says just that?"

He speaks Greek that is a little bit more difficult for me than I'm used to. The very little I know is a lot more ancient. But I know *what* he's saying.

"And what is it?"

He nods at the same time tightening his mouth almost in a single line, shapeless. "Sometimes it's just that, a fire. Certainly. Other times is this. Wouldn't be able to tell how many cases our fire department slept over because they thought it was just that. See, right now there is nothing to extinguish. No fire. Nothing for them to do. But oftentimes it is a fire, too, a regular fire. That is what it is, and yet oftentimes it is something else and then, if the fire department s mistaken, people's property burns…"

"Houses?"

"And whatever else!" "Like what?"

"Who knows exactly? But it is here and now. And what you're looking at now never needed a definition to be anywhere. Just like us—it just is."

At some level up there seems to be a suck of some kind, that's where the soot-black stream of smoke suddenly ends. "Everything ancient enough attracts that presence. We can only pray. I tried to find another solution, but there is none. Not really."

"Everything ancient enough…"

"Yawp!"

I was trying to look around, but he didn't give up.

"Did you now that Homer resided here? Homereum is nearby."

"Yes," I said. "My father told me that. He loves Greek and Greece. We finally talk Greek, don't we?"

"I was about to ask, where are you from?" "I'm French."

"Oh…"

And then it's Father. I hear his voice at first, voice only, as if coming from behind the wall, but then I can see him too. "I try to teach. I try to make them sensible to the stuff their lives are made of. Tell them stories. Tell them about Greece, about what a myth represents, how far deep that stuff can go if one knows how to read it. I tell them the story. I look at my daughter, Alva, and I feel exactly, how listening to me now, she will tell about it in the future."

He laughs (and suddenly it is the story I know so well, I remember the details now…)

"The very moment Zeus gave the order to spread the contents of the basket—the virtues, that is—it was Epimetheus who wanted to do that. He would be the one to give creation what it deserves, what's it been waiting such a long time for. Now, we can't forget: Prometheus has an excellent memory. He never forgets anything. Epimetheus has a very bad memory. He forgets everything. But precisely because of that Prometheus treats him a bit like a cripple, with particular politeness, so this time too it is 'Sure thing, you wanna give them this stuff, go right ahead…' Funny thing, huh, Zeus commands that the beautiful ones gather on the right side and the wise ones on the left, which gives the frog a dilemma and in the end makes the poor thing cry out, 'I can't rip myself apart…'"

We were laughing for a moment—well, I've heard the joke before, but I too was laughing (didn't want to spoil anything). He takes a bite of meat from his stick, chews at it for a while, and then keeps going.

"Whoever approaches Epimetheus gets something out of the basket. He's not saving anything. And then, when man approaches him to get his thing, whatever it might be, it turns out that there's nothing left. The basket is empty."

Father coughs, clearing his throat.

"Now think what the consequences of such a predicament might be. Huh? The fact that the basket is empty is a reason for developing the word *techne*. Kids, that's us. We have to make everything ourselves, we've been given nothing. No fur, no claws, no particular sense of smell or hearing. No, we have *techne*. If we want something, well, if we need it—and at times badly—we have to make it ourselves of what's available around. We have the question we use quite often: 'Is that good or bad?' At first glance everybody will say it's great. That's how we are human. Right? Yeah…That's true. But even today I can see certain indications of our techne outgrowing us. Superstition which today puts people at stake will someday become a joke and then entertainment. Don't ask me how, please. Or how I know. I remember the antiquary in Smyrna I talked to. Some would even say he was Joseph Cartaphilus himself. He told me a lot of things. He seemed to have a particular interest in the future of mankind, and he saw it rather gloomy. Techne would outgrow us and we would start serving things we have made. There shall be no other way. Religion shall die. Or maybe just get reduced to gestures and formulas still recited but meaning nothing. In the end even the evil spirits will be reduced down to a joke. That's the end. There's nothing after that."

His head fell on his chest and for a moment; I thought he was asleep. But he wasn't. He lifted up his head and looked at us, and it was a sad look. He put some meat on his stick because there was none left. We ate in silence.

"See, I have this knife because Epimetheus had such a lousy memory. A small bear would be defenseless if he attacked m, or if I were hungry. But in the long run, this knife will be my end. All the gifts we have are like that: impossible to tell if it comes from god or the devil. If it's a gift of love, in other words, or one of hatred…"

He puts the piece into his mouth and starts chewing. "It's all been describe in the library of Alexandria. Well, that one burnt, but there shall be more like that. Yes, there'll be an ocean of libraries."

I know they listen to me.

OUTREMER

GISCARD

I'm sitting at what's left of the bonfire (ambers, that is, red, although not very much of a glow in them anymore), most everybody went to sleep, and I can hear snoring from most everywhere. The worst at it is probably the Ormian priest who'd stopped by yesterday in his travel to Jerusalem, to the grave of the Lord. That didn't die. Not altogether anyway. He has few people with him; they were armed, which makes me think that Julius's calculation as to what were we gonna do down here were not mistaken, not mistaken altogether anyway. About that later, though.

Above me is the infinity of the night without clouds, dwarfing my soul's feeling of infinity down to nothing, giving me sense of the very contrary: superfluousness—secondhand meaning in being future of an insect. I just had to take a deep breath. I don't feel like being an insect. No, I'd like to be me, and the only problem with that is that I have no idea what that is.

I stood up. Julius told me, yet before he went to sleep, to brush his horse—doesn't have to be perfect, just the big spot under the saddle, thoroughly, to remove even the smallest rests of sweat from there, the rest of the animal's back superficially treated or not at all. I don't want to get his reprimand tomorrow when he would be talking to me, his voice artificially lowered, holding my ear between his index and his thumb, and nobody (maybe Alva, she is the saint here) would say a word for me. So I do it now, as best I can, until I have the prickly feeling under my eyelids.

The sleepiness is overtaking my senses to the point where everything seems indifferent, even the morning's reprimand I may receive from that big brute. I still manage to put a piece of wood into the former fire, and then I just lie beside it, covering my poor body with a camel wool blanket as best I could. Nights get cold here; one wakes up stiff and sore, and tomorrow we have the last piece of our journey to what's left of Alva's and her brother's castle from the past (if anything—they have no idea). And according to what they say, that'll be some journey. I definitely need to rest as best I can during the few hours left till morning. I fall asleep in an instant. I dream of Paris, I have to flee and I do. Prosecuted by the king's people, I have the feeling of an impending doom, I'll be burnt at the stake, in front of a friggin' crowd. I don't want to. I haven't done a thing, there's no reason…When I managed to open my eyes, it is already the crack of dawn. I still lie without a movement, using the rest of the night for my sleep's last seconds; they are truly sweet when I think about getting up. Rare moments when life is worth living.

Then Alva got up. She made the fire, and then went over to the mule with our provisions: two bags, now on the ground, which the animal was touching with its hind leg. She took out a clay pitcher with eggs and started beating out a portion for each of us into the frying pan hanging over the fire, in which the butter just started sizzling. Her brother was cutting bread and putting it onto a tray. And then we started eating. I wasn't hungry, in fact I wasn't hungry at all. But I also knew, knowing Alva's brother, that we would stop next time probably toward the evening. Have you ever spent the whole day in the saddle? You know how you feel? How your butt feels? I can easily recall days that I fell asleep on the saddle, and I shall never know by what miracle I fell *not* off the horse. They don't seem to feel tired, ever. And if one says one is, they just look at you like you are from another world, some kind of a poor misfit in this one. Goes without saying we keep going; nothing changes in that department. So I ate what I was given, the whole portion. Bread from the tray has been eaten down to the last crumb. We all had tea. And then Alva and Julius started cleaning, which wasn't much: wiping off with a rag that later item, as soon as we would encounter a creek (they knew the area, or thought they did—there was supposed to be one, not that far away, which would serve our washing purposes as well as to replenish our water supply), and the rag then would be washed. For now doing the dishes was over. The frying pan as well as the tray we were using for bread were wrapped up in a rag and stored in a bigger bag, which then ended up hanged on the supply mule. Same goes for the teacups, pretty beautiful ones, family heirloom, made in France—Sevres, I think. We were more or less ready to go.

All of us knelt down with our hands together and prayed, silently, from our hearts, for guidance and protection. Kneeling, I was trying first of all to imagine Mary's face. I always do that, and then, already seeing her, my eyes closed tight, I asked the same thing: Please lead me away from danger and toward where we set out to get to. Stand between me and the evil one, lend me just the hem of your divine mantel, oh, mother of God. Please don't let him destroy my life...

Then we travel through the country of mild hills, covered with fresh, green vegetation—at least this time of the year. It is late afternoon when Alva's brother visibly changes his attitude; he starts looking for something—not just correcting our direction but obviously looking for something he knows it's there. Alva looks kind of nervous too. And then, yet some time later, we all see what's left from what a long time ago was most probably exquisite property: mounds of rock, stumps of former buildings covered with soot, although not quite. If we didn't know the history of the place, I realize, we wouldn't know what that actually was—soot mixed with dust and sand, sort of sunk overtime into the sandstone, just giving it a strange nonexistent in nature color of a body...

Alva dismounts. Then it's her brother and then Julius, and after him his wife. I just followed suit. We kneel and pray, right there, amongst the strange-colored stumps of the past and our horses, in the air which slowly goes over into the evening color and evening length of the shadows. Slowly, not talking, we start building the bivouac; a beam is fixed to which our horses are tied up to, bags with our stuff necessary for the cooking and then sleeping on the ground under the open sky, which yet a moment after shall be filled with stars, just like that is taken out and spread on the delicate grass. And we eat, sitting on the skins, on which we shall then sleep.

Alva, sipping tea, addresses Gabrielle. "This here used to be our home. I was little at first, then just a girl, grew up here. I had a dog I loved. Died right there." She points her hand. "Right there. I'd call it ridiculous, if you can use a word like that relating to death. A bit to the left I saw my mother die too. An arrow got her. She just knelt at first and then fell altogether. Died. There was a building, right there, with a basement I was hid in, watching it all. The Mamelukes haven't found me. And then they came." She points now to her brother. "Dad was alive, of course."

We were all eating in silence. Then Gabrielle says, "Just out of curiosity…why did you come here? I know I wouldn't…"

"I think we are the criminals," Alva says, "who have to come to the place of crime. Attracts us like a magnet. We just cannot not come."

"Yeah…" Julius says. "Life is what's happening all around, so we think we understand it, you know? Because it's an everyday thing. And it doesn't stop. Doesn't change much, just goes on and on. We get used to it, like pigs. Or some such."

"Yeah…" Alva says. "That's what it is. I guess." And then, "That's why we came… That too."

ALVA

'm here all by myself, on top of the hill, in the dugout they had made—the bottom of it is stone, sandstone, made almost polished, so smooth in fact, that the cart I'm sitting in can move every which way I want it to, with no effort, or almost none. Brother considered this position of mine the most important thing at the moment since we have landed at Acre. Everything would depend on the accurate and timely information, and this being the highest point of the terrain we are interested in it could provide such information…I can move, as said before, every which way I find fit, thus providing insight about our situation at any moment. They can work quietly, undisturbed, knowing about any movement around us.

Above me there's a roof made of wood and supported by five also wooden columns, just in case we have rain. To one of the posts a thin rope is attached going from here all the way down to where they are working. There's a tiny bell; if it rings, well, that's me telling them that something has changed, something or somebody new has appeared: stop and grab the weapons, be ready. That: be ready! A thing which is the most frequent here, the most typical, although not always signifying the same thing. A lot of people, totally different people, pass through the area: commerce, exploration, religion and spirituality of any possible kind. And then thieves. Scum, seeking easy prey, ready for anything to whom killing means next to nothing. Now for meeting with the latter, you need the weaponry and being in general good shape. I still remember our first days here, and even though nothing really has changed the time we've already spent here all by itself has the strange gift of changing how the old stuff feels now (maybe that's our life in general; we just have to get accustomed to it). We still live in the same tents we bought yet in Cyprus—one small for me and my things (Gabrielle's personal things fit in there too), one just like that for Giscard, one much bigger for brother and his wife as also one of the same type for Julius and me. We still cook on bonfires and keep our supplies in a hole dug out in the dirt covered with a small type of a tent—well, not really; it looks like a little mound of dirt under the cowhides getting clearer and clearer from the sun. That didn't change. None of it. And yet there's a difference: any of it and all of it looks a lot more familiar now. We are used to it. And the place itself has changed too. They took apart the small mounds of dirt and rock of strange color like that of a dead body assumes certain time after death. They've cleaned the pieces of rock and restored the square in the middle of the "plaza," which is to be the future floor in the main room—well, it is different now. It is. Almost every single day brings changes in that sense—I can see the old place, our former place here we proudly called back then the castle, revive at an accelerated pace. Sometimes I even try to think farther into the future what's it to be like when we finish. Brother says it's gonna be bigger this time, more impressive and more comfortable to live. The smithy shall be farther up the hill, built only of wood. Time and again they had to travel down south to get the stuff they needed, and those were also moments of greatest uncertainty. I was left here with just another woman and Giscard, which isn't much in terms of defensive strength. But so far we got lucky. Oh, they had to fight, they had to defend our little treasure time and again, and they fought like devils too—the cemetery is our old one in the north, now with a collective grave, accommodating all those bodies left after the fighting was over each of those times.

During the second year there was a battle I will never be able to forget: a detachment of Mamelukes, some fifty of them, came and at first asked for water and some food, with the time, though, beginning clearly to express their disappointment and then just rage. One of them hit Julius in the face, and I think now, that was it: the battle flared up. The first guy who started it died that very instant; and then the two, brother and Julius, back-to-back, started fighting. It took all night. With the rack of the dawn the whole terrain was covered with dead bodies. Brother had a bunch of injuries of a lighter caliber of which I then was taking care for a while. Julius, as soon as there was nobody left from amongst the Mamelukes, collapsed. He had a crossbow arrow under his right shoulder blade, several punctures in the area of his belly done with a sword; and the moment I got to him, I thought he was dead. He regained consciousness only several days and several cups of sage brew later. Yet quite some time after that, they both looked like their own shadows, hardly able to move, their movement limited to the basest of all we can perform. I remember my reaction to their health: I couldn't care less. What it was basically: if they live, I'll live. Should they die—hell, so will I.

Enough! I've seen enough of death. I simply wouldn't allow it to bug my mind anymore. Oh, I know today back then I meant it! Enough! The bodies all around us started to rot and to stink, and so Giscard and I, as best we could, started on our part cleaning up, bury the bodies in the soil. That was so far the worst of our experiences down here. Then slowly (and I think that is the keyword here, *slowly*) it all started, or should I probably say restarted, getting back to normal: full days of work, dawn till sunset, with pauses for eating, a short nap in the afternoon, and then the rest at night.

Toward the end of the third year the castle was, give or take, finished. We could (and we did) move in. I was happy beyond measure. I kept kissing everybody like I was crazy or something of that nature. I wasn't my usual self. And then the days started their usual trickling again, reminding me of the fact that our life is but hanging on to our daily stuff, hanging on spasmodically to all of it, which then, after finally lost, doesn't look worth all that obstinacy at all. But for now we hang on. Oh yes, we do. We fight. We give our lives, we write sermons and preach, built churches, some of them truly magnificent; and only with the flow of the time our loneliness envelops us tighter and tighter, taking from us that illusion of sensibility. The mouth is bitter, the tongue dried up—all of it has the aura of putrefaction.

Something just told me to turn around, and I did. I saw a pillar of dust approaching us from the south, and I yanked at the rope. Almost in no time brother and Julius appeared in front of the castle, and yet a moment after that they started to run toward me. We were then sitting and waiting. Ready.

GISCARD

One more time, before the curtain falls down for good and I'll be left alone and unable to speak, I intend to show no less than William of Paris, the grand inquisitor, talking to me; well, because he did. They brought me to him—the guards, nighttime— and he spent major part of that night with me. And here it is, against anyone I tried to consult. Here he is; I think a fragment that does him justice better than any of them so far—the grant inquisitor, William of Paris.

His hand, now reaching for the bell on the table, reminds me of something I've once seen at home when I was yet a little boy—a hand of my father's friend, much older than himself, looking like made first and foremost of extremely delicate lacework of some kind. Looking up an encyclopedia I found Brabant as the place famous for that kind of work—then I thought wrongly; Father's friend must have been from Brabant. He rang the bell, and the servant entered, pouring each of us our sherry.

With him gone, I picked up again (all this time I was answering his question): "His high esteem is spread very, extremely unevenly. Barely known to his own, he is appreciated by the Christians and some Greeks. We'll have to resign ourselves to the very little we know about individual character of Ibn Rochd. Almost all of what's said about him pertains to the legend and gives witness rather to the opinion that has formed over time than to himself. The great mass of his work could testify to the fact that his capacity for work has been enormous. His assertion that he did not pass without studying more than two nights since his prime: the night of his own marriage and the night of the death of his father. We can't say that Ibn Rochd gets out of the typical scheme of an Islamic scientist. He knows what others, very much like him, know also: medicine, hence Galen; philosophy, hence Aristotle; astronomy, hence Almageste. But he adds also certain degree of critique rare in the Islamic approach, which goes a lot farther than the horizon of his times. Like every good Islamist, he joins to his secular studies the jurisprudence (he knew *mouata* by heart) and like every Arab really, distinguished, very much so, poetry. The poetry in that time wasn't much more than an ingenious combination of syllables; one should then not be surprised seeing that she was cultivated by people of so little lyricism like Ibn Sina and Ibn Rochd. Leon of Africa tells us that Ibn Rochd had composed a few pieces of poetry moral and gallant, which he burnt in his old age. Leon conserved for us a fragment which could testify to the fact that wisdom wasn't for Ibn Rochd anything but the fruit of years. Quotes from d'Antara, d'Imroulkais, d'Asha, d'Abu Temam, de Nabega, de Montenabi, out of Kitab el—again (echoes of the ancient chanson Arabic). That paraphrase accuse, on the other hand, ignorance most complete possible of the Greek literature. The Arabs knew Greece only through philosophers and other authors scientific. Not one of the writers in real characteristic of the Greek genius did get through to them and, no doubt, they were unable to appreciate the beauties so far different from those they researched.

I've been trying to concentrate, gather my thoughts…

He reaches now for the bell, and the servant entering and pouring our drinks asked one more time, simply repeats itself. Then the servant gets out, leaving us to ourselves. I know that my task is to diminish Averroes's importance, decrease the significance of his work—God, significance for whom? He says now that so deep in the night we should be able to feel more of our freedom and less of the life that is pressing us down, toward the earth…

"Why do you think we have such profound reception of the Greek theater as opposite to them? They don't seem to have basic understanding…You know Euripides, in French, of course, Aeschylus, Sophocles?"

"Yes, sir, I do, of course. And…"

"And? See, the Greeks have their Bachanalia, they have Dionysus cult, they have Dodona and Diana there, they love wine, they love drunkenness, drunken chant…For a Greek, there is nothing out of the ordinary, if a god finds himself on his way, don't you think? Arab? No celebrating. God is one and mighty from the very beginning, sullen, all puffed up with pride, and he says clearly thou shallst not drink. You drink, you get puffed up, you offend me, you hear about it, you bloody worm. On your knees! Beg! What do you think?"

Then I keep going. "Averroes, says d'Herbelot is the first who has translated Aristotle from Greek into Arabic, and that yet before the Jews have done their work, and so for the longest time we had no other text of Aristotle than the Latin version, which has been done on the base of the Arabic text from this great philosopher who has added broad commentaries to it himself, which then have been used by Thomas Aquinas and other scholastics, all of which took place long before the true Aristotle originals in Greek have been known to us.

"D'Herbelot could not have known the history of the Latin versions of Aristotle, whom nobody studied in such a detailed manner so far: but in what concerns his quality as before Averroes, that the translations of Greek authors into Arabic have been accomplished almost all of them by the Syrians, and that may well be that no learned Islamic man, and certainly no one from Spain, knew Greek. Ibn Rochd never read Aristotle other than reading him in the ancient versions done in Syriac through Hunayn ibn Ishaq, Ishak-ben-honein, Yahya ibn Adi, Abul Bashar Mata, etc.

He knows how to utilize in the best manner the means of exegesis that are in his possession. He compares the different versions Arabic, he disputes the valor of lessons, and even at times he makes critical observations which would suggest he knew Greek. But the text really stayed closed to him."

We are looking at each other; he is smiling, I don't dare. "See." I pick it up instead. "I really tried to stay close to it, once I got to this point. I would pay I had friends bringing me paperwork from Cairo while I was in Smyrna and from Spain while I was in Jerusalem. I studied. Compared. And I was more and more shocked.

He would mix Protagoras with Pythagoras, Cratyle with Democritus; Heraclites becomes a philosophic sect, the Herculeens. First philosopher of that sect was Socrates, just as Anaxagoras is the chief of the Italic school. These errors would of course accuse of an awful ignorance, if we didn't have to recognize the fact that they result for at least in a part out of the translations Ibn Rochd had in his hands."

"Albert thought a lot of him…He did."

"I think that the doctrine Albert represents at the time doesn't offer the same firmness, which later on shall characterize the doctrine Dominican. Time and again the theories of the Arabs surprise their own orthodoxy. His doctrine of the creation is vacillating. Intellect at times seems to be the source from which emanate the intelligences. Influence of the superior beings upon the human intelligence is explicitly reckoned with. In the womb of the active intellect, the intelligent and the intelligible are identical. And in the passive intellect, as opposite to that, the intelligent and the intelligible are identical. Agent attract specimens of the matter, cause them to be simple and general; thus prepared, they move and inform the intellect possible. Agent joins the possible, like light joins the diaphanous, and raises it up to the dignity of the intellect speculative. The latter in its turn serves the soul to get up to the level of the intellect acquired (*adeptus seu divinus*). That last term is reached when the intellect possible has received all the intelligibles and attached itself in a manner indivisible to the active intellect.

"Man is thus perfect and in some manner resembles God.

At this stage, he acts divinely and becomes able to know it all, which is the sovereign contemplative happiness. I told you all this to show how the Arabic doctrines have penetrated the Albert's doctrine, although they are so distant from being it. He writes, 'Possibilis apeculativa recipiens cum eis lumen suscipit agentis, cui de die en diem fit similior; et quum acceperit possibilis omnia speculate seu intellect, habet lumen agentis ut formam sibi adherentem…'"

He was now looking at me smiling. "Can you think in Latin, Giscard?" "Not quite yet. But I am close."

He points to the glasses and the decanter on the table, and my question is, "Could I do it this time?"

"It's divine, isn't it?"

"Yes, it is," I said, already pouring.

Then we were having it, slowly, letting the wine spread on palates.

"Tell me about Thomas… whatever you can…"

"It's first of all against the theory of the unity of the intellect that Thomas deploys the resources of his dialectic. Not content to return to the subject without a break in *Summa theologiae, in Summa contra gentiles*, in the commentary *Questiones disputate de Anima*, he composes in the end one of his most important works, *De unitate intelectus, adversus Averroistas…*"

He doesn't look good. His mouth moves as if he wanted to say something, but he just takes another sip instead. I keep going.

"The form of his polemic exhibits us sufficiently the fact that he wants a school well organized, pretending to represent the true spirit of peripatetism against the Latin philosophes, which is to say against the orthodox scholastic, and he does that attaching himself to Averroes like to the greatest authority, superior even to that of faith…"

"Parbleu!" He throws he glass against the wall, but I manage to remain composed.

"Unide erum est quomodo aliqui, solum commentum Averroys videntes, pronunciare presumum quod ipse dicit hoc sensisse omnes philosophos grecos et arabes , preater latinos…" We look each other in the eyes.

"You came here to mock me? You think you can?"

"Truth is what I'm telling you, sir. You asked me the question, and I am answering it according to my best knowledge. I'm truly sorry that the truth mocks you…"

"Want to try something that would suit me better? Huh? The night's young…" I have the last sip that is still in my glass.

"Saint Thomas becomes indignant himself seeing that the Christians thus become the disciples of an unfaithful and prefers over the authority of a man who deserves more than the title of a peripatetic, that of a corruptor of the peripatetic academy. He then tries to refute him not by means of the authority of the Latins, that does not collaborate, as he tells everybody, but by means of philosophical arguments borrowed from the Greeks and Arabs. Not the Aristotle, not Alexander d'Aphrodisias, not Avicenne and not Algazel, not even Theophrast and Themistius whose thoughts Averroes once changed, did not dream of this strange doctrine of the unity of intellect. The same form belongs to many, but matter belongs to only one. Hence it's matter that makes the quantity of beings, not the undetermined matter which belongs to many and is still the same, but delimited matter, the quantum individual."

"How do you arrive at ideas? Do you take long walks?"

He smiles. "Talk to yourself?"

"I have a friend." A quick, malicious maybe idea crosses my mind quickly. "We talk. Walk. Or sit at the river. And talk." I imagine him hanging from the ceiling, his hands tied up behind his back, nothing drips down 'cause all already have, I imagine the misbelieve after he says he's never even heard of Averroes, or any of those…guys—never, fuuuuuck! I'm no saint. No, sir! It makes me feel really good. I look at the guy on the other side of the table, at his face; well shaven, his head. Well, this time I'll know about the saint (with no doubts, absolute certainty) who will turn my old friend Guy (the guy who grabbed Alva's breast and then did some stuff too) into something on the floor one could step into. Who knows, saints may still have plenty of use. Friggin' plenty!

He asks me if I would like to stay for the night (it's very late already); he may order a cart for me that would bring me right to my door, and I tell him that there's no need for that, I love to walk. And why should Paris be worse than Athens? We get a chuckle out of that, and then he just accompanies me to the door. To the main entrance I am accompanied by a huge servant, walking on the side of whom I have the impression to still be a little boy. Then it is the night I walk into.

ZWEIFLER

feel that we are alone here. Now and then somebody gets of the main track to what's left of Acre traveling from Jerusalem or the other way around, but that doesn't change the basic feeling of almost splendid isolation we experience down here. Those rare guests come here for water (we have excellent source—a creek flowing right through the middle of our property; water is perfectly clean and rather cold). Some would like to buy some food—for themselves or for the animals—and we do whatever we can, considering the fact that we too have to buy it. We grow a little bit of wheat, but that doesn't suffice to become business selling supplies. People who come here in good faith understand that without much ado; against those who don't, we have to defend ourselves, and so far the cemetery in the north of the house has gotten substantially bigger. There's another thing—mail; I know that in Europe it still functions relatively well, but not here. To get a letter or parcel, no matter how small it might be, you have to use services of someone who travels absolutely privately to a place near you and then compensate. So much more of joy was the letter from Meister who is now in his Thüringen, healthy and well, although, as he says himself, aging considerably in the old house where he seems to have been born too, if memory serves.

The person who has brought me the mail from Meister has actually already been in the vicinity, except a bit eastern of us, already passed our property in his way to Jerusalem, and only on the basis of mathematical calculation (time since they left Acre as compared to what Meister had told him), and so that discrepancy made him turn around and go a little back up north, this time though on the western side of the trail, and at some point they just rode into us. He says he remembers me from the times when I was in Meister's company in Paris, but I have no recollection whatsoever; I could swear I'm seeing this guy for the first time in my life. Be that as it may, it is still great joy to see an old acquaintance like that here, in this almost complete wilderness.

What Meister sent me is a parcel, quite thick, containing letters. He writes about everything, Europe from the last decade, give or take, writes me in detail about King Philip de Fair's death, exactly one year after Jacques de Molay's burning, as the latter predicted from the fire. And the pope too died; well, that one had always, from the very beginning just a lousy health, and there's no surprise in his leaving this world. What made anyone move their heads in astonishment was the accuracy of prediction made by the dying man, fighting the flames: a year did not pass by as they all stood in front of God to answer for their deeds. The Knights Templar ceased to exist. Those who still wanted to be knights were free to join the Hospitallers, and they did that too, unhampered, left to themselves.

They had now houses in Jerusalem and, supposedly, Acre; but then again, what's it to me? I certainly won't be a knight ever again defending whatever…except my own family and my own business. Julius thinks the same, so we won't be joining anything anytime soon. Next month maybe we shall start the smithy, and then, once that is built, we try to make weaponry of the quality Father once made. Back to Meister now! He writes me about his Thüringen, it's warm, beautiful weather; he used to take a stroll, hours sometimes, to the water where he would sit long time, warming up his bones getting older. But now he doesn't have any more strength to do that. Surely he takes a short walk…hell, he has to sit down almost right away because of the muscles in his lower back, his buttocks, as well as the backside of his tights. It's not even pain in the regular sense of the word; it's more like those were slowly burning, whatever might cause that. A time comes, he writes, when one knows that one's stay here touches its end. See, and here is what he wanted to actually write about. He doesn't have any riches, goodness, the few trinkets—you people have ten times that. No, in that sense he doesn't have any riches to bequeath. And yet from the time when he was in Köln teaching as *baccalaureus* only on Peter Lombard's sentences, and long before all that later stuff came, he met a person who decided what his later life was going to be. That was Albertus Magnus, who would talk to him and listen and, devastated by Aquinas's premature death had given him, copied by himself on the best parchment with the best ink he was able to produce the five proves of the existence of God. Well, here they are copied by Albert and at some point written by Thomas. He, Meister, knows that this is something that will warm up your heart. That's one thing, and another is that after he, Meister, is already dead, this stuff here won't perish. It'll be with you, and then with whomever you choose. And thus he, Meister, will have his rest uninterrupted.

A thick leather etui containing few pages of thick, certainly very expensive parchment—I hold it in my hand and think. I imagine him, Meister, as a young man talking to the greatest authority of this world, all impressed by those moments, unforgettable and so full of hope and joy. He, Meister, is almost a boy (but it could have been later too, we will never know; we can only imagine what's outside the documents, and those documents, so few…).

So he can't make it even to the water anymore…

> *Quinta via sumitur ex gubernatione rerum. Videmus enim quod aliqua que cognition carent, scilicet corpora naturalia, operantur propter finem, quod aparet ex hoc quod semper aut frequentius eodem modo aperantur, ut consequantur id quod es optimum: unde patet quod non a casu, sed ex intentione perveniunt at finem. Ea autem que non habent cognitionem, non tendunt in finem nisi directa ab aliquo cognoscente et inteligente, sicut sagitta a sagittante. Ergo es aliquid intelligens, a quo omnes res naturales ordinantur ad finem, et hoc dicimus deum.*

I see his hands, full of pronounced veins, his skin with moles, as if too big for his bones and muscles holding it; there's a smile on his face. He has a cup of wine in one of his hands, gold covered with white enamel, made in one of the Saxon southern duchies, an object of luxury and beauty, one of the few he allows himself to have. It is more respect for an *object d'art* than the will for the riches of this world. I know that, he doesn't have to tell me. When a friend departs, his life hence missing gives one the sense of loss; the world isn't what it used to be. It's lonely and cold. Well, Meister is still here—then how do you know? Do you know? Do we know anything?

Otto died a while ago and was buried at the local cemetery; the inn has been sold to new people, and Carla and her husband, now entering the age where they'll have to think about their old age, are still employed there. When Meister wrote his last letter to me, she, Carla, was serving him his wine and keeping the tables in the inn clean. Her son, Günter, was there too. He was just sitting at one of the tables and watching things. He is now *bacalaureus* accepted as such at the monastery up the hill, teaching on *Sentences Peter Lombard's*. He speaks fluent Latin and Greek, and his mother is very proud of his position. Meister asked her once (he writes about it) if she had ever given a thought her resting time, the period before she goes altogether; and she answered him, very serenely, there was no anger in that at all, that she still has time, still strong, moving like when she was twenty, and only Günter smiled at it delicately.

Meister awaits the verdict concerning his hereticism, and he is serene about it too. He suggest delicately that they have a very little time; he can feel the weakness approaching at an accelerated pace. Once he is out, they can use their verdict…

I think about those moments of life which then, *ex post*, are considered the most important ones, moments after which life was never the same. I wonder about the fact that the only love Meister ever got to know was God; he is quite clear about it, no mistakes. And yet there was that moment in his life I never stopped wondering and pondering about, when he was standing there, on place de Grève, under that pyre, and watch the woman of his life die one of the most horrible deaths man invented for man. How can there be talk of love after that? But there are so many things I don't understand. I struggled all of my life and never got even close to understand. I look now one more time, before I put it back into its etui, at the black-gold letters written on the most expensive papyrus by Albert the Great half destroyed by Thomas's premature death, with the best ink made also by himself:

> *Ergo est aliquid intelligens, a quo omnes res naturales ordinantur* ad *finem, et hoc dicimus Deum.*

GABRIELLE

rack of dawn. I get up and go out, because it is the only time nobody is at the creek and I can take a bath with nothing on, without having to count on somebody looking. The creek would be a lot more accommodating in, let's say, three hours, with the sun up; but then everybody will be up, and I can just wash (with everything on).

I took all of it off and entered the water. It's ice-cold. It makes it hard to breath at times, but I am submerged all the way up to my chin. I needed that. Oh yes, sir, for the longest time. One doesn't feel fresh; one's body begins to smell, and the thought about a bath becomes an obsession. It seems at times that waiting any longer is simply impossible, first of because of the people around one. The place I am at is a deeper spot on the creek where I can even make a few breaststrokes without hitting anything, so I swim a little, slowly, taking my time. But then I get to the shore and use soap: on myself and on my cloths—well, some of them. In the meantime water doesn't seem so terribly cold anymore; my body is getting used to it. Then I decide to get one more time into deeper water and do a little swimming, even risking being seen as I am now, with nothing on. And that risk grows with every minute. They most probably do not sleep anymore. I'm absolutely certain of Julius; Alva is an early bird too…Would that be a problem, though, if Alva saw me naked? Certainly not. I should ask a question entirely different: would there be any problem if anyone from amongst them saw me naked? And the answer should also be the same: of course not!

I get to the shore and rub my body with a towel, watching the skin get red. Then I put my clothes on. I sit down on the sand, and everything gets so comfortable and so quiet that for a second I think I'm gonna fall asleep. I don't think about the breakfast now, although yet a moment ago I felt hungry. I feel someone's eyes on me. I can't see him (whoever it might be), but I know he's watching me. And only a little later I see him move quickly along the bushes—I actually don't see him; what I see is a quickly moving shadow. Then he stops and I see his face; for one brief moment I see his face. It's Lionel. Born French, then a goldsmith here, in Outremer. He lost everything—wife and kids murdered, his psyche broke. Brother and Julius built for him a room with separate entrance, which he almost never used. He lived outside, in the bushes I just saw him in, and such. He couldn't talk, except when he would, standing in the midst of us, prophesy. He would talk about the future, what's coming and what's not, and nobody would interrupt him. We would all be quiet, listening to him. Times were coming when education was going to be a joke; new sets of values would be established, and the ones we cherish now trampled into the ground. God would be replaced by what's gonna be called science. Religion shall be named prejudice and fought down with a vengeance. Poverty and misery would reach the sky. Judicial system would be there only to make life even more miserable than ever.

I see his face, unshaven, of course, moving quickly on the backdrop of the bushes. He wants, obviously, to be left alone; today is not the day for prophecy. I wish I could tell him somehow that I am not after him and that he doesn't have to try to escape each time he sees me. I don't wish him anything bad; he was always good to me.

My husband comes out and seeing Lionel invites him to have breakfast with us. From the bushes emerges slowly the silhouette covered with dirty rags, actually close to naked, and stays immobile, right about the center of the yard.

"Come on, Lionel," says my husband, "you don't have to be a wild creature. You know us, right? All of us. Come on!" He won't sit at the table though, no matter what. He finally sits right there, right where he stands, and when he gets an omelet with ham, he starts eating it also right there. Small pieces. Bit off, chewed, swallowed. There's an obvious delight on his face all along. At some point he farts loudly, not paying us any mind. Then he burps, stands up, and disappears into the bushes. Julius makes another omelet, picks it up with his wooden spatula after he throws it in the air a couple of times, eats it piecemeal until there's nothing left in his plate. So much for breakfast. We remain sitting there for yet a while, letting our stomachs perform their function on what we just delivered to them, and then the usual day of work starts for everybody. I go to the creek to fetch the water to wash the plates and the frying pan. I feel pretty good, fresh and young; there is a lot of hope ahead of all of us. That's how I feel. I know it's just the bath I have taken this morning, I'm not naïve, and yet I feel like whistling a melody I remember still from Paris. I start whistling and then I suddenly feel like crying. I see Seine, the boulevard along the river, I'm walking on it; the day is just like it is here— sunny and clear, just a few clouds on the otherwise azure sky. I had to kneel down because of the pain in my lower belly. I took a deeper breath. One and then another. And it was slowly over. I don't think I've ever realized how I miss France, my life over there. I don't want to admit to that. We want to persuade ourselves that France was bad, dangerous—that it meant a terrible death in the end. Sweet Jesus, maybe it did. Sure I know it did. My memory isn't so short. And yet…

I see Alva's brother and Julius walking together toward the smithy. Ahead of them there's an exhausting day of work on a new sword; the oven has been built, and they will set the fire today because they also got the good steel—pieces looking like small stones—from somewhere past Jerusalem. That's a journey in itself. The steel is made somewhere around Damascus, and it's very expensive, as I understand; it actually makes me laugh—the few dark, little stones, wrapped around in a rag, being the greatest investment in the whole process. From that moment on there'll be no interrupting the process until at least that part is finished and they shall have the ingot of a steel which is worth it. The work shall be incredibly heavy, that steel ingot is the hardest thing a human being probably ever produced while living on Earth.

Our job—that is mine and Alva's—is something else though. The castle before it was destroyed and outside the wall there was a moat for which the water could have been delivered from the redirected creek. Now that is what I am busy with, having Alva with me at all times. We don't build the stone wall, but we do empty the moat—with our shovels, buckets and a set of pulley blocks that has to be reset each time we change place. It works slowly like molasses, but it works. By the end of the day there's no difference. But by the end of the month—oh yes, sir, even a blind man could see. As Alva laughs, we are definitely not wasting our time, the progress is obvious. I think by the end of the summer we'll be able to start digging a ditch for water, which is to say the moat shall be so far advanced that we'll start filling it with water from the creek. It'll be funny—a castle with moat (knowing Alva's brother, he'll come up with some kind of a drawbridge) but no walls. And yet Alva's brother maintains, whenever it comes to talking about it, that the moat is more important for the defenses of the castle than the ramparts. Particularly in a case like this: very few people defending. Those who are coming out of the water are truly defenseless. It's the moat what renders them useless as attackers. The moat has to be at least seven feet deep, so it's a lot of work. My hands have blisters all over, and I know Alva is in the same predicament; she's just too tough to complain loud.

We both now, Alva as well as I, go down into the pit and start digging. I trust Alva's brother as far as fighting defending the castle. He fought so many a time already that if there's anyone anywhere who knows how, it's him. One more time I recall the defense of Rochester, where King John's question was that how could a thousand people armed to the teeth fail so miserably against twenty? Somebody answered him, "But the twenty, Your Highness, were knights Templar..." Let's hope it's not gonna come to that down here, Templars or not. I for one wouldn't wanna see that with my own eyes. Oh, Lord, have mercy on us! On the Abbasids court, changes took place that may raise some hope, and Alva is of good cheer, but I am more skeptical and that is because so far (and it hasn't been all that long) they were forced to fight and I don't know (I honestly don't) how many times. What if one of them gets injured permanently so he can fight no more? What then? Are we gonna go back to France? We were having this discussion yesterday at the fire, and it was Julius who brought that up.

Two are no sufficient force in a region like this, even the best. There are bows and arrows and knifes thrown with precision that takes one's breath away? What if?

Hell, where is my freshness from morning? I told that Alva, but she doesn't seem to be any better. We just kept on working.

Most probably all of us lost in the same thoughts; and if there are memories emerging, those are also the same memories. By the same token we are, all of us, too disciplined to change anything in our outside attitude. Yes, sir! Nothing changed.

GISCARD (THE NIGHT)

I t's me again, my voice. In the last fragment I thought I was a-joking talking about the curtain getting down; hell and way, as long as I have a voice.

I remembered watching once a big cat, like a leopard or cheetah, playing with its mistress and going too far at some point; the play with the cat would have gotten dangerous for the woman, and what saved her was the fact that she knew how to react properly: she grabbed the cat's mouth with her hand exactly like the mother would have treated the nursling back when it was yet little; and the huge predator, capable of killing her with a sneeze, was suddenly down, flattened on the ground. I thought the same happens with us. We think we can do something and it's life that proves us wrong, usually in some ridiculous manner like I just have described—or the opposite; we think that something is not for us (too big, too difficult, too dangerous), without trying at all, so we leave it untouched and just turn away, with a little shame, dissatisfied, a bitter taste in our mouths, only to find out later, somehow, how little it would have taken to really do it.

I remember the day we were attacked; I remember the guy on the horse attacking. Julius threw him off almost right away, the sheer strength of Alva's husband made his horse stumble away; but I also saw his sword's end touching Julius's breast (one of the several times that day—I shall never know how many times that was—many a time—by God). And then it was Zweifler: they fought for a moment, standing in face of another one, surrounded by the halo of lightning-fast-moving swords, only to see the Arab in the end thrown back together with his horse, just as it had happened before with Julius. I saw that from my hiding place. I saw that he kept avoiding those two until the very end, when the band, what was left of it, finally took off. Some of ours were heavily wounded but still upright and fight-ready. Not many though. And I saw their horses galloping, getting dust up in the air, farther and farther away from our place—just one more low cloud over time. I saw Julius getting off the horse and approaching Alva and then almost right away after that, her brother did the same thing going up to Gabrielle. And the poor me watching them, how they were moving—I knew it all in that one glance: our time here was over, the two women and I, we were children lost and wandering again. The rest of the day was going to be fear and despair, although silent, subdued perfectly. Then the night came. The worst one of them all down here probably, I still remember that. Then the absolute silence set in; slept crept to those whoever could, and who couldn't was, I think, just lying down and praying. I started looking for the knife Zweifler made once for me—from a leftover of the great steel they had made their commerce of down here. I found it in the leather pack with my few things that were not scripts and scrolls, and I got up and started walking south. The starry sky with no ceiling and no bottom was right above me, encapsulating me like a point, making me truly feel in the middle of nowhere, like moving ahead would cost me really no effort at all, like I was just carried by some kind of a current. Having left behind me what I just have left, I felt pretty good (considering).

I found them several miles south of our place, on a creek, shore of which had bushes on both sides. The night seemed deeper now, and yet there was somebody coming toward me just a moment after I had spotted them. I could hear his steps. He wasn't paying any attention; he wasn't there for me, maybe just taking a piss or something. I fell down, my face in the measly grass. I let him find me. He wanted to look at my face after the discovery that there was a body, and so he tried to turn me around, and I felt like helping him with that. Then he helped me get up, made sure

I wasn't injured, and we walked for a minute or so toward their camp. And there he was, their friggin' big boss, cowardly murderer. I could feel hatred growing in my breast, like one can feel a rock in the dark. His black hair falling onto his shoulder, his black eyes trying to pierce me through, although his mouth was smiling at all times. He just wanted to know if anyone might recognize me in association with the place they just had turned into a graveyard. But nobody did; of course not, I was at all times underground, in our hiding place with the women. He then told them to give me something to eat and drink and show me where I would sleep. We ate. I was listening to the talk, to the bragging, I should probably say, about what has been done and in what manner, how was that a proof of heroism, impossible to subvert. I didn't feel anything most of the time. Well, I felt that I was alive, that I was slightly… not much different from them. I felt that I was hungry, and I felt the gratefulness for the food—yes, I'm certain of that. After eating, some of them were still talking for a while. Others went to sleep right away. I didn't have anybody to talk to, so I stretched on my back and closed my eyes. But the light of the stars troubled my eyes even if closed. I threw the camel wool blanket away and slowly stood up.

"Where you goin'?" That was the boss himself. Which I did not expect, of course. Undaunted, I just said, as indifferent as I could, "To take a piss."

"You know what?" "What?"

"I have to myself!"

We left the place close to the fire and walked a little farther in the night. We stood there, I'd say, at a yard distance maybe from one another. I felt him rather than saw getting ready, and then I could hear his piss hitting the ground. I pulled from my sock the Zweifler's knife. Without any further ado, I just plunged it into his throat. We were standing there for quite a while, and I was stunned by his lack of any defense. He seemed (he was very much alive for quite some time) to be concentrated on getting air, and nothing else was of any interest to him—well, maybe my hand with the knife, which he seemed to be trying to hold back in a strange way, like to push it all the way in, trying to breathe all the time. Then he fell. Like a tree. All by himself. He looked kinda funny with his trousers' fly open, his dick in the air. In that position I couldn't see his face; his head went back. I left him there and went back toward the fire, to my place at first, but then I changed my mind: I went around them, almost to the other side, across the fire, where the one sleeping snored most. He really reminded me of some kind of a machine. I hit him with the knife, with whatever I got, into the heart. He got halfway up with my hand on his mouth, making strange noises. Lord, he was fighting with me, and then a guy from across the fire (now I wonder if it had been my former neighbor) got also halfway up and, seeing us like that, he shouted (Lord he did—that was a shout), "Don't bother, he always does that!"

"Sounded like a wolf or something, didn't it?"

"I told you, with him it's always the same. Go back to sleep."

"Got me shitless scared, you know?"

"At some point I was like that too." He said that and lay back, wrapping around his body his camel wool blanket as tight as he could.

I was sitting on the ground. The night was very warm. I wondered why he wasn't sweating. Nobody, I mean nobody, was paying me any attention; they were all asleep and with the exception of some of them, one would be able to track them down on the ground by their snoring. I thought about doing one more at least. And I did. And it was the guy next to me, whose throat I just slashed, and then I lay on top of him, my hand on his mouth, until the kicking stopped. Leaving their camp, I promised myself to do one more: same thing. Standing up and starting my walk back to the castle, I said under my breath, "I'll see you…"

Why didn't I do any more of them that night? I think I just got scared—at some point, one's imagination starts working and one sees one's self in their paws, one's body taken slowly apart, and that is the paw on the cat's mouth. Enough! Mommy doesn't like what you're doing. Stop! That's us. It's always me, may always be different, never the same, and yet the same me in the end, unmistakable. Once coward—well, stinking coward—and once a hero. Do heroes stink too?

SMITHY (ZWEIFLER)

We rebuilt it in the same spot it was before it got burned down. Smithy is supposed to be our source of income. It was the idea why we have come here. I know it is Julius who will claim the authorship of the idea, but it is also mine; I thought about coming back here yet at the time we had not left Outremer for France, believe it or not. It's always been, somehow, in the back of my mind. The environment here is based on fighting; war is the main article of the trade, and so I thought a sword or dagger of the quality known to me only would be something that we could sell without much ado for lots. People would buy anything that relates to their lives so closely. I thought we would make swords of the highest quality, just as I have learned from Father, and—overtime—we could sell them here (that would be living the dream) or go down, like to Jerusalem, get a stand where things like that sell, and sell it there. I did not expect failure. Every person here in Outremer wants to have a sword they could depend on.

We were building the oven, bricks made of clay in wooden forms we then dried in the sun (that's the preforming, which allows you to build something, which then the fire shall finish), and the joints between bricks were made of clay—just our dirt here mixed with water. Inside we stored the ingot—a round form of a crucible containing steel with high content of slag and other impurities, on top a measure of carbon (that's possibly the most important ingredient and the final strength of the blade we intend to make will depend on that carbon content; I use here the amount I know from Father—we did this time and time again with the encouraging results), and in the end small broken glass to help absorb the slag and also a measure of sand. Then I cover the crucible with sunbaked plate-form, glued to the crucible's body with the clay mix, and position carefully the whole thing inside the oven, which is then filled with charcoal to the brim. The oven is then covered with bricks glued together with clay. An oven like that was found—well, dug up, according to what Father told me—in Southeast Asia. The crucible steel secret must have been known to the people of Damascus in that region and on the other side of Mediterranean, in Spain, Toledo. Weaponry famous for its strength, although strangely different shapes the craft produced here and there. Then we start working with the bellows, soft, made of skin of small animals—very soft, pleasant to the touch. Each of us works for about half an hour, after which we're replaced by another—this will go on for two days. One of the things decisive is the temperature: it has to be high enough to separate the slag and the rest of the impurities from the steel. The fact that the steel from that period was so weak and brittle was due to the temperature too low; they had no means to heighten the temperature to experiment to fully remove impurities from their product. Did they understand it? Some may have but had also no means to change the known technology and so produced a product only mediocre then used as equipment by most everybody in most battles around. Only very few could afford weaponry my father and only few other blacksmiths produced. Those products were purchased at their exorbitant prices because it was very easy to prove by proposing a duel and, once accepted, in front of those watching slice to pieces the opponent's weapon. They were ready to sell a few villages to have a weapon like Father made them. It wasn't only the steel and its chemical composition; it was also the shape of the sort and certain details in the final execution that would have incredible influence upon the sword's performance. Truly little things, subtleties nobody would think could be of any importance, and those were precisely the ones of incredible influence upon the final performance of the sword.

And then it comes to that one moment when the oven is cooling down and the smith starts taking apart the whole construction brick by brick. The crucible was there, in one piece, emitting a strange, as if magic, bit of light that makes everybody apprehensive. With several hits of the hammer, a bar of steel is laid bare. That looks like we've got a good ingot. Almost right away we started hammering. Very little amount of sparks (after only a very short while literally none) is indicative of also very limited amount of impurities. It is extremely hard to reshape the ingot into a bar, which would be the beginning of the sword shape. It takes us days of hammering. The sword starts showing, as if painfully, slowly emerging from somewhere else into the dimension we are in. We hammer the fuller into the blade then— it is an indentation along the blade that allows the sword to be longer and wider without increasing the weight. Okay, time's come for quenching, an operation which is the most dangerous out of the whole process. Everything done so far can be ruined, leaving the blacksmith with just a piece of metal he could recycle, if he still felt like it. The sword has to be heated up until it is dark orange, evenly along the blade, and then submerged in liquid—in our case here, oil. There is mystic to it as well: the fluid (and blacksmiths do it all over the place) can be the blood of a dragon, for instance, or blood of your enemy. If it cracks, well, I just said it: the sword then is a piece of recyclable metal. But if it doesn't ping, it is the final product—a sword of the Toledo's best class, something we are after from the beginning, something my father developed technology to produce that, give or take, took his entire life. This one is not my first. And yet when I quench it and it doesn't crack, I feel like it was, for whatever reason. It's come to polishing. Using different stones, differently shaped and of different grade, I sand the blade by hand for days on end. Very hard work. But this is the stage where beauty appears, too. The last stage. First judgment of the potential buyer will be based on how this stage is accomplished; how much effort, in other words, went into it. I rub it using different stones as already said until I can see my own face reflected in the blade without any distortion. Then I know we are ready.

That night, we get drunk with Julian. And just a few days after that, a caravan passes by and the main guy buys the sword, after only a few demonstrations. I proposed a little duel and cut his sword to pieces. Each time our blades cross, his is getting shorter. He was ready to pay a bag of gold for the sword. Lamentably, after departure, he wanted his gold bag back, and so we had to dig graves again, which is something I hate. We put the sword for sale again, this time with a lot more luck: the sale is final, the buyer disappears with the sword, and we can start making another one.

This is how I imagined the whole story. This is our life down here. Won't be any different from this, and if we don't like it, we can go back to France. Thinking about it, I suddenly reflected that if I said that aloud, nobody would probably mind. That's our human nature, isn't it?

ALVA

'm making an omelet. I can't stop thinking about France. It's a fact that I'm bored with the life down here. Financially, it's okay, we have enough. And yet can anyone imagine themselves on the desert with a bag of gold. What would you buy? And where? And yet the guys don't stop working, from the crack of dawn till sunset. What for? The idiot just came, stopped, and now just stands there, looking at me. I asked him if he was hungry, and he nodded in the affirmative. The room is filled with smell of eggs. So the omelet will be his once done. The moment it was ready, I gave it to him and started then making one for myself. He ate with vengeance, like I was about to take it back from him, but I didn't say anything because I know how terribly easy it is to spook him. If I say something improper (whatever *proper* means in this case), he might leave his food on the ground and run. To where? We don't know if it is a specific place out there he runs to or is it just away from here…We don't know actually anything about him, except the prophecies. In fact right now, eating, he is mumbling something over his plate.

"What?" I asked him. "What is it?"

He was looking at me like he saw me for the first time.

"You're saying something there, under your breath. I can't hear the words, see?"

He still didn't react. "What?"

"It's going down…" "What is?" "Everything!"

"The world?"

"Yeah, the world! Down…" "This here too, then?"

"Most of all this here. Not a stone on top of another."

"What will you eat then?"

"The dead don't need to eat."

That made me pensive. What then is our history? We have discussed time and again the nature of a prophet. Brother came up with hypersensitivity, and that there's something in the air that it (that sensitivity of theirs) picks up. Wouldn't that mean that whatever happens down here is only secondary to happenings somewhere outside our world? What then is this world of ours, what for? Because the tears are real; time and again I would get up against those tears, I would have my soul stirred to the point of open apprising against the order of our world itself…

"Why don't you finish that for now?"

"Oh, I will. Don't worry."

He seemed to be closer to me than he was to the others. Our conversations took on the tone of casual, which was something that could not be said (not even close) with the few furtive words he would squeeze out of himself when whoever else tried to talk to him.

I stood up and went inside to get the bag with the dirty linen. I put it on my shoulder and went over to the creek to wash it. Once there, I beat the pieces at my full strength, first of all to wash it as best I can and then also to deaden something inside of me, something that is there and growing, something that I'm beginning to be afraid of. I remember myself as a little girl, right here, at this very spot on this creek's shore, when I was washing brother who had sullied himself badly (there was a suspicion of dysentery and that he, my brother, somehow had contracted it). I had him in the water and was washing his privates to the accompaniment of his howling; the water in this creek is cold, summer or wintertime, as an old man I'd never seen before that told me (he was right there, suddenly standing, towering above me) that brother was gonna live, that he was gonna be a great worrier. I shouldn't worry.

Then a lot of years had to pass by; he became a great worrier, so the prophecy turned out to be true. Involuntarily, my memory passes through all of what we had to go through so far all the way up to now. There's an instinct in me, a drive I should probably call it, to change place, go somewhere else—a drive I've also spotted in Gabrielle. She is as unquiet as I am. She's all moving when simply sitting at the able. But she never says a word about it to me. Gabrielle isn't an easy person to get information from, and I have to skip questioning her because it simply leads nowhere. Guys don't talk. Period. They work—dawn till sunset. A recipe for not thinking too much. Question is for what else. Somehow I cannot stop thinking there is something else they are trying to avoid, they don't want to talk about.

I just started cooking dinner; it'll be a roast beef, boiled potatoes, cabbage, and for after dinner, a vanilla custard. I do what I have to do, sitting down now and then, and those are the moments of the greatest disquietude. I go back to thinking about things.

Yeah…I was about to hit the bell calling to the table when a sound that wasn't from around here hit my ears. Almost the moment I got to the door to look outside, I saw the detachment of Mamelukes pouring into our yard and in the middle of it two people on horses: brother and Julian, swords drawn. I didn't go out anymore. I remained standing there, in the door. Just watching. Watching the battle flare up, brother and Julius back-to-back, or rather since they were both on horses, watching each other's backs as best they could, surrounded by a halo created by their swords, moving the way they were moving: incessantly, at an incredible speed, constantly fending off the hail of attacking blows that created a sound I will never be able to forget and watching, which I'm trying to persuade myself it is one of those demonstrations brother performs to sell a sword. Those who were out were replaced by others coming from the back, and only brother and Julius remained irreplaceable. Five hours? Six? That long it took for our enemies to realize that they are no match here; and, trying to preserve their good name, they still fought although backing up slowly—slowly but perceivably. And soon the yard was empty, and I heard the hoofs of horses getting away. Julius got off the horse. I thought he did that strangely. In a way that seemed crooked to me, him holding his saddle, not letting go even when his feet were already on the ground. Brother motioned me toward him, which was strange too. I obeyed. He just let himself fall on me and was then standing there, his hands on my shoulders. And when I looked at his face, I knew he didn't quite know where he was, his eyes not really his anymore. I bent and let him settle on my back; and then when that was already accomplished, I headed with that weight, enormous, way too big for my little strength, toward the house. I wanted, once we got there, to take his chain armor off him, and I wanted him to give me a little hand with that, and that was when I realized that he was unconscious.

Gabrielle called me over because brother had lost his consciousness too, and she couldn't do a thing by herself without my help. We took care of brother first, and when he was naked, we went over back to the room where I had started the thing with Julius. We got his armor and the rest of his clothes off too, and only then I could see how badly wounded he was, his body covered with blood as if he had taken a shower in it. I started washing him up. The blood already started solidifying, and it wasn't all that easy. Long time after that I had it done though, his body looking normal again—well, almost. All normal, except for the wounds. And all this time he didn't give me any sign of life either. I just held my ear to his chest, and that was how I knew that he was alive. Days and days on end passed by. One morning I woke up kind of lost. I truly didn't know for quite a while where I was. I was trying to concentrate. And then it came to me: I turned around and put my ear to Julius's chest—and what I got was deadly silence. I changed the position of my ear on his chest—nothing. I sat up on the bed. I thought. And I thought. And then I tried one more time: my ear to his chest, stop breathing, listen—nothing. Only then I knew: Julius died last night in his sleep. He died not having regained his consciousness. Just departed like he'd got bored or something like that.

Departed crossing the barrier I couldn't cross—not yet anyway—and now he was…who the hell knows?

Brother lived few more days longer. Then the same happened in that room too. We were left, Gabrielle and I, and Giscard. There was also that poor idiot out there who would most certainly wanna stay with us. Here or elsewhere. He couldn't be all by himself. He ain't gotta full deck. We did. Hell yes, we did. Have we been asked if we wanted to or not, we did. One would like to…The voice in my throat is breaking and makes a strange bubbly sound I'm not used to at all. I'm trying to subdue that to my will, but is doesn't quite work. I then addressed Alva, and the strangeness almost made me fall. Alva told me it was okay. And I told her it wasn't.

GABRIELLE

Yet a moment ago he was here, his voice is still here; I can hear his laugh, I could stretch my hand and touch him, and then I know it's not true and have to force myself not to howl like a wolf. Oh, God…you give, and it is like you give only to take away, to make us feel the loss as such that cannot be taken. God, where is he? Why did you take him from me? He was here, warm, smiling, talking to me, telling me jokes that would make me laugh, and now…Where is he? What is that place he went to? All I want—add that to the pain that cannot be borne anymore, a pain beyond anything I've known so far—all I want is to see him again, to love him. To tell him that.

His shirts I put exactly one on top of another, pressed, fresh, and clean, smelling a meadow under the sun. I know he'd like that. I have to do something not to lose my mind. I know perfectly well we should have expected that; we came here against all the advice we could get from whomever, to the place to some extent consisting of danger and anyone's death shouldn't come as a surprise. I know. And?

I walked out. Alva was in the yard too. She was sitting on a stone there, and I approached her.

"You gotta be outside? You too?" "Yeah…Inside is too heavy. I can't." "Same here."

"You have experience. People died in your family. Your dad, you told me about that yourself, remember? I want to ask a question… Can I?"

"Go ahead, ask!"

"Is this ever gonna be different? Am I gonna stop wishing to rip my own heart out to make it stop?"

She looks at me, silent. Only after a while she answers. "Won't be as bad as it is now. It's like all wounds. You may not know it, but this is a wound. It is. But you'll never forget, all the same."

The day was idiotically sunny, the sky idiotically blue. It was warm. I had on a robe with no sleeves because one with sleeves would've been too much. Giscard was cooking like nothing happened, and I hated him for that, I hated the thought that anyone would be able to even think about eating.

"Where he went," Alva said, obviously addressing me, "thither you cannot come."

"Is that supposed to warm me up?"

"This is the moment which is critical for your faith," she said.

"If you could talk about faith…"

"See what I mean?"

And then she was folding Julius's shirts in the box they keep those in and I was standing there, watching. I saw that she had to do something—as life approaches the barrier of pain, one can't remain unoccupied. I thought that the "thither" they went to is separated from here and now with a wall made of our despair. Suffering takes us out of the world so that the world isn't there anymore. I had that impression as she gave me water from the creek and that water seemed to come from some heaven, so distant in fact that it did not have much in common with my own being anymore. I held the golden cup she handed me with the water in, in my hand, wondering and pondering. I did not know what to make of it. Then we both just sat down on the shore, right there, straight on the sand.

"What now?"

Alva shook her head.

"Give me some time. It's too early for anything. I still didn't get it, you know?"

"I know. Me neither."

But more than a month passed by and we still have no idea what we are going to do. Bodies are buried. We got that accomplished. The castle is there just as it was since it got finished, our things unpacked. But we can't stay here. The first detachment of the Mamelukes (common erring robber, for that matter) will finish us off in no time. We offer no defensive strength. None. We have money. That's our strength, and we have to make use of it. I think, and Alva agrees, Cyprus might be our first choice, at least for the time being. We'd go back to Acre at first, and then we'd pay a boat to take us over there. By now it should have reshaped, and towns most certainly offer opportunities of a business we three could manage. Alva is, for instance, pretty good at tailoring. And I could learn whatever it takes to help her. Giscard could be a writer, preparing legal documents and such. We could live there. That's for sure. In my opinion, there is no sense in going all the way back to France. We have nobody there. Well, we talk. We talk and we shall see soon what will transpire, where shall life take us. As it always does. It always takes one for a ride and show one things one did not think where there, opens doors that never looked like doors, makes you meet people who whisper solutions into your ear you yourself would have never arrived at. So the general idea was to give it a little bit of time; let's wait and see. And then we'll see whatever choices we may have ahead of us. Right!

And right then a caravan arrived. They had something from Europe, Thüringen to be exact, to Alva's brother. When I heard the guy telling me that it was like he tore apart a wound freshly healed and still extremely tender, the pain overwhelmed me again. I sat down, taking a deep breath, fighting nausea. And he kept looking at me, without any understanding, not asking any questions, though, which I appreciated, of course. Alva came out, and she was more together than I was. She invited them inside to rest and to eat, and to tell us the story of their journey so far (they wanted to get to the holy sepulcher in Jerusalem). We were sitting at the table, and Alva was serving. I wanted to help, but she just motioned me to sit down and eat with our guests. I was listening then. Now that the first shock was over, I felt a little better too. Less shaky. And no more butterflies. I even managed to have some wine and not throw up. I found true interest in the story I was listening to, even that the story did not represent a thousandth of what happened to us on our way here. How often it is that somebody else's life impresses us so that we can't talk and only much later we realize that it should have been our own life which was the one to impress... That the fact we are still alive is actually a miracle.

GISCARD

The box is open, its lid with bas relief lying now on the floor. I don't know how to make an estimate as to its material value; prices vary and they also fluctuate, and then there is also the question of the place. The value of anything written will be different here (where it's literally worthless) and Paris, for instance, or Köln, Strasbourg, and other centers of European schooling, where a private library like this would be of incredible value. This much I know. What is that value, though, well, that just beats me.

The night outside gets ripe, all filled up with the voices of cicadas; and listening to it, I stop reading for a while. I just put aside a letter written in Latin in Eckhart's hand telling Zweifler that he shall be the heir as far as the writings in the box.

There's almost complete Aristotle. I never thought it would be as much. Goodness...

Plato, basically the same thing—the same impression of being overwhelmed without limits...

One of the things I noticed first and now just went back to was the book: stitched papyrus between to wooden covers (thin, sculpted wood and leather on top, pressed and glued, lots of gold adornment, title and author's name also in gold leaf, two basic tones—reddish and then more silvery—handwriting easily surpassing everything I've ever seen, incunabula throughout the text at the level of the true art). The mirror of simple souls by Marguerite Porete. I read for a while, and it made me pensive; they not only knew each other, Margo and Eckhart, but according to what Zweifler (Alva's brother) told me, they were lovers. I know that when she had been sentenced and then burnt on Place de Grève, he was also there, standing at that pyre and watching till there was nothing more to watch. Zweifler was very simple (not to say simplistic) about it. How could he (Eckhart) still pray after that let alone write about the greatness of God...? Talking to me, he was trying to be as explicit as he only could be trying to present as clearly as possible the cruelty of the moment—the tears, the anger, and the spiritual uprising of the soul, telling me to imagine my mother up there (he didn't know I already had a lover in my short life), fighting flames until she is a charred, black shapeless form held to that soot-covered post by what's left of the carbonized ropes, smoke of that terrible stench slowly rising toward the sky wherefrom He sends his silence down to us.

I just sat back, my eyes closed. I think. And the whole night seems to be getting filled up with my thoughts.

I find then Eckhart's sermon composed in great Latin, as far as I can be the judge of that, written in Strasbourg after the year 13, which is exactly what I'm talking about here: the greatness of God, infinite goodness and love. Goodness, how little I have understood of everything! And I have tried. God be my witness, I have. I read the sermon I opened sort of mechanically, not really trying to understand. Then I just put it down. I go over to the kitchen and cut myself a piece of roast beef and pour a glass of white wine. I eat. I drink. I don't try to listen to anything. The torch makes everything shaky, and it also makes a sound that now, in the silence of the deep of the night, is perfectly audible.

He had a mild death, quiet. He just stopped breathing at some point, and that was all. I wish I could get to know where he was now. But where he went, thither I cannot come and that can't be helped. Until the very end he was rather active, reading and writing his thoughts down, discussing stuff with his servant. (He was a big guy, responsible for the entire Thüringen as far as the Dominican cloisters were concerned. He was the one responsible also for the women religious activities; paradoxically he must have helped a lot of Beguines. The only one truly important to him, he couldn't help…

Then I find the letter to William of Paris, concerning religious freedom and, as opposite to that, imprisonment because of religious views. I have the impression that he wanted to talk about Templars and just didn't dare. The letter is halfway finished. Halfway only.

I rubbed my eyes. I am slowly getting sleepy, and my thoughts behave respectively. I think about what I just read, but I also see faces I've never really seen and I hear voices unknown to me. I put my head against a head support of this chair—it has a beautifully sculpted head support.

This is our last week over here. Alva has already spoken with the cart owner who shall take our belongings to Acre; and over there, at Acre, she has hired a boat too that will take us to Cyprus. Will I regret this here? I think so. I already got used to it. To its comfort. To my ability to read, unmolested, never hungry. To the smiles of people here, well wishing…always.

Tuesday or Wednesday the cart shall come, and I should see this castle in the middle of nowhere one last time. Then it'll be Acre and yet a bit later the sea and then a city I probably have already been in, and that should be the place we will look for a lodging in. We're not starving. I know Alva has more money than I shall ever see in my whole life, what's left of it.

I nodded to myself.

Then I was back to Aristotle—calm, majestic text, telling me what poetry is, what tragedy is. I smile. I love the voice coming to me through the distance of almost two millennia. And then I pick the text fifteen hundred years younger and read it. It's in Latin. It was banned in Europe because it doesn't seem to agree with what Europe accepted. I see slight possibility of fun. Maybe it is; oftentimes I thought it might be like we are the tin soldiers and it is fun playing the battles with us, now and then ripping off a leg here, a head there. Isn't that fun? I keep on reading and then I write a sentence, in vernacular, which I would have a problem to explain, except I feel it belongs to this night: "S'imaginant que la tragédie n'est l'autre chose que l'art de louer et la comédie l'art de blâmer…"

ANNEX

P.4 The first and more manifest way is the argument from motion. It is certain, and evident to our senses, that in the world, some things are in motion. Now whatever is in motion is put in motion by another, for nothing can be in motion except it is in potentiality to that toward which it is in motion; whereas a thing move inasmuch as it is in act. For motion is nothing else than the reduction of something from potentiality to actuality. But nothing can be reduced from potentiality to actuality, except by something in a state of actuality. Thus that which is actually hot, as fire, makes wood—which is potentially hot, to be actually hot, and thereby moves and changes it. Now it is not possible that the same thing should be at once in actuality and potentiality in the same respect but only in different respects. For what is actually hot cannot simultaneously be potentially hot; but it is simultaneously potentially cold. It is therefore impossible that in the same respect and in the same way a thing should be both mover and moved, i.e., that it should move itself. Therefore, whatever is in motion must be put in motion by another. If that by which it is put in motion be itself put in motion, then this also must be put in motion by another, and that by another again. But this cannot go on to infinity, because then there would be no first mover and, consequently, no other mover, seeing that subsequent movers move only inasmuch as they are put in motion by the first mover—as the staff moves only because it is put in motion by the hand. Therefore it is necessary to arrive at the first mover, put in motion by no other; and this everyone understands to be God.

P.44 The second way is from the nature of efficient cause.
In the world of sense, we find there is an order of efficient causes. There is no case known (neither is it, indeed, possible) in which a thing is found to be the efficient cause of itself; for so it would be prior to itself, which is impossible. Now in efficient causes, it is not possible to go on to infinity because in all efficient causes following in order, the first is the cause of the intermediate cause, and the intermediate is the cause of the ultimate cause, whether the intermediate cause be several or only one. Now to take away the cause is to take away the effect. Therefore, if there be no first cause among efficient causes, there will be no ultimate, no any intermediate cause. But if in efficient causes it is possible to go to infinity, there will be no first efficient cause; neither will there be an ultimate effect nor any intermediate efficient causes—all of which is plainly false. Therefore it is necessary to admit a first efficient cause, to which everyone every one gives the name of God.

P.110 The third way is taken from possibility and necessity, and runs thus. We find in nature things that are possible to be and not to be, since they are found to be generated and corrupt and consequently, they are possible to be and not to be. But it is impossible for these always to exist, for that which is possible not to be at some time is not. Therefore, if everything is possible not to be, then at one time there could have been nothing in existence. Now if this were true, even now there would be nothing in existence, because that which does not exist only begins to exist by something already existing. Therefore, if at one time nothing was in existence, it would have been impossible for anything to have begun to exist; and thus even now nothing would be in existence—which is absurd. Therefore, not all beings are merely possible, but there must exist something the existence of which is necessary. But every necessary thing either has its necessity caused by another, or not. Now it is impossible to go on to infinity in necessary things which have their necessity caused by another, as has been already proven in regard to efficient causes. Therefore we cannot by postulate the existence of some being having of itself its own necessity and not receiving it from another but rather causing in others their necessity. This all men speak of as God.

P.167 Ciax qui vienent plus que le pas…
a French poem by Chretien de Troy:
Those who come more frequently than frequent
They wonder saying: by my soul
Let's look at mother, our lady
Who tells me that the devils are
More common than all else in world
And if that's said to educate me
It also has for us to sign

P.156 The fourth way is taken from the gradation to be found in things. Among beings there are some more and some less good, true, noble, and the like. But *more* and *less* are predicated of different things, according as they resemble in their different ways something which is the maximum, as a thing is said to be hotter according as it more nearly resembles that which is hottest; so that there is something which is truest, something best, something noblest and, consequently, something uttermost being; for those things that are greatest in truth are greatest in being as it is written in Methaph. II Now the maximum in any genus is the cause of all in that genus; as fire, which is the maximum heat, is the cause of all hot things. Therefore there must also be something which is to all beings the cause of their being, goodness, and every other perfection; and this we call God.

P.225 The fifth way is taken from the governance of the world. We see that things which lack intelligence, such as natural bodies, act for an end, and this is evident from their acting always, or nearly always, in the same way, so as to obtain the best result. Hence it is plain that not fortuitously, but designedly, do they achieve their end. Now whatever lacks intelligence cannot move towards an end, unless it be directed by some being endowed with knowledge and intelligence; as the arrow is shot to its mark by the archer. Therefore some intelligent being exists by whom all natural things are directed to their end; end this being we call God.

P.252 Imagining that tragedy is nothing else but the art of praising and comedy art of blaming.

Sentence from Ernest Renan: "Averroes…used also by Jorge Luis Borges as introduction to his short story about Averroes's "Divagations."

9 781950 596577